What the critics are saying...

ஒ

5 *HEARTS* "Lise Fuller is a very talented and witty writer and I laughed so hard reading her novel: CUTTING LOOSE that I almost cried! Ms. Fuller took me through so many emotions as I read the book that I wavered on sympathy, agreement, enjoyment, and as a woman I completely understood Miranda's dilemma." ~ *The Romance Studio*

"Sexy and funny, Cutting Loose is a book sure to please...Readers who have never read Lise Fuller will want to pick up this book...With talent like this, Lise Fuller is an author to watch. I will be anxiously awaiting her next offering!" ~ *Joyfully Reviewed*

"Ms Fuller shows a rare talent for writing a story that readers will easily relate to. I could see this tale playing out in front of my eyes like a movie. As the tension built between Mira and Gary, my reading picked up pace and I devoured this book...I recommend this book to anyone who enjoys contemporary romances with a dash of comedy thrown in. So, take a walk on the wild side and grab CUTTING LOOSE" ~ *Romance Junkies*

"This was a fun story from beginning to end. You laugh, you cheer, and you feel the love in the air. The vines of this story wrap you up and keep you held tightly until the very end. I enjoyed it thoroughly." ~ *Coffee Time Romance*

Cutting Loose

Lise Fuller

Cerridwen Press

A Cerridwen Press Publication

www.cerridwenpress.com

Cutting Loose

ISBN 9781419956034
ALL RIGHTS RESERVED.
Cutting Loose Copyright © 2006 Lise Fuller
Edited by Sue-Ellen Gower
Cover art by Willo

Electronic book Publication February 2006
Trade paperback Publication March 2007

Cerridwen Press is an imprint of Ellora's Cave Publishing, Inc.®

Also by Lise Fuller

৯৹

On Danger's Edge
Intimate Deceptions

About the Author

৯৹

This award winning author, after writing and producing a neighborhood play at the tender age of six (earning all of twenty cents), took a sabbatical of many years before she found the love of creative writing again. Now, having earned her MBA and CPA, raised four children (three as a single parent), Lise brings her adventurous spirit and extensive experience to her captivating stories. Lise has traveled to several countries, studying the culture and enjoying the native way of life, and has explored our world from the watery depths of the Caribbean to the heights of the Rocky Mountains. Having married her hero, an ex-82nd Airborne paratrooper, she devotes her time to writing, raising the couple's teenager, and her own personal accomplishment—body sculpting. Some comments of her work include:

It's the BEST I've read...in a very long time!

The emotion! Fast paced and sexy.

You just know it's going "to be Hot."

Great hooks! Drew me in right away.

You have a great voice. Love your characters!

Lise welcomes comments from readers. You can find her website and email address on her author bio page at www.cerridwenpress.com.

CUTTING LOOSE

ɞ

Dedication

∞

*To Mom,
and to sisters everywhere.*

Trademarks Acknowledgement

∞

The author acknowledges the trademarked status and trademark owners of the following wordmarks mentioned in this work of fiction:

Band-Aid: Johnson & Johnson Corporation

Barbie: Mattel, Inc.

Batman and Robin: DC COMICS composed of Time Warner Entertainment Company, L.P., Warner Communications, Inc., American Television and Communications Corporation, Time Warner Operations Inc., Warner Cable Communications Inc., and Capital Cablevision Systems, Inc., and People's Cable Corporation

Corvette: General Motors Corporation

Nike: Nike, Inc.

Super Bowl: National Football League

Tarzan: Edgar Rice Burroughs, Inc

Chapter One

ഇ

"Unbelievable. And from my own flesh and blood."

Miranda Harper flew off the elevator. "Bad enough Dani sets me up with a guy. But a hockey player?"

The man her sister had sent had cornered her as she rushed between a sick hippo and a constipated elephant. The guy even followed her into the large animal yard, grinning with all thirty-two pearly whites. When Mira snapped on her gloves and asked if he'd help, the man asked her how. After describing the process, which included reaching into the animal's rear, the player bolted.

Mira's anger notched higher. A jock from her formative years caused her the greatest embarrassment of her life. She'd shunned any guy with triple-sized biceps since. Not that Dani knew the specifics, but damn, her sister still knew Mira wanted nothing to do with air-headed athletes. Any *other* sibling would respect the opinion, but oh no, not Danielle. Her younger sister insisted on playing the caped crusader of lonely hearts—with macho men her specialty. With this last fiasco, Mira had reached her limit. High time that girl got a piece of her mind.

Mira glanced around, trying to remember the name of the company where her clever sister worked. Spying the floor directory on the corner wall, she walked toward the sign, pointing her finger like a dagger. "There it is. Market Dynamics. Room 504."

Without looking, she whipped around the corner and rammed into a brick wall.

Or, at least, the impact felt like one. She wobbled and a pair of powerful arms wrapped around her as she tried to steady herself.

"Doctor Harper, are you okay?"

The warm, deep voice came from above. Woozy, she let her head drop against the man. The muscles in his chest bulged under her fingertips. "I...ah..." Mira looked up to see Danielle's hunky, blond boss, Gary Staunton, an ex-pro football player. God, talk about jocks. Could she faint now? Either that or she'd die for sure.

How embarrassing.

She backed away and managed to tangle herself in a tall plant that stood beside her, something she hadn't noticed before.

Gary's brows knitted. "Maybe you ought to come in and lie down."

His voice flowed over her like melted chocolate. Before she could argue, he swept her up and cradled her in his arms. Looking at him, her mouth went desert-dry.

"I..." She wanted to apologize for banging into him but the blood rushing to her temples prevented the words from coming. Instead, she stupidly bobbed her head in agreement.

The gaze in his light blue-green eyes sparkled.

A sudden surge of hormones ripped through her telling her he wanted her. But somewhere in the foggy, logical side of her brain, she knew that was a lie. Still, she wondered why no SOS sign flashed hard and heavy behind her eyelids in warning, shouting "Danger, Danger" like the robot in that old TV series. After all, Gary Staunton was a jock to beat all jocks.

He smiled and her pulse skipped a beat, her libido working hard and heavy. "No, no, no..." she mumbled. She knew a testosterone threat when she saw one.

"Are you in pain?" Gary pulled her against him.

Every synapse in her body fired, and the way he held her, she had no choice but to lean her head on his shoulder. At least, that's what her muddled gray matter reasoned.

floor-to-ceiling windows. Several trophies lined the case at the other end of the sofa.

Rising, she walked over to the display and fingered the glass, staring at Staunton's awards. This man had no place in her life. She forced her faithless body to get control. Later, when alone, she'd forgive herself for this temporary lack of good judgment.

Lifting her chin, she strolled past the couch and touched her cheek where he'd brushed it. Her body burned again.

She cursed herself and hurried out the door, thinking that running into a brick wall would have been safer by far.

* * * * *

Gary steadied his rapid pulse. Something happened back there and the feeling scared him. Mira's long, dark hair had tangled in his fingers, giving him a funny sensation in the pit of his stomach—the one that said he needed, wanted a steady woman in his life, a woman who would stand by him no matter what. His parents had that kind of relationship and he'd always thought he'd find the same. But the freak accident he'd had, shattered his dream. He'd been on the verge of breaking the NFL sack record. His career had skyrocketed and he'd captured the heart of Darlene Woods, queen of the Denver social set. At least, he thought he had. Darlene proved otherwise after she saw the physical damage he'd suffered, a permanently busted knee, and…

Well, she wanted to be married to a sports pro. He couldn't be that anymore. He closed his eyes. They were to marry two weeks from the date of the incident. The next summer she married some baseball player with good stats.

He bit his lip, steeling himself against the pain of her rejection. Far better he'd found out then what she wanted. If the accident had happened a few years into their marriage, he didn't know if he could have survived the heartache her leaving would have brought.

He grumbled, knowing better than to dwell on Darlene's abandonment. But it took effort. Darlene had used him for her own deluded purposes, pursued him like a trophy, a thing to show her friends what a good catch she'd made. When he couldn't fulfill her fantasy of being married to a professional ballplayer, she left him. He'd decided afterward he'd never again let himself fall into such a deceptive relationship. A shallow life in the romance department suited him. After what Darlene had done, he wouldn't risk his heart again.

Besides, too much of him had changed to suit any woman who desired a family, especially a woman like Mira. She exuded sex, intelligence and sensitivity—the type of woman a lucky guy spent his life with. She didn't need a guy with a bum knee and a crushed testicle.

He rubbed his face, erasing the memories. He had goals. As an established businessman, he had a plan, which didn't include love and forever after. Not now, not when he had too much to do, too much to accomplish. But for some unknown reason, he wanted Mira, wondered if he'd had an unmarred body, if she would have wanted him too. He swallowed and wrestled with the tormenting thought, knowing a woman that great wouldn't want the damaged goods he carried. The horror on Darlene's face had testified to that.

He punched the down button and berated himself as he waited for the elevator. He should have watched where he was going. Instead he mowed down the most attractive woman he knew. He'd put men in the hospital for less.

He blamed the run-in on his preoccupation with the problems and potential of this latest ad job. Sam Carter, the ad exec for Fast Drive, Inc., had called and confirmed the piece would go nationwide—Gary's first coast-to-coast spot, a job that would open several doors for him, making him millions. He wouldn't blow something this big, not again. He'd washed out of football because of a stupid fluke. He wouldn't wash out of advertising. The time for action was now.

Growling, he watched the indicator light for the elevator as the lift moved from floor to floor. He didn't mean to take his pent-up energy out on an innocent bystander, especially one who affected him the way Mira did. She seemed okay. He at least got that much by getting lost in the brown specks of her hazel-green eyes. He'd never been so close to her before, and the way her soft body molded into his...

The elevator door opened. Guilt-ridden, he stepped inside and jabbed the lobby button, trying to forget what bothered him most was how she felt in his arms.

* * * * *

"Mira, get a life. A date. Get something besides those blasted monkeys. You're coming up on the big one. The big three-oh. Hit the celebration with a bang."

Mira mashed the cell phone against her ear, trying to mute the noise from the chimps scurrying through the trees. "Look, Dani, I already hit your boss with a bang today and ended up on his couch."

"And in his arms." Dani snickered. "The receptionist told me. She saw the whole thing from her desk. Said he carried you into his office. You should have closed the door and taken advantage of the opportunity. I would have."

"Well, I'm not you," Mira stressed, still embarrassed from knocking into Gary. At least she thought that's what the emotion was. Another sensation nagged at her she didn't want to name, *especially* to her meddling sister. Dani understood lust only too well.

"All right," her sister said. "Forget Gary. What about your birthday?"

"Dani, it's just another day. What won't be another day is you setting me up. *Capische?* And don't get any ideas about your boss. He's the *last* guy I'd want to spend my time with."

Dani sighed then blessed silence reigned for a sheer moment. "Fine," she said. "I hear you. Clear as a bell. But *somebody* needs to grab you and put you back in the human race. You've become too much of a recluse. Your birthday's my biggest chance. You know, someday you'll wake up and realize those monkeys have taken over your life."

"They're chimpanzees, Danielle. A form of apes. A form I find preferable to some humans, especially sisters."

"You would," Dani protested. "You're lonely, Mira."

"I am not. I date."

"Who? And the last guy you went out with doesn't count. He was even nerdier than you. I think Gary would be perfect."

Mira bit her lip so hard it started to bleed. "Don't even think about it. I have my work, and that's all I want."

"Your work is studying apes, Dr. Harper. You're in a zoo. This is Denver. There's more to do than play with lower primates. You need to get out, as in o-u-t. You're not one of the inmates. Find a wild life outside those cages, and, God forbid, a man—any man. Just make sure he doesn't have a thick layer of hair all over him."

"I know the difference between an ape and a man." Mira bit her lip to keep from cursing. "Besides, I have a life."

"What? Nursing Sara? I know the matron of ape virtue is one of your best friends, but she's a chimp, for God's sake." Dani paused. "I've never known anyone who didn't have some problem over turning thirty. In a few weeks, you'll be an old maid."

"How would you know? You're only twenty-six. Wait four years and then you can tell me if you feel like a spinster."

"Mira…"

"Look, I have you to pester me. What more do I need? Besides, I have better things to do with my life than to look like Barbie."

"Ouch. Okay, so maybe getting old is bothering you more than I thought."

"I'm not old," Mira protested. "Just seasoned."

"Seasoned my behind. You've always been dynamic—in every way that counts except for intimate interactions with male Homo sapiens. Get my drift—Doctor?"

"You don't need to talk to me like an anthropologist."

"Hey, anthro is one of my favorite subjects. And you won't listen unless it's clinical sounding. Now, about tonight. You *are* coming, right?"

"Didn't I promise?"

"You promised to come out and play with us girls last week but Sara's problems got in the way."

Mira frowned. "She's having a hard time right now. She's going into some weird version of primate menopause."

Dani snickered. "You know, I've heard that lack of using certain female equipment can cause early menopause. Are we studying apes, Doctor, so we can get an opinion?"

"Very funny." Mira sat on the brick wall that lined the interior of the ape house. "I'll be there. Promise."

Dani sighed. "Mira, *they* are your friends. It's time you let your hair down and had some fun."

"Okay, okay," Mira said. "I'll loosen up, at least for the night. Might even talk to a few dudes."

"Dudes." Dani clicked her tongue. "We'll have to work on your lack of modern language. Tonight—wild, promise?"

"I promise I'll relax."

Dani laughed. "Okay. We'll work on wild. Hey, it's worth a try." She paused. "Gotta go. Gary's rolling on a new project. A big one. Might go nationwide. I'm helping with the artwork and talent. We've got a great shot. I'm psyched."

"I can tell." Sara scrambled up to Mira and stared at her with those chocolate, soulful eyes.

"Give Sara a hug for me," Dani said, as if she knew the chimp hung around. "I'll see you tonight. *Ciao.*"

"*Ciao.*" Mira shook her head and pushed the off button, wondering why her sister had so many concerns about her sex

17

life. Dani had always been the wild one, not her, but in some sense, she reminded Mira of their mother. Mom always worried about when she'd get "attached", her word for married. The older woman believed the key to a happy life included family, and occasionally she'd pester both her children. Now, Dani took up where Mom left off, except in her case attached meant a steady lover. Well, the FDA daily nutritional requirements didn't include sex and she had a family. She was happy — she just wasn't "attached". So why couldn't they leave her alone?

Mira shoved the phone in her jacket. "They say I'm not wild enough, Sara." She stroked the fur on the old girl's head. Sara took the movement to mean she could crawl onto Mira's lap. "What do you think?"

The chimp moaned and nodded, making the crooning sound the animals were famous for.

Mira chuckled. "I thought you'd say that." Per Dani, her big sister spent too much time at work to find a decent man. Maybe, Mira thought, but more likely she just didn't have a "to die for" body. No movie star here. Not that she was fat, but her body would have fit better when women with voluptuous curves were the thing. Curvy and soft. That described her.

Desperate to get Dani off her back, Mira had asked the last guy out herself. He'd had good possibilities, characteristics she'd appreciate. The man had been kind, witty...

Lifeless in the romance department. She groaned, remembering the wet, tepid kiss he'd placed on her lips when she'd dropped him at his mother's. Yuck.

Mira shook it off. "There has to be somebody out there for me, Sara," she mumbled. But where? After all, she had needs, didn't she? But Mira wanted a man who could stir her body *and* her mind. Someone who wanted more than a quick roll in the bed sheets.

Someone like Gary Staunton.

She sulked, reminding herself he couldn't be her type, even if he did make her pulse jump enough to fry her brain. As an ex-pro football player, the man had brawn. Tough guys like that she didn't need. At six feet five, his athletic body towered over her. And from what she'd touched of the muscled form underneath… Oh God.

She groaned and Sara patted her on the back. Figures the old girl would be the one to console her. She hugged the chimp then sat back and looked at her.

"Okay, Mira, forget it. The guy simply isn't for you." She wouldn't be jock bait, not again. Besides, the guy could get any dopey fan who tagged after him. She swallowed, hoping to banish the thought of him and reminded herself that most men like him were only interested in themselves and what conquests they could make. She, for one, wouldn't be conquered.

Still, Dani had a point. She was lonely. Except she'd choke before she'd admit the fact to her meddling sister. Mira guided Sara's hand away and stared at the ape's face. The old chimp still had a better sex life than she did.

Sighing, Mira moved Sara off her lap and went to give some of the other chimps their monthly once over. The crowds dwindled after Labor Day, giving her some respite and some time to examine the apes and their dwellings. The warm sun banished the coolness from the morning so she removed her jacket and dropped it on the rocks. "Okay, George, your turn." She walked over to the young male and picked him up. "Let's see how you're doing."

Behind her, the door squeaked. Candy Thompson, one of the zookeepers, entered. The chimps scurried, squawking to let everyone know someone else had come into their domain.

"Hey, Doc." Candy raised her bandaged hand in greeting. "Doctor Death wants to see you."

"Charlie? Why?" She lowered George to the ground, reminded of the worker's angst with Dr. Burrows, the zoo's administrator. "How's your hand?"

"Better." She smiled. "Should have this thing off by the end of the week."

"I'm sorry about Anthony. I didn't know he would bite."

She nodded. "I should have been more careful. Those Rhesus monkeys can be vicious. What I hate most is those dang rabies shots. Although, the intern who gave the injection to me could bite me anytime." She waggled her brows.

Mira shook her head, wondering what it would take for her to make such a wild move. The effort wouldn't be much with someone like Gary.

Ouch. Didn't she dismiss him for life? "What does Charlie want?"

Candy pursed her lips. "Don't know for sure. I think he wants to talk about Sara."

Mira tensed. "Why?"

"You know, Doctor Burrows. Once an animal loses its value, he looks for other ways to make up the money. Sara can't breed anymore and we have more than our share of chimps." The zookeeper shrugged. "I hope he isn't thinking about selling her, but he might be."

"Over my dead body. Sara has other value than that of a brood female." Mira stomped toward the door, halting at the entrance to glance around the cage. Why was everyone obsessed with sex? Didn't she have enough problems?

She slammed the door shut behind her, determined to change Burrows' mind.

* * * * *

Gary rubbed his palms together, pleased with the way the new ad came together. This was it. His big chance. What he'd worked so hard for. He wanted national recognition for his firm, Market Dynamics, almost as much as he'd wanted the Lombardi Award he'd won for best college defensive end several years ago.

Until the accident, football had been his whole life. High-school team captain, state championship... The football scholarships he'd been awarded could have paid for college. Instead, he chose to use his scholastic ones. Football had been fun. School had been work. And he figured what he took the time to work for should pay for his education.

An education that became critical much sooner than he'd planned.

He looked at the Lombardi Award in his trophy case. Actually, he'd been one of the lucky ones. He'd achieved a dream—and still found a successful life outside the football field. Many of the guys he'd played with would never be able to say that.

He studied the ad campaign. His success depended on this spot. He'd started the business. Brought it from the ground up. A lot of hard work and sweat went into it. Still did. He examined his palms. With the company's future uncertain, his fate was in his hands. How did the old quote go? He was the master of his fate, captain of his soul. He'd be damned if he'd lose. After all, besides the business, what else did he have?

A knock returned him to the present. His tawny-haired assistant opened the door and poked her head inside. "Ready when you are, boss." Dani Harper winked at him.

Sometimes Gary wondered about the innuendoes she threw out but, hell, he liked her energy. She'd been fun to have around and, over the years, she'd become a close friend and ally. "I want to apologize for running into your sister. Is she okay?"

"Yes, she's fine." Dani grimaced, twisting her lips in a way that said more than she did.

He wondered what the gesture meant. "You're sure?" he asked. "I thought so, but…"

"She's fine." Dani pasted on a grin.

"Good." He relaxed, glad Mira was okay. He could still see Mira's hazel eyes staring wide at him. He rested his hands behind his head, trying not to think of the sexy brunette. "You find the voice talent yet?"

Confusion etched itself across Dani's face. "I thought we weren't going to spend time looking anymore unless…" A genuine grin grew over her classic features.

"You got it, lady. Sam called. The campaign is on."

"Yes." She clenched her fist and punched it into the air. "This is awesome. I do know someone who could do it." She winced. "Although I'd have to get her to buy into it."

"Sounds like an amateur." He leaned back.

"Well, sort of. Actually, she's someone with a lot of speaking experience. Everyone says her voice is sexy as hell. You game?"

Gary nodded. "Sure. They want to use a local if we can to cut costs. We don't have much time. You really think this gal will do it?"

A mischievous look came into Dani's eyes. "I'll work on it. Trust me?"

Gary smiled. "You know I do."

His cell phone rang and he flipped it open. "Hello?"

"Oooh. Ahhh. Ohhhh…"

"Who is this?"

"Mmmmm."

"And I think you're okay too, darlin'. Let me know when your mom catches you, okay? If she does, I might have a deal for you." He hung up.

"Who's that?" Dani's brow arched.

"Some kid who's been calling me for the last few hours. All she does is moan. I've been trying to ignore it, hoping she'd give up. I have to admit, though, she has one seductive voice." He sat up, appalled at how that might sound to Dani. "Ah, no offense. I mean, don't think…"

Dani laughed. "Gary, I don't, whatever it is your male mind is thinking. You're an ad exec looking for a voice. Maybe you found one?" She whirled around and headed out, stopping at the door. "In the meantime, I'll check my other source. So far, our preliminary search of the talent agencies around here hasn't turned up anyone either of us likes. I'll check again, but I think the lady I have in mind might do the trick. If not..." She pointed to the cell phone he'd dropped on the desk. "Maybe your mystery lady will give it a go." She winked again. "Think about it." She breezed out the door and closed it.

Gary frowned. The voice had to be a kid, some teenager or something, which was why he wouldn't do anything about it. The prank was harmless. Why get the kid in trouble? But use her voice? Absolutely not. Unless it was a woman, but he couldn't imagine any woman making a prank call except as a joke. Maybe one of his ex-teammates put her up to it? Could be. Many of them were still close friends. They knew his days of chasing wild women were over. Now, his choices were more selective. He wouldn't put it past them to pull this kind of stunt.

Before he could reconsider, he turned on the phone and punched star-six-nine. "Let's see what number this girl is dialing from."

* * * * *

Sara stared at the small box her large friend often talked into. She tried to eat it again, but it didn't taste good. Still, the funny button she pressed always gave her the warm voice she liked. "Oooh..." she moaned. She'd tried to talk to it. Like her friend did.

Ringggg...

"Ah, ah..." The noise excited her and she dropped the thing.

Ringggg...

"Oooh, oooh, oooh, oooh, oooh." The other apes in the cage began to scramble.

She headed for the highest tree, but stopped halfway. Would the voice be there?

She eased herself toward the box. Picking it up, she pressed the button.

"Hello?"

The voice. "Aaah…"

"Okay, look. You know who I am, don't you?"

"Mmmm."

"I figured. Listen, I don't know who put you up to this, but I'm in desperate need of a voice like yours. I think you might be the ticket. How would you like to be in a commercial?"

"Ooooh."

The male voice sighed. "Great. Can you meet me at Schinnery's Bar & Grill tonight? About eight?"

"Aaah…"

"Just curious, but one of the guys put you up to this, didn't they?"

"Mmmmm."

"Thought so. Look, don't be afraid of upsetting their joke. In fact, you don't need to tell me your name if you're worried about breaking some strange code of silence. Not yet, anyway. Let's see if we have some mutual interest first, okay?"

"Kaaa…"

"Good…um, you are over twenty-one — aren't you?"

"Mmmm."

"Great. Eight, then. And don't worry about the guys. They won't mind that the jig's up. They'll just laugh harder. See you later."

Sara heard a click and the deep, soothing sound went away. "Mmmmm." She eyed the box and stuck out her bottom lip.

"Eee, eee, eee," she shouted and ambled over to Mira's odd fur she called a jacket, fingering it as she put the phone away…just before her friend came through the door.

* * * * *

"Sara, what are you doing?" Mira picked her up and sat on the stone wall. "Did you miss me?"

"Mmmmm." Sara stuck her lip out again and handed her friend her fur.

"Thanks." Mira stroked her head and laid the coat on the wall.

"Ooooh, ooooh."

Mira hugged Sara then put her down. Sara scurried off.

A deep breath allowed Mira to think. Candy had been right. Dr. Burrows wanted to sell Sara. In fact, he insisted. There would be an auction soon, but as strange as Sara had been acting, probably only a medical research facility would buy her. They would torture the chimp. Eventually Sara would die.

Mira had protested. Vehemently. She'd bought thirty days to come up with some alternatives. Thirty days to find a way to keep Sara at the zoo.

Thirty.

She was starting to hate that number.

Sara ambled back and cocked her head to one side, giving her an odd look. "Eee, eee, eee," she squeaked then took off and ran back and forth across the compound, screeching and stirring up the others.

"You're right." Mira studied the racing chimps. "Time for action. Why am I sitting here pouting?" She tugged at the right pocket of her coat and searched for the phone.

"Funny…" Didn't she put it away?

She looked around her feet, thinking it might have fallen on the ground. Nothing. Picking up the jacket, she felt the heaviness on the other side. "Humph, I'm really losing it," she mumbled and pulled the instrument out.

She had confidence in some of the zoo's board of directors that they wouldn't want to lose Sara, but the directors had limited say on the subject. She needed more clout. And who was the *only* person she knew with influential contacts?

She flipped open the phone and dialed.

"Hello?"

"Dani. It's me." She paused to get her breath. This would be the worst thing she'd ever done. "Sis, do I have a deal for you."

Chapter Two

ജ

"So…" The smugness in Dani's voice came through loud as a bell. "You need my help."

"Yes. This is important. Sara's life is at stake. If she's transferred to another zoo — or God forbid, a research lab — she'll be locked up, maybe tortured. It'll kill her. She needs the other chimps. I don't know how many years she has left, but she needs her loved ones around her."

"Loved ones? Mira, they're chimps."

"They're family," Mira insisted.

Dani sighed. "Okay. I'd hate to see my sister Sara shipped away and put in solitary. Besides, you know me and deals. I love 'em."

Mira groaned. "That's what I'm afraid of."

Dani laughed. "Mira, I'm doing this for your — and Sara's — own good. Now look, you get wild with me for, say, seven *full* days. I mean hours, minutes *and* seconds. Since both you and I are busy, we can spread it out over the month — an appropriate amount of time since you *are* turning thirty about then — and we'll settle. Plus, you have to audition for this part in the ad."

"An audition?" Mira held Danielle's old cell phone away from her ear for a second, sorry she'd ever accepted the dang thing from her a month ago. The flipping phone would have to be red. She put the receiver back to her ear. "Dani, now I know you're crazy. What ad?"

"The big ad Gary landed. The one I told you about. We need your voice."

"My voice?" Mira briefly stared at the receiver again. Her sister had gone nuts. "Why? I'm sure some sex-starved maniac would be happy to put their voice on for your boss. Probably not much else, but…"

"Oh Mira, really. Gary isn't interested in groupies. Besides, your voice is sexy as hell. When Gary hears you in the ad, he'll think so too." She paused. "It's this or nothing."

In her mind's eye, Mira could see Dani standing in her office, hand on hip, and acting like a stone wall — not budging a bit. "What *exactly* do I get in return?"

"My help and the help of my friends," Dani said. "Of course, that includes Gary and some of his athletic buddies."

Mira groaned. "Why them?"

"Duh. It's because they've got the political connections needed to make an impact on your zoo board." She snickered. "Trust me, you'll like working with Gary."

Mira ground her teeth. "Fine," she mumbled.

"What? I didn't hear you…"

Mira listened to the teasing in her sister's voice. She took a deep breath and sighed. "I'll do it."

"Yes," Dani shouted.

"But on certain conditions. I'm not going to do something I'd abhor or have moral principles against."

"Mira—"

"Danielle, I'm not getting my body pierced."

"How about a tattoo?"

Mira sighed. "Nothing permanent. And no jumping into bed with any man of your choice, especially Gary Staunton. Got it? No matchmaking."

"Oooookay. It's a deal."

Too easy, Mira thought. Dani had something up her sleeve.

"Well?" Danielle asked. "I don't have all day." She paused. "It'll be all right, Mira."

Mira rolled her eyes. "You know, you're a pain."

Dani giggled. "Yeah, but you love me."

Mira huffed. "Fine. It's a deal." She'd have to figure out later what idea cooked in Dani's head. She hoped she didn't figure her scheme out too late. "When can you talk to your boss? We need to get to work. I've bought a month. His supreme highness Charlie is giving me the chance to figure out a way to keep Sara without breaking the budget."

"Tomorrow," she answered. "Gary's gone again. Won't be back until after we're out on the town, chicky."

"Chicky?"

"Yep," Dani replied. "Tonight we are gonna have the time of our lives. See ya, sis. Love you."

"Love you too, Dani...and thanks."

"No prob. I'll meet you at my place. *Ciao*."

"*Ciao*." Mira clicked off the phone, half in shock. Did she really commit to such an insane deal? Promising to get wild with her sister? God only knew what went through the crazy girl's head. Mira flinched. She didn't look forward to fun, Danielle-style. The deal committed her to a whole week of unadulterated wildness.

Seven days.

One hundred and sixty-eight hours.

Ten thousand and eighty minutes.

She didn't know if she would survive. Shoot, why talk about her sister? Mira was the nutsy one. She pressed her lips together, trying to grip the fear threatening to overtake her common sense. She needed to do this — for Sara — yet she abhorred mixing social situations and politics. Polite banter simply wasn't a skill she had. The worst part would be the introductions to those people she hadn't formally met — people like Gary Staunton.

Oh God. The Neanderthal.

Heat rushed to her cheeks. If Gary hadn't caught her when she ran into him, she'd have been flat on the floor. She should have apologized. That would have at least been better than gawking at him.

But when he touched her...

Okay, so no one could blame her for gaping. Gary Staunton made an impression on anyone who saw him—much less ran into him. Yeah, she'd been a little ditzy, but he sure as heck didn't need to sweep her up and carry her into his office. This was the twenty-first century, for heaven's sake. Not the Jurassic era.

She rubbed her arms, replaying his deep, smooth, sexy voice in her head. He'd been so close, she could feel his warmth. She swore he knew the effect he had on her. He'd grinned, giving her that slow, saucy smile which said—"Hey, I know I turn you on, babe. I turn all the women on. It's my job."

She hated that.

Still, somehow she'd learn to deal with Gary—for Sara's sake. She shivered. By himself, he would be bad enough. His overconfident smile would raise her ire. But to deal with a whole roomful of oversized Neanderthals? They would be her downfall. The egos on those guys were bigger than their bodies. Her foot would be in her mouth in no time. Then where would she be?

She sighed, not sure what to do. Being too direct, politics had never been one of her strong points. Dani had the ability to play to their egos, not her.

"Be subtle," she mouthed. "Docile. Compliant." She forced a smile. "Be a dumb Barbie."

She plopped on the short retaining wall and planted an elbow on her leg, letting her chin drop into her hand. She could do this. She had to. She needed all the help she could get. Besides, her sister had faith in Gary. Lots of it. And as much as she wanted to ridicule the guy, she couldn't. To Dani, he'd been the best boss in the world. Her sister never stopped bragging about him, about his company, about the fact he'd won some national award in college as a defensive end. Personally, Mira found that fact more offensive than defensive. From her sister's description, the man's only job in the pros had been to flatten whoever had the ball. How many brains did that take?

Yet Dani's excitement still reverberated in their everyday talks—about Gary and his company. Dani loved her work and she and Gary had become very close. Mira wondered if her sister had a thing for him.

Sara moaned and sidled up to her, reminding Mira that she sat in the middle of the ape house. She patted the chimp's head. "It's all right, girl. I have a solution." She grimaced. "One with a weird twist. I hope the plan works."

She gave Sara a crooked grin and rose, feeling a bit scared and—yeah, she'd admit it—excited.

Tonight would be a new beginning. The start of seven full days of lost virtue.

* * * * *

"I can't meet tonight." Dani plopped herself in one of Gary's overstuffed chairs, surprised he had come back early. "I'm going out with my sister. I promised. Can't your mysterious woman come into the office?"

Gary wanted to get everything for the ad moving. He tossed a pen onto the desk. "She seemed skittish. I didn't want to frighten her off."

"Hmmm. Sounds like an odd one."

"She is, but it's the voice I'm after. Nothing else matters."

"You sure you don't mind if I pass on this one? I hate to, but this thing with my sister…"

"It's fine," he replied, recalling how the soft curves of Mira's body intrigued him. "Mira seems like a nice lady." His voice sounded gruffer than normal.

"Nice isn't the word." Dani frowned. "Stodgy. Straight-laced. The woman needs to realize she isn't ninety-two."

The corner of Gary's mouth twitched. "She's pretty. Why would she think that?"

"Because she can. No one has ever called her on the carpet for it."

"And her baby sister will?"

"Yep." Dani nodded. "I'm working to loosen her up. By the way, what did you think of *her* voice?"

"I…" Gary rubbed his chin. "You know, she's never really talked to me." He shrugged. "Even this morning, she didn't say much. Our run-in stunned her so bad she only mumbled. Why?"

Danielle bit her lip. "Because I think her voice would be perfect. She's spoken across the country on chimp behavior. After one of her local lectures, I overheard some of the male students say they would never miss one of her talks. They would close their eyes and…" She cleared her throat. "Well, they would imagine other things." Her face reddened.

Gary smiled, sure he'd think the same. "I can imagine. You go to all her lectures?"

"Try to." She shrugged. "She's actually one of the coolest ladies I know, once you get past her massive set of defenses. You see, she has this social issue. She's great with lower primates — chimps, monkeys and whatever — but with the higher level of apes — men, to be specific — she turns into a geek. The only guys she's gone out with are dweebs or old men."

His grin deepened. "Defense is good. I understand that game."

Dani glanced at his award. "I heard that."

"You think she'll talk to me? I'm not a dweeb or an old man. Not yet, anyway." He sat up, giving her his full attention, wondering if this would be a good idea.

"Oh yeah. I'll make it happen." She drummed her fingers against her cheek. "How about tomorrow?"

"You're on."

"I'll set the audition up," she said rising and walked out of his office.

*　*　*　*　*

"You are *not* wearing that."

Dani fussed at her again. Her sister stood behind her as Mira stared in the mirror.

"Why not? I thought we were going to get wild. Jeans are the best thing to do that in."

Dani rolled her eyes. "You're exasperating. How do you expect to bait a guy in that thing?"

"I'm not a fishing lure." Mira planted her fists on her hips.

"Argh, look, a deal's a deal. You're about my size. You're going to wear one of my come-on dresses."

"I'm not. I'm nowhere near your size."

"Yes, you are. Besides, this one's a little large on me. It'll fit you perfectly. Now hurry. I made a hair and nail appointment for you."

"You what?"

Dani smirked. "Part of the deal, remember?" She yanked a short, red dress from her closet. "Here. Try this on."

Mira winced as she grabbed the garment. It took a few minutes to change. Dani had a new pair of hose—black—and a pair of pumps that fit her perfectly. With her flat feet, she wondered how long she could stand on the things. She never knew how Dani did it.

A few minutes later, she looked at herself again. Gone were the loose-fitting jeans. Instead, she looked like a woman on the prowl. The neckline dipped to expose her cleavage. The material clung to her ample curves.

"Wow." Dani stood behind her and turned Mira around. "You look terrific."

Mira squeezed her eyes closed. "I look fat."

"No, you don't. You're a fit woman, Mira."

She sighed. "I don't have the right kind of body for this dress. You do."

"Bull. You look great. Come on." Dani threw her purse to Mira. "Let's go. We have fifteen minutes to get to the salon."

"I can't. I...I need to go home and get my jacket. I'll freeze in this skimpy thing." She said a silent prayer, hoping the stall would work.

"You wish. Look, you left your jacket at work, remember? Besides, it's warm out, and even if it does get cold, there's always those great guys who'll offer you their sports coat." Dani wiggled her brows. "Now, come on. Let's go." She handed Mira her purse and rushed to the door. "We're going to be late."

Mira moaned. Taking one last look at herself, she followed her sister. It couldn't get much worse, could it?

* * * * *

Gary stared at his watch and sipped his beer. The dark lager tasted smooth as it rolled down his throat. Nine-thirty passed and the mysterious lady hadn't shown.

"Losing your touch, Roller?" Derek Branson, a lineman with the Denver Broncos, sat down with him, a grin pasted on his face.

Gary tried to think of the last time a woman had stood him up. He couldn't remember. "Guess so. How'd training go?"

Derek nodded. "Good, but God, it gets tougher every year." He stretched his back. "Still missing it?"

"Yeah." He took a drink and stared in the mug as he swirled the few inches of brew left.

"Well, your absence is noted."

Gary huffed. "Even after five years?"

"Never stood next to a better man."

Gary clapped him on the shoulder. "Thanks, Derek."

"I bet you're making almost as much as you would in the pros. And you haven't sacrificed your body. Some woman will appreciate that at some point."

Gary smirked. Little did Derek know. If his knee wasn't bad enough, there was always his...

He refused to dwell on it. "How's Brenda?" Gary asked. Well beyond married, Derek had two boys and another on the way.

"Fine. She's hoping for a girl this time. Says there's too much testosterone in the family. Even our dogs are male."

Gary laughed. "Can't blame her. Sounds like a plan—"

"Wow." Derek cut him short and his attention wandered toward the door. "You know, I'm glad I'm married. Otherwise I'd be in a whole lotta trouble."

Gary looked. Some women were debating whether to enter. He noticed Dani among them. Would Mira be with her? He studied the group, trying to find the dark-haired beauty. If she hadn't been Dani's sister, he'd have asked her out on the spot. He liked something about how those khaki pants fit her.

"Man, give me that brunette any day." Karl Larson, a rookie, came up to them.

"Huh?" Gary turned to him.

"The one in the red dress."

Gary looked again. The women were heading out of the bar, but he caught a glimpse of the brunette hidden behind the rest. *Mira*. Man, did she look different in a dress.

"Hey, doesn't one of those ladies work for you?" Derek pointed to Dani.

"Yeah." Gary gulped the last of his beer.

"Oh man. Introduce me," Karl asked.

"Later." He broke away. "Good luck in the game next week. Gotta go." Gary rushed out of the tavern. Why waste time? His number one voice pick had stood him up. It may have been because the guys were there tonight, celebrating the almost nonexistent break after preseason. It didn't matter. She was unreliable. He needed a talent he could depend on. Didn't Dani say Mira was responsible? If she had a voice that could stir a man like Dani said, he just might have his ticket.

* * * * *

Thank God her friends talked Dani out of going into the sports bar. Mira had spied Gary, and if Dani had seen him, they would never have gotten out of there. That would have been all she needed, being prodded by a bunch of jocks, and what kind of statement would that make to Gary? She needed his help in a professional way, and right now she didn't like the kind of business her image portrayed.

Mira studied the street. The city hosted a midnight arts fair of some kind and the sidewalks were crowded with vendors hawking their wares. The yakking of her friends and the noise from the street reminded her of the ape house. Passing under a streetlight, she caught her reflection in a shop window. The bit of wind tossed her new hairdo around her face, making it stick to her glossy red lips. A man strode by, eyeing her like a side of beef. Why did men do that? She walked faster.

Her foot caught and her body jerked forward, stopping her. She looked down. The heel of Dani's strappy shoe stuck in the grate. She pulled at the sole but the shoe wouldn't budge. The others were getting further ahead. Maybe she could slip away?

"Come on, Mira. We're popping in here for another round," Jo Devereux, her friend and neighbor, yelled.

"Another? Haven't we had enough?" she shouted back. Her friends only waved her on.

She slipped out of the shoe and bent over, pulling it from the grid. Standing too fast, she got a little lightheaded. What was that last drink they had? Sex on the Beach or some such nonsense.

A well-dressed man brushed by her and his hand slid along her derrière. "Dammit." She turned, wanting to punch him. The man winked and hurried by.

Growling, she put on her shoe and walked toward her friends. The others crowded through the doors and she filed in behind them. Inside, Dani ordered a round of drinks. The bartender lined them up and Dani slid a group of three toward her.

"What's this?" She glared at her sister.

"Stoplight shooters. You start with the green. Unless of course…" She downed one. "You want to keep going. Then you end with the green."

"Geez." Mira grabbed the green and sipped it.

"Throw it back, Mira," Jo urged her. "None of us are driving tonight."

She gulped the sweet liquid. "Dani, this is the last drink. I thought you gave up these idiotic binges."

"None of us are drunk. Tipsy, maybe." Danielle giggled.

Mira glared at her.

"Okay, no more," her sister promised. "But the night's still young."

"Young?" She glanced at her watch. It was nearly ten. Her mornings came early. She always went to bed by ten-thirty.

"And I have another idea." When Dani downed her last drink, a dangerous sparkle came into her eyes.

* * * * *

Gary ran down the street looking for Dani in the crowd. People filled the Sixteenth Street Mall, making it difficult to find someone. Luckily, his height gave him an advantage. Still, he couldn't find them. He cut between some of the booths and displays, about ready to give up.

"I don't believe I'm doing this."

He stopped, listening to the sultry voice. It would be perfect.

"Oh Mira, it looks good. 'Romeo, Romeo, where art thou, Romeo?'"

The tinny voice that replied didn't sound like Dani's but how many Miras could there be in Denver?

He ducked around the corner of the tent and went through the opening. Dani stood shoulder-to-shoulder with her friends. They were huddled around something—a piece of sculpture, maybe? The artist, another woman in front of them, moved her arms in circles.

"Oh." One of the ladies, a redhead, noticed him and turned around, exposing the table. On it rested a very nicely formed, real-life buttock. "Hi." The redhead sauntered toward him.

The derriere squirmed. "I'm almost done," the artist said.

Gary looked again. Painted roses adorned the pale skin, the words "Romeo, where art thou?" laced through it. His temperature jumped at least ten degrees.

"This *will* come off, right?" the sexy voice spat out.

"Oh yes, ma'am," the artist replied. "It'll wear off naturally in about six weeks. That's the nice thing about henna. There." The artist made one last stroke. "That's it. Keep it exposed to the air for a few minutes to make sure the dye dries."

The rear end squirmed again and he heard a sigh. The girls chatted with the artist and Gary looked away.

"So, you *are* Romeo, aren't you?" The redhead rubbed her palm along his chest.

He attempted to speak but could only jerk his thumb toward the opening.

The artist looked up. "Whoops."

Gary glanced from the painter to the woman in front of him. "I think I ought to go outside."

A small screech rent the air and Gary looked at where the naked flesh had lain. In its place sat a very angry Mira.

"I, uh, well…" He pointed to the open flap. "I didn't know. I heard the voices." He dropped his arms. "I'm sorry."

"Gary!" Dani bounced up to him. "Oh, don't worry about this. What's a tattoo, even a temporary one, if people don't get to see it? How'd you find us?"

Gary didn't want to take his eyes off Mira, but the look she sent him promised something other than a welcome. "I'd better go."

Dani grabbed his arm. "Come and meet my sister— officially. You remember her, don't you?"

A noose seemed to tighten around Gary's neck. He could smell the sweet liquor on Dani's breath as he let himself be dragged along. "I remember." He nodded and tried to stop his gaze from wandering to Mira's hip. When she yanked down the minuscule dress, he looked into her face. Big mistake. If her eyes could throw daggers, he'd be dead. "Hi," he said.

Mira folded her arms across her chest, causing her cleavage to deepen. He gulped.

"Hello," she clipped out.

"I didn't mean to barge in. The flap was open. I heard your voice and thought I'd stop." The explanation sounded lame, even to him. "I didn't know…" He wiggled his finger at her backside.

The other girls giggled.

Gary cleared his throat. "I would have left but the shock of, well…I couldn't move."

Shock wasn't the word for his sudden shutdown. Only luck allowed him to stand on his own two feet. Who'd have known she'd have such dynamite legs and an inviting behind?

"She looks damn good, don't you think, Gary?" Dani winked at him.

Uncomfortable didn't name what he felt. He didn't want to get caught in one of Dani's schemes, especially one involving her sister. Now what should he say? Anything that came out of his mouth would kill his chance of getting her voice.

"Very nice." He jerked his chin in a nod, not able to think of anything else. He turned to Dani. "Did you set up the meeting?"

She pressed her lips together then wet them with her tongue. "Not yet." Dani looped her arm in his. "Why don't you escort us around? We could use a big, strong guy to chase off the maggots. Mira's attracting all kinds of them."

"I bet," he grumbled, but not softly enough. Mira's scowl grew. He cleared his throat. "I'd love to, if it's okay with your sister."

"Fine." Mira jumped off the table and straightened her clothes. "Keep up." She slung a purse strap over her shoulder and rushed out.

He watched her go. "First down and fumble. I think I lost ten yards."

Dani giggled. "Have faith. Now, come on before she leaves us. Would you mind sticking to her? She's a little upset with me right now."

"Really?" He stuck his hands in his pockets. "I wonder why?"

"Thanks, Gary." She patted him on the arm.

"Welcome."

"Take it slow with her. She's a running game."

"I can do that." He smiled at Dani then hurried out of the tent, the ladies' voices fading as they moved away. He rushed to catch up with them.

* * * * *

"I can't believe it. I'm baring my backside and Dani's boss walks in. Why didn't one of you warn me?" Mira stomped ahead of the pack, her friends right behind. They snickered again.

"Oh Mira, don't sweat it." Jo caught up with her. "If it was me, I'd drop my drawers in a second. God, he's sexy."

With Jo's sleek looks and dazzling red hair, Mira doubted she'd drop her panties for just anyone. The woman never had any problems getting a date, but her friend was more than tipsy. That last drink had done them all in.

Mira rubbed her hip, wondering what possessed her. It had been Dani's idea to get the henna tattoo, but Mira had insisted on the design and location of the supposed artwork—except for the Romeo addition. That too, had been Dani.

She sighed. Mira loved roses, and putting the tat on her hip would let her hide the design, but a declaration for Romeo? What Romeo would come looking for a squirrelly zoologist? She walked faster. She shouldn't denigrate herself, but she'd been doing some weird things lately—like watching those beat-'em-up, bang-bang type movies hoping she could see the hero's naked chest and thinking Gary Staunton would look better than all of them. 'Course, that was only in her dreams, and those she wouldn't *dare* mention to her sister.

She bit her lip. Dani insisted the behavior stemmed from a lack of companionship. Was she lonely? Or was her internal female time clock ticking? "Romeo, Romeo, where the hell are you?"

She stumbled.

Someone's arm came around her and snatched her up before she hit the ground. "You called?"

"Don't tell me." The familiar hold reminded Mira of her earlier collision. She turned and looked into Gary's blue-green eyes. His arms wrapped around her and pulled her close. Mira's breath caught and liquid heat replaced the anger burning inside. The thought itched at the back of her brain that if he hadn't held her, she'd be flat on the ground, as her jellied legs would never support her now. She stared at his strong jaw and resisted the urge to run her fingers over his face. How many times had she fantasized about the tall, built, ex-*football* player?

Too many, she decided and tried to rekindle her ire. Most jocks went for one thing, and that had nothing to do with her brains. Besides, intelligent men were safe.

She backed away. "Romeo? I thought your name was Gary."

"Sweetheart, my name can be anything you want."

"How about butthead?"

He winced. "That hurt."

She grimaced, remembering this was Dani's boss. "Sorry. My mouth tends to get me in trouble."

He stepped so close their bodies touched. "I'm going to see you girls get home. I don't think any of you are in good enough shape to do that. There are too many idiots running around tonight."

"You can say that again." She looked at him for what seemed to be the longest time. What else did she see in his face?

He cleared his throat. "From everything Dani's said, I didn't think you had a wild side."

"I…" She licked her lips. Some perverse side of her didn't want to deny it. "Wild?" She leaned into him. "I'm a zoologist, not a zookeeper. I study the wild, not cage it up." She ran her hand up his ribs and taut torso. "Maybe I have more life in me than you think." She could feel the rise and fall of his chest. Its rhythm came faster. She stood on her toes, wanting to put her lips on his.

Ringgg…

She backed away as he lifted the cell phone to his ear. Her spell broke. What kind of crazy thing did she do now?

"Hello." Gary eyed her under half-closed lids. "So, it's you," he muttered into the phone and covered his other ear.

God, and she'd almost succumbed. This was Dani's boss, for pity's sake. Had she lost her mind?

A small voice inside her brain nagged at her. *So what?*

Gary turned his side to Mira. "The guys pay you more not to come?"

Mira ran her tongue across her lips, trying to think. Gary's mouth parted as he watched her.

Why not? she thought. Could she remember the last time she'd been with a man? And when had she been with one that was so, well…big. Besides, Dani was right. Her last date had been a dud. The guy actually lived with his mother.

Gary juggled the phone between his ear and shoulder and removed his sports coat. He turned his back and her eyes roamed over his body. She got a great view of his well-developed rear and broad shoulders. He flipped the jacket over his arm then faced her, a wicked gleam in his eyes.

"Look, you stood me up."

Stood him up? Did he have a girlfriend?

Of course he did.

"Mira, you are an idiot," she said, convincing herself she'd lost any common sense she'd had left. She looked around for her sister. Farther down the street, the all-female troupe crowded into a cab. They were leaving her.

She glanced at Gary, her nervousness spiking. *Now* what would she do?

Chapter Three

∞

Gary flipped the phone closed and watched the cab pull away. What was Danielle doing? Did she want him to do the interview now?

He looked at Mira shivering under the street lamp, watching her sister and her friends. Gary walked to her and draped his jacket over her shoulders. "Where to?"

She threw her hands in the air. "This is a nightmare. I can't believe they abandoned me."

"What's a nightmare?"

"What? Everything." She slapped her hands against her thighs and paced. "First, this thing with Sara. Then I call Dani, hoping she'd help. Why did I let her talk me into this? Oh, and the drinking…" She stopped and looked at him. "You know I don't approve of that." She threw her hands in the air again and stomped around. "I can't believe it. Plus…" She pointed at him. "I'm getting groped by dirt bags on the street…"

She rambled, although the part about the dirt bags had his ire up. He shoved his hands in his pockets, thinking the tirade may go on a bit. She needed to let this out. How many times had he done the same thing with his older sisters?

"And I'm sorry we didn't come into the bar. I saw you." She frowned. "I don't think Dani did, but I did. I just couldn't handle being looked at like a cheap snack by a bunch of jocks, especially…"

He really liked the way she looked in that outfit. The streetlight shone against what showed of the red dress from underneath his jacket, highlighting her well-formed curves, especially her breasts, which looked soft and inviting beneath the clinging material.

"Then I bare my *behind*, thinking just once I'd do something weird and wild, and what happens? *You* show up. My sister's boss. Jock à la mode. Then, of course, your girlfriend calls you, even if she did stand you up. Geez, could my day get any worse?"

Jock à la mode? He didn't know whether to laugh or be insulted. "How about some coffee?"

"Coffee?" She stopped pacing.

He nodded. "My treat. No dirt bags—promise."

She wiped a large tear off her cheek. "Okay."

He walked toward her and placed his hands on her shoulders. "Look, whatever it is, it'll be all right. And let's get one thing straight. I don't have a girlfriend."

"Not one? Not even a recently passed one?"

"Last time I looked, all my ex-girlfriends were still living."

"Funny." She frowned and teetered a bit. "I probably could use that coffee."

He put his arm around her and pulled her close. "I think I can manage that."

They walked along the mall. If Gary hadn't supported her, she would've been flat on the sidewalk.

"What did you girls have to drink?"

She looked into his hypnotic eyes—at least they seemed hypnotic. She had trouble focusing. "I'm not sure." The sparkling lights on the vendor's cart caught her attention. "We started slooowww—one of those microbrews—then we grad-geated."

"Grad-geated?"

She nodded. "Last time there were three…" She looked at her hand. Did she hold up the right number of fingers? "Shooters."

"Good God, woman. I'm surprised you're standing."

She laid her head on his chest. "You do have a girlfriend, don't you? She stood you up tonight." She lifted her head and ran a hand up his powerful arm. "I'm sorry. I know what it's like to be rejected."

"No, no girlfriend." He put a warm cup in her hands. "Here. Drink this."

"You know, I'm really not like this. Well, normally anyways. You see…"

"Drink." He put a finger under the cup and lifted it to her lips.

The warm java tasted bitter. "No cream?"

"You want cream?"

"And sugar."

He looked at her funny. It made her body burn.

"So, when was the last time you made love to a woman?" God, did she say that?

He coughed as he poured the cream and stirred then gazed at her. Even in her haze, she recognized the yearning in his eyes.

She sipped the coffee again. "Better." The drinks were really kicking her hard. "It's scientific interest, you know. My question."

"Drink some more." His finger lifted the cup again.

She wobbled.

He placed his hands on her waist and steadied her.

Closer. She wanted him closer. She pressed her hips against him.

He swallowed and she fingered his Adams apple when it moved. "You want some coffee?" She held up the cup.

"No." With each word from his low, raspy voice, the want in his eyes deepened.

She ran a hand along his cheek. "Thanks for staying with me."

"No problem," he whispered, his face much closer.

She cradled the coffee against her breast and leaned into him. Closing her eyes, she did the unthinkable.

She kissed him.

Her senses reeled. His spicy aftershave tickled her nose. His chin sported a hint of stubble. His warm lips thickened with desire.

She was lost.

She delved the tip of her tongue into his mouth then ran it along the edge of his lips. He moaned and pulled the cup away. His arms came around her and held her body flush with his.

He took over the kiss, his touch a mixture of tenderness and strength. She reveled in it. Her body grew hot, alive. Something she hadn't sensed in years. Her knee lifted, as if it had a will of its own. She ran it along the inside of his thigh.

"God, woman, you're killing me."

She rubbed her hips against him, feeling the length of him harden, and ran her hand along his erection.

"Jesus." He covered her fingers with his. "I thought you were the tame sister."

She laughed, exhilarated, the heady sensation making her realize he wanted her. "Get me out of the zoo, and look what happens." She gazed into his face. "Haven't you ever, just once, wanted to break out of the mold life put you in?"

His gaze grew intense. "Mira, you don't know what you're saying."

"Yes, I do. I want you. One night of wild, passionate sex." She paused. "You are healthy, aren't you?"

"Very." His mouth crushed against hers and he moaned. His lips traveled to her temple. He kissed the soft spot then looked at her. "The first time I make love to you, I want you to remember everything I do—everything that happens between your body and mine. As much as I want this—need it—I'm not going to. You aren't sober."

Erotic thoughts crossed her muddled senses, stimulating her already keyed up libido. "You...you do want me, don't you?"

He laughed. "Honey, you don't know how much."

She backed away, confused, trying to regain her equilibrium. "What makes you think you'll get another chance?"

He gave her his "I know you want me, baby" smile. "I will."

Her body trembled, need and anger fueling her. Did he tease her, trying to make a fool of her before they became intimate? She walked off. She wouldn't let that happen again.

He ran to catch her. "You're mad at me."

"That's not the word I'd use."

"Okay. What word would you use?"

"Look." She spun on him. "I don't ask just anybody to bed, you know. In fact, I've *never* asked anybody."

"Then why me? Why tonight?"

"Because, I..." She waggled her finger at him. "Ohhhh."

He grasped her hand. "I'd bet it's the drink making you do this. You've been caged up with those chimps for too long."

"I have not."

"You need a break, Mira. But if we did what you want, you'd wake up tomorrow hating me."

"I would not."

"Yes, you would. You don't understand this yet, but I can't afford a one-night stand with you."

"You can't?"

"No." A corner of his mouth turned upward. "Tell you what. Come out with me tomorrow night and I'll explain everything."

"A date?"

He paused. "Yeah."

"I…"

He kissed her, deep and hard, his body flush against hers. She could feel his desire pulse against her. "Tomorrow night?"

She backed away, trying to figure out what messed with her mind. A date with Gary Staunton?

Her stomach rumbled, interrupting her thoughts. She barely made it to a nearby tree before the last of her dinner hit the dirt.

He came up behind her. "I hope that wasn't your final answer." He held onto her until the wave of nausea passed.

Mira braced her hands on the tree and straightened. Examining her wet dress, she realized she'd landed some of the mess on his jacket. She wiped her mouth with the back of her hand and looked at him. "I'm sorry."

Half a grin came on his face. "It's okay. I'm used to sexy women getting sick of me."

"I doubt that."

He pulled out an old-fashioned hanky.

"You're kidding." She leaned over to look at it.

"Nope. Mom always insisted. Never got out of the habit. Besides…" He wiped her off. "It comes in handy sometimes. Like now."

When he finished, he took her arm. "Come on. I'm going to take you to my place. It isn't far. You can clean up there."

"Your place?" The fear and excitement combo gripped her again. They were becoming a duo, sorta like Batman and Robin.

"Yeah." His voice had been soft and even, but the look he gave her said he wouldn't take no for an answer.

Did she want to argue?

"Okay." She nodded, unsure but willing, and wondered if she really wanted the night to end.

* * * * *

He'd handed her one of his shirts and a pair of shorts, figuring he could tie the waist of the shorts long enough to make it to her place. The shower still ran and if he didn't hear from her in a few minutes, he would break the door down to make sure she was okay. He let his head fall back against the sofa, wondering what the hell had happened. He certainly hadn't meant to kiss her, but damn, she played him—played him like a pro. He was a normal red-blooded man. Of course he reacted. What the hell did he expect?

So why did he promise her one night of erotic passion? Especially when he knew he wouldn't do it.

The fire in his blood rose another notch. He knew why. Her body.

Frustrated, he ran a hand through his hair. He liked Mira, what little he knew of her. She was different, far different from her sister. In fact, the two didn't even look alike. Dani was blonde and slight, Mira a built brunette. He liked brunettes. He'd like to run his hands through her long, dark hair.

Admit it, Gary. He'd been thinking too much about the sexy zoologist. Maybe because she *was* different? Intelligent— obviously. Vulnerable—definitely. Perhaps those qualities hooked him. He liked the innocence surrounding her, the sincerity that tempted him. It'd been a long time since he'd been around a woman who thought about more than how her makeup looked and what clothes she wore.

Whatever the attraction was, he'd had dreams since he met her, with a rating way beyond triple X. Yeah, it'd been a while since he'd had sex—there were too many things that could happen in a casual affair, and he didn't plan on catching any of them—but he'd always wondered about the fire he thought boiled under Mira's cool exterior.

Now he knew. Or, at least, he thought he did. Drink made people do strange things. "Damn." His below-the-belt companion started to get ideas again. He couldn't stand the pain and stood to walk it off.

She was Dani's sister. Maybe someone he would work with in the coming weeks. They were on a deadline for this spot. There's no way he would blow this.

Of course, afterward...

He grunted. It wouldn't work, couldn't. He rubbed his knee and knew he would never saddle a woman like Mira with the half of a man he had become. If anything did develop between them, Mira would get hurt because he'd leave, not wanting the relationship to linger and fester. Or his ego would take a hit again. She'd leave after seeing his injuries. He didn't think he could withstand the bruising.

No, a shallow life in the romance department suited him. After what Darlene had done to him, he wouldn't risk his heart again.

Besides, Dani made a great assistant. She'd make a great ad exec someday. Showing more than a passing interest in her sister might not sit well with his protégé. When Mira got hurt, Dani would leave. He wouldn't risk losing his potentially best ad exec for a passing sexual interest. His business would suffer. He couldn't tolerate that. He'd excluded failure from his vocabulary. He rubbed his knee again. It always reminded him he'd learned his lesson the hard way.

He took a deep breath to steady his nerves. He'd make sure Mira dressed and would get her home pronto. Then tomorrow, they'd talk.

The water stopped. He looked at the bathroom door. Within minutes, Mira came out, dressed in the ridiculous garb. Strands of her upswept hair fell around her face. Her color didn't look good. "Why don't you sit down? I'll get you some tea."

"Tea?" Her body wavered and she loosened whatever binding held her hair. The tresses floated to her shoulders and the wildness of them stirred him.

Steeling himself against his physical reaction, he grabbed Mira and sat her on the sofa, focusing on her care. "Yeah. I actually drink the stuff. Maybe some peppermint tea will soothe your stomach."

She nodded and he rushed into the kitchen. "How long have you been at the zoo?" He put a cup of water in the microwave.

"Five years." Her voice sounded weak. "I interned there."

"Interned?" Stick to the small stuff, he thought. It's safer. "I bet interning is like being a rookie."

"I guess. It's a little longer. Aren't you only a rookie one year?"

Good. Keep her talking. "Sure. You know, I had the best stats for a rookie in the NFL? The following year I led in sacks. 'Course, I crashed my knee the season after that."

She grunted.

He pulled a tea bag out and looked at the timer. *Fifty-six seconds.* "That had been a killer season for sure. Don't know what I would have done if I hadn't stumbled onto an old friend. He pointed me toward advertising. Been doing it ever since."

"Hmmm."

"It's a good business." The bell dinged. He pulled out the cup and dunked the tea bag in it. "Dani's good at it too. A natural. I really see her making the distance."

Silence.

He peeked out the door and didn't see her. Dumping the bag in the trash, he rushed the hot cup out to her.

She'd slumped against the side pillow of the sofa. "Mira?" He put the cup down and checked her breathing. It was steady.

Mira moaned once and snuggled her head against his hand. Her hair draped over his fingers. Yeah, the strands were nice. And that wasn't all. An open button near the top of the shirt exposed the silky skin of her breast. If he stood here too long, he would get a cramp—in the wrong place. "Okay, Gary. Cut it." Horny thoughts he didn't need.

"Mira?" He shook her once. She slept. Now what would he do?

Her cheeks had paled and he wondered if he should move her. He glanced at his bedroom then at her.

Take her home, dammit. What was he thinking? She couldn't sleep here.

He moved his fingers, trying to free them, but they caught in the soft tendrils. Her hand caressed his forearm then she draped it over his arm, tossing her body and giving him an even better view. A dusky nub peeked out from the shirt, as if begging to be kissed.

He groaned. "Forget it." Picking her up, he cradled her in his arms. He had no idea where she lived and his tired body ached. "Face it, Gary. If you take her home, she won't talk to you in the morning. She'll be too damned embarrassed."

On the other hand, if she stayed in his bed, she'd have to talk to him, wouldn't she?

He stared at her. Guilt drove women to do strange things. He'd seen it in his sisters.

She stirred, purring as she snuggled against his chest. "That's it," he muttered and took her into the bedroom, thinking this may work to his advantage. After all, they didn't have much time, and he'd already fumbled once.

He laid her on the unmade bed and removed the baggy shorts, letting himself admire what he could see beneath her lacy underwear. He left the shirt on. He wouldn't dare mess with it. Another peek at what lay underneath would drive him crazy. Swallowing, he tucked her in and paused to study his handiwork, hoping like hell this might work. She slept soundly, a good sign she'd sleep it off without any problems. Walking out, he partially closed the door, wanting to hear her in case she did get sick again.

Although late evening, his body tautened like a bowstring. He stared at the only option left to him. The couch. Looking back at the bedroom door, he grumbled. The solid sofa didn't look anywhere near as inviting. "This better work."

He grabbed a blanket and plopped on the cushions, his feet sticking over the edge. Now, if he could get some sleep, maybe the night wouldn't be a total bomb.

Closing his eyes, he tried to rest, but a certain part of him would only let him think of Mira.

* * * * *

Her eyes hurt. She hadn't even opened them and they hurt. She thought for sure a drum beat in her brain. The steady rhythm pounding behind her eyeballs clued her in.

"God, what did I do?" Her eyelids were swollen shut. She rubbed them and forced her lids open, blinking as they broke apart. Sitting up, she glanced around. Where was she?

The noise of clanging pans brought her back to reality. She'd been with Gary. Threw up on his clothes if she remembered right. Now she slept in his bed? She glanced briefly under the covers. Bare to the bone, except for her underwear. The shirt she had worn lay on the floor and the shorts were folded and stacked on the dresser. "Oh God," she moaned and plopped her head back on the pillows. What had she done?

The memory came back to her like a freight train. She'd come on to him. Didn't he say no? She buried her face in the pillow. The fabric smelled like him. "Guess not."

The door made a small squeak when it opened. "You okay?" Gary's voice floated through.

She pulled the pillow over her head. "Probably not."

His deep chuckle rumbled. "You'll feel better after you eat, if you can."

She couldn't look at him. "You mind telling me what happened last night?" She changed her mind and peeked out. He'd dressed in boxers, just boxers, and almost every sculpted inch of him showed. Did she breathe?

His brawny arms crossed and he leaned against the doorjamb—smiling, of course.

"Oh God. Never mind." She released the edge of the pillow she held, causing everything to go dark. "I don't want to know."

"Why?" His voice sounded closer. The bed sunk under his weight.

She peeked out again. "Because I think I'll hate myself."

He lifted the pillow. "And here I thought you'd hate me."

She swallowed and looked at him. "Why would I hate you? I'm the one who asked. You just accommodated."

"Accommodated?"

He looked confused. She covered her eyes, embarrassed. "I hope we used a condom, assuming we got that far." She looked at him again. "You are responsible in that department, aren't you?"

His brows arched. "Very, look…"

"Just tell me one thing." She pulled the sheet to her chin and propped herself on her elbow. "I wasn't that bad, was I?"

He closed his eyes and touched his forehead as if he had a headache. Then he started to laugh. "You don't remember anything?"

She shook her head. "Last thing I remember was lying on the couch."

He brushed her cheek with the back of his fingers. "Would you believe me if I told you nothing happened?"

She lifted the sheet and peered at her nude body again. "No." She covered herself.

He looked at the floor then at her. "You had my shirt on when I put you to bed."

"Yeah, I bet." She clicked her tongue.

He laughed and studied his hands. His lip jutted out when he looked at her. "Did you have fun last night?"

"No." She'd almost cut him off before he finished. "I mean…" She dropped back against the pillow. "I have no idea."

The baby-you-love-me grin came on his face again. Her body flushed with embarrassment.

"My offer from last night is still open. How about I take you out tonight, and we talk about it?"

"Tonight?" She arched her brows. "You want to take me out?"

He nodded. "Believe it or not, Mira, I find you fascinating. And I need your help."

"My help? But, I'm…supposed to be doing wild things with my sister."

He leaned nearer and placed both his hands on either side of her, studying her. "What if I help out? We can do wild things together."

Her libido went nuts. She coughed, trying to buy time. He came *way* too close. "Why would you want to?" She inched farther under the sheet, trying to regain control of her faithless body.

He inched closer. "Mira, we're adults. What's wrong with us getting to know each other?" He eyed her. "I promise we won't do anything you don't want."

She licked her lips.

Longing came into his eyes again and he kissed her. Slow. The tip of his tongue painted her lips then delved briefly inside.

She let him. God, did she let him. In that second, she'd have let him do anything he wanted.

When he pulled away, she heard herself moan.

"Tonight, then?"

His baby blues pierced the shredded armor she'd welded around her sex drive. Blood rushed to her head and she couldn't think.

"Mira?"

Instead of speaking, she nodded like a spring-loaded doll.

He grinned and kissed her neck. "I'll pick you up at seven. Why don't you get dressed? I have breakfast waiting for you." He paused. "I'll have an aspirin waiting for that headache too."

He left, closing the door on the way out. She inched herself up and looked at the oversized shirt on the floor.

Okay, so what *did* happen?

* * * * *

Nothing. Nothing happened.

Gary marched into the tall office building, which housed his office, almost running into a crowd coming out. He apologized and moved on, his thoughts jumbled. He wanted to tell Mira the truth, but something stopped him from an all-out push to convince her. Maybe because he didn't know how much of "nothing" was true. Something did happen—to him.

The thought pestered him after he'd dropped her off at her place. His jaw clenched. Yeah, he'd kissed her, even held her tight. And the view…

"Oh Christ." He took a breath to steady himself. He hadn't touched her, not in the biblical sense anyway. But he wanted to. God, how he wanted to.

He ran a hand through his hair. He figured she'd gotten hot during the night and stripped. That had to be it because as much as he wanted to see what hid under that shirt, he sure as hell didn't walk in his sleep and take it off. Fact was, he'd grown hot during the night too, and he'd made certain to keep his clothes on. Once naked, the temptation to crawl in bed with the beauty would have killed him.

He exhaled and tried to relax. Much as he wanted to, tossing around in the sheets with Mira wouldn't be a good business decision. A good businessman didn't let anything jeopardize a major project. And he was a good businessman. This was the game for him, the Super Bowl of advertising. He intended to win.

He hit the elevator button and glanced at his watch. His body still thrummed with sexual tension. Dani had better be in because the longer he waited to talk to her, the more of his mind he'd make her hear.

* * * * *

Exhausted, Mira sat and studied the chimp area. Her world had become very weird. She couldn't quite put her finger on why, but it had something to do with Gary and whatever happened last night.

He'd promised to tell her. At dinner. She was nervous. If he kissed her again, would her body betray her?

Would she even go?

She growled at her stupidity. What *had* she done? And was it really so bad? She was a normal woman with needs. Needs sometimes had to be fulfilled. She could accept that. So why not fulfill them with someone she found attractive?

Because he was a jock and jocks only cared about their own egos. And boy, did they talk. Even if what they said wasn't true. She'd found that out the hard way. Would all his locker-room buddies know?

She hoped not. She needed to talk to some of them about Sara. God, she prayed the man had some integrity—the kind of honor that would keep his trap shut about whatever happened.

But had something happened? Somehow, she trusted Gary to tell her. Why, she didn't know. But why wouldn't he? He hadn't been quite the Casanova-devil she'd imagined. At least she learned that much over breakfast.

They'd talked about trivial things. Family life, what she did at the zoo. Small stuff. He didn't acknowledge her slip into sensuality the night before, and for that, she was grateful.

Before she woke up, he'd even called her in sick. His chivalry had impressed her. She'd never found musclemen to accomplish heroic actions.

She called her work later to tell them she would only be late instead.

Looking around the cage, she realized she needed to be here now more than ever. Not just for Sara. She needed the familiar place. Last night had been too different for her to feel comfortable, but even now, she sensed something wrong, something missing.

One thing she could identify, though. Guilt. That and the drink still kicking her gut.

"So, who's the guy?"

Candy's question pulled her from her daydreaming. The zookeeper had taken Gary's call. That she wasn't grateful for. The zoo loved rumors, and Candy was an expert at them.

"A friend."

"Sure." Candy winked at her. "Never heard that friend's voice before. Deep and sexy." She shook. "Gave me chills all over."

Mira sighed with exasperation. "Trust me, it's nothing. Nothing I want to think about anyway."

Candy giggled. "Yeah. So why are you sitting here staring into space? Doc, you need to lighten up. If you have a man in your life, I'm glad. As much time as you spend with these apes, you deserve it. And don't worry about me. I won't say anything to anybody."

"I don't have a man."

Candy held her palm up. "Okay, Doc. I won't say another word. By the way…" She held up Mira's jacket. "I found it this morning. Sara slept with it."

"I wondered where I'd left it." She took the coat and felt the pocket for the cell phone. "Well, I guess my sister will be happy. Her old phone is still here." She pulled it out.

Candy shook her head as she swept the cement walk. "I don't know why you don't keep the phone turned on. She gave it to you so you could use it."

"Then I'd have to recharge the battery all the time and wait for more badgering calls from Dani. No thanks. Besides, I don't even really know how to use the dang thing. Give me biology over technology any day."

Candy leaned on the broom. "Heck, give it to me if you don't want it. I could use another one."

Mira let herself laugh. "No, better not. Dani would have a fit."

"Then do you want me to show you how to use it? It'll only take a second." Candy grasped the phone. "Look." She pressed a few buttons. "These tell you who called last." She pushed the button again and a list of numbers popped up. "I think this one programs."

The number at the top of the list looked familiar. Had it been the cell number Gary gave her? It resembled Dani's but the last digit ended with a one not a five. "I'm sure those are Dani's work numbers." Mira dropped the idea of finding out whose numbers they were, not wanting to talk to Gary by mistake.

"You want to put some new numbers in?" Candy asked.

The phone rang and saved her. Since Mira didn't like to use the thing, instruction didn't rank high on her "to do" list. She couldn't care less about the whole button sequence thing. She took the phone back and pressed talk. "Hello?"

"There you are. I've been trying to get you all day."

Dani. Mira rolled her eyes. "Really? Because I don't think I'm talking to you right now, especially after you left me."

"Oh, come on. You were in good hands."

Mira wondered how good they'd actually been. She cleared her throat. "What did you want?"

"I wanted to find out about last night, of course. How did it go?"

"How did *what* go?"

"Well, either your date or your audition. I don't care which."

"Audition?"

"Didn't Gary explain it?"

"Explain what?" Mira's irritation raised another notch.

"Your voice. Using it for this spot we're doing. I told you about it. Your voice will be on a national ad. Isn't that the bomb?"

"What?" She'd forgotten about the ad. Is that why he wanted her? And here she thought he might have been interested in her personally. Fury lit into her like a fire. "You're kidding."

"Nope. And you can do it too. Your voice is sexy as hell. You'll be perfect."

"Well, somehow Mr. Macho forgot to mention it."

"I can't imagine why." Dani giggled. "I think your looks blew him away."

"Right," she spat.

"Mira, you don't realize how attractive you are. He would. Trust me, he's all male. He noticed big time. So what happened?"

"How would I know? I could hardly remember my name after those drinks you shoved down my throat."

"Oh c'mon. Tell all. I know Gary's interested."

Mira huffed. "Interested in what? My body? Aren't you concerned about that? You act like you have this hot thing for him."

"Me? Absolutely not. He's my boss and I love him like a brother. But that's as far as it goes. He's too conservative for me. In fact, he's more like you."

"Me? We have nothing in common."

"Mira, you have two feet, two hands—and no one in your sex life. You have that in common." She sighed. "You know, he asks about you all the time. And quite frankly, I think you have a thing for him too."

"I do not. And since you aren't interested in him I guess you won't care that I slept with him last night. I hope that's wild enough for you."

"What?"

"Bye, Dani. Give Gary my love, especially since I won't be seeing him again—ever." She punched the button, turning the phone off before Dani could say another word.

The nerve. Telling Dani he needed her voice when his interest lay in...

She looked up and found Candy staring at her. "What?"

"Nothing." Candy raised her brows and bit her bottom lip. It still didn't stop the upturned corners of her mouth.

Mira shoved the phone in her pocket. Now rumors about her "affair" would be everywhere, if such a thing actually happened. But did it? Gary said nothing did. If that's the case, how did she wake up almost totally naked and in his bed?

"The big deceitful jerk," she fumed, mumbling under her breath while she tried to put a wall around her insecurities. No way would she meet with him now, but how could she get out of it? And how would she ever know the truth?

She gritted her teeth, knowing she couldn't avoid the meeting. She needed Gary right now, at least to keep Sara safe, and he needed her, at least for this ad.

Sara swooped down from a tree branch and picked her pocket, pulling out the phone. The chimp handed the thing to her.

"Thanks, girl." She took it and rubbed Sara's head. "I wish you'd keep it. It's caused me more problems than what it's worth."

The chimp moaned and Mira picked her up. She showed Sara the dialing pad. "See this? This modern marvel is the bane of my existence. You're my friend. You could at least lose it for me."

Sara oooo'ed at her as if in reply. Mira smirked. If she did lose the thing, it would put Dani in a tizzy. She'd *never* be able to get a hold of her, and…

The idea struck like lightning. "Candy, you've done the major cleanup for this week, haven't you?"

"Yeah, why?" The zookeeper stopped sweeping and leaned on the broom.

"I think we should minimize contact with the chimps for a while. Maybe Sara will calm down."

Candy's mouth quirked. "But she doesn't bother us. It's the guys she comes in contact with she keeps hitting on."

"Yes, but we're menstruating females. There isn't another one in the cage. Maybe something about it is what's upsetting her."

Candy gave her a look that said she didn't believe any of it. "Whatever you say. By the way…" She finished sweeping then pointed to her cell phone. "You better watch that thing. I think Sara's been playing with it."

"Sara?"

"I know it sounds weird, but it's this gut feeling I have." Candy finished and left with the broom.

"Sara, have you been playing with my phone?"

The chimp moaned.

"Good girl. Break it next time, okay?"

Sara aahhh'ed.

Mira doubted the chimp would want to mess with the electronic marvel. The phone made too much noise and it didn't taste good. She scanned the rafters. "Okay, where should I hide this?"

Sara eeked and pointed to the tree.

Mira looked. A hole in the trunk faced the wall. "Perfect."

She set Sara down and went to study the defect in the tree. The gap opened just enough. She popped the phone inside and covered it with some leaves. "This'll learn you, sis. You want something wild? Just watch your elder. Between you, me and Mr. Staunton, wild will have a new meaning."

She brushed off her hands, thinking the phone would be safe until she needed it again. Dani would turn the rest of Mira's life upside down looking for the cell phone, except for this world at the zoo. Now, Mira needed to make herself unavailable for a while until she put a plan in place—one including the elusive Gary Staunton. She'd find out what had happened last night one way or another, and on her own terms.

One by one, Mira thought of the Dani-type things she could do—without Dani. The more she wrapped Gary Staunton within them, the better. He had wanted her last night, said he'd help her. Why not use his desires to her advantage? Having him along would nix the need for Dani to be present and make things even worse with her meddling. Gary could verify what Mira did and report her activities back to Dani, and bingo, her sister would be out of Mira's personal life and Mira would still be able to complete the deal.

Mira let the smug sense of satisfaction roll over her. The football he-man wanted a voice.

She'd give him one—for a price.

Chapter Four

ℬ

Gary stopped at Danielle's office and peered through the open door. She was talking on the phone. Figures.

He waved at her, telling her to come see him when she got finished.

Nodding, she mouthed "okay". She smiled and he didn't like the gleam in her eyes.

He stomped off. What had she been thinking? Last night he fumbled in the end zone. He'd recovered, he thought, but Mira doing the piece would be a long shot. If she didn't, he'd have to settle for something less. Otherwise, how were they going to get the ad done on time?

He greeted Laura, the receptionist, and walked into his office, shutting the door. He would take Mira out tonight and spill his guts. Everything. Well, almost everything. He wouldn't tell her he'd lain awake all night thinking about her. She'd been liquid heat in his arms and when he'd touched her sweet lips…

He grunted and sat behind his desk, not wanting to think about the way her body molded into his. Mira was one of those classy ladies who should have a guy to take her places—opera, lectures. Someone secure in his profession, a man with whom she could have a family. Not some guy with half his testicles. Not that he couldn't function, reproductively that is. The doctors had told him he could have children. But from his experience, he was sure no woman would believe that. They were too put off by the scars and missing equipment.

"My, we're running late today, aren't we?" Danielle stuck her head in the door.

Gary glared at her. "You mind telling me what went through your perky brain last night? Mira was drunk as hell."

She bopped in and closed the door. "Hmmm, maybe I should apologize, but by the way you looked at her I didn't think you'd mind."

He paused. "You set me up?"

"Well—" She squirmed. "Yeah." She bobbed her head. "My sister too."

"I like your sister. You ought to watch the type of creeps you put her with."

"You're not a creep."

"I'm not the guy I was five years ago either."

"And what's that supposed to mean?"

"I lost my knee, Danielle. And my career. Mira deserves better."

"Bah, you have a new knee." She leaned on his desk. "Gary, if you'd lost your whole leg you'd still be the sexiest thing in town. As far as your career, you're the president and owner of a very successful company."

"So?"

She shrugged. "I think you and Mira look good together. You didn't seem to mind being near her last night."

"I don't mind being near her, she's..." He swallowed. "An attractive woman. Have you forgotten we have an ad to do?"

She straightened. "Look, if it works for you guys, great. If not, fine."

"That isn't the point."

She pursed her lips. "Okay, scratch my first stint at matchmaking. Maybe I'm not so good at it."

"That's for damn sure. It's bad enough you mess with your sister's life but to mess with mine..." He stood and leaned on the desk, towering over her.

"Oh, come on, Gary." She eyed him dead on. "You like her. Admit it. You want to get to know her better—well, other than enjoying the comforts of her body. I can't think of any reason why you shouldn't."

"Danielle, you've lost it."

"I'm your friend." She got in his face. "And I tell things like I see it. You know that. I love my sister. She wants you and you want her. What's wrong with that? So tell me…" She sat and snuggled back against the chair. "What *did* happen last night? Other than you slept with my sister."

"I didn't." He thought he might be blushing, but he couldn't be sure. He'd never done it before. "She just thinks I did. Whatever else happens between us is none of your business."

"How can she think you did?"

He grimaced. "She passed out on my couch and I put her to bed."

"So you made moves on her."

"No, I… Well, I didn't try to. She didn't make it easy."

Danielle laughed. "Good for her. This is working."

"What's working?"

"Nothing." She smiled like the Cheshire cat.

"Look, Danielle. We have a spot to do and I want to use Mira's voice. We're having dinner tonight and I'm going to talk to her about it. Until then, keep your paws out of this. You know what this job means to the firm and to me."

"I know, but I think you might have a problem."

"Why?"

"I mentioned the ad to her this morning. She says she's never talking to you again."

"Oh God." He plopped in the chair, dragging his hand across his face. "What did you say?"

"I just asked her about last night." She shrugged.

"And what exactly did you ask?"

She smiled. "To tell me about her date or her interview. I didn't care which."

He grunted. "Her date? Good lord." He rubbed his head. "Now what are we supposed to do? We need her talent."

"You're going to have dinner with Mira. You need to figure out how to get her to go out with you. I've got some calls to make. Besides not all my cards are played. Mira will do it. She has to."

"Why?"

"Because you're going to use your influence to help her to keep her chimp."

* * * * *

Danielle left Gary with his mouth gaping. Closing the door, she walked back to her office, worried. An upset Mira would sink into social oblivion and Danielle couldn't afford the pain of seeing her sister become a recluse again. Did Mira regret what she thought happened with Gary?

Danielle hoped not. She knew Mira liked him, but jocks like Gary were piranhas to her. Sitting behind her desk, she plopped her chin in her palms and glanced at the pictures she kept there. The one of Mira receiving her doctorate seemed to glare at her. Danielle frowned and turned the picture facedown. She didn't need more derision from her sister, especially from a photo. Instead, she looked to the family picture where they were young kids. Her older sister had her arm around her shoulders and they were smiling. Mira had always been good to her. Helped her with homework, made her feel good about herself. Now she wanted to return the favor and make Mira felt good about Mira. Her sister was a beautiful woman. How many guys had told Mira they desired her? She wanted her sister to like attractive men. Nice attractive men, anyway. Even touching a good-looking guy started Mira in the right direction. After last night, she'd been sure Mira had touched Gary, several times. Didn't he say she hadn't made it easy?

Unsure of her judgment, Danielle still made moves to get them together. So far her efforts only worked this once. But they liked each other. What could be wrong? And she trusted Gary. Trusted his judgment. He was a gentleman, a big guy with an even bigger heart. If things clicked for them, he would do right by her. She wanted to give the two of them a chance.

Fingering the picture, she stared at Mira. Social boundaries were a real thing for her. In high school, some crappy football player had embarrassed her sister. A few years older than Mira, he had been her first date. They'd gone somewhere after school. Something happened. Danielle didn't know the specifics but she'd been old enough to realize the jerk and what happened became the crux of Mira's problem. Hurtful things escalated afterward. Mira became a wallflower. Then their father died. That had been a bad year.

She touched the photo of Mira's face. A "significant event" is what her psychology professors would have called what happened. Before she'd stumbled onto that tidbit of science, her primary target had been having fun, but Mira's problem grounded her. She loved her sister, and she didn't like seeing her embarrassed in male-female relationships. Mira needed to get over whatever happened almost fifteen years ago.

"Okay, Danielle, what next?" she mumbled and tapped the panel of glass on the photo. She had to keep Mira moving. Just being with Gary last night signaled a good start. Yeah, she cared about the ad piece, Gary being so damn particular. But they could find someone else. He just didn't see it that way — yet. And he probably wouldn't need to. Mira would do the piece. Danielle was sure of that. Of course, his mysterious stranger could do the job, if needed.

Danielle took a breath. She played a dangerous game with Mira and her boss. Gary usually dated these stuck-up, ditzoid chicks. Women who Danielle thought only cared about his money and prestige. Cold as ice ladies who pursued him with gusto until they got the pleasure he offered. The ones wanting more, Gary cut off, as if knowing what their scheme had been. She shivered, remembering the last frigid one. The woman stormed into the office, looking for her "fiancé". Gary cleared her out, fast. She'd never seen the woman again.

Frustrated, Danielle stared at Mira's picture. Her boss and close friend needed a good woman in his life, not these crazy chicks. Gary wouldn't like her meddling, but what choice did she have? High rewards often required significant risks. For Mira's and Gary's happiness, she'd pay the price.

She glanced at her watch. Ten o'clock. Maybe Mira would meet her for lunch? She could explain last night before her sister's imagination got out of hand.

She lifted the receiver to her desk phone, tapping her pencil while the phone rang.

"We're sorry, but the party you are dialing has moved out of the calling area or has reached their destination. If you would like to leave a message…"

"Damn." She hung up. Mira must have turned the phone off.

She heard footsteps coming down the hall then Gary appeared in her doorway. "I'm going out."

"Out? I thought you needed to coordinate with the studio?"

"You can handle the details. I want to find your sister and explain things to her. We'd planned to have dinner tonight and I, for one, am still counting on it. She is at the zoo, isn't she?"

Danielle nodded.

He took a step away then stopped. "I'd appreciate it if you didn't call her. I'd like to handle this myself."

"Yes, sir." She grinned as he walked away, quite pleased. "It is working," she mumbled and picked up the cast-off picture of Mira. She giggled, thinking this progressed much better than she'd ever dreamed. "Sis, you definitely have the brains, but let's see how you do against the sexiest brawn in town."

* * * * *

"What's this?" Mira stared at the list Charlie Burrows put in her hand.

"The zoos interested in buying Sara." Charlie adjusted his glasses and all five feet four inches of him squirmed. "I thought you might want to see those inquiring, since you're interested in Sara's wellbeing."

She glanced at the first name on the list. "Abilene?" her voice rose. "You've got to be kidding. What kind of a zoo is that?"

"A very fine one. Granted, it's small—"

"I bet they don't have the space the chimps need—"

"But adequate." Charlie glared. "They have giraffes and other large game."

"I thought I had a month?" She shook the paper at him.

"You do." He bobbed his head.

"Then why the list?" She stuffed the pad under his nose.

"I...I have to plan. With Sara's problems, we may be hard pressed to find someone who wants her."

"We want her, Charlie. The Denver zoo. Her problems aren't insurmountable."

"But..." He waved his hands in the air. "She jumps on every man who goes into the cage and...and tries to..."

"Kiss them?" She arched a brow.

He tsked. "Miranda, you know keeping her isn't possible."

"Keeping her is possible, and I'm going to prove it."

"How?" He shrugged. "The board members understand, at least most of them. And the city needs a top-notch zoo."

"We have an excellent zoo. Yes, the grounds could be bigger, but—"

"We need to raise the zoo's standards and new attractions keep the public coming."

"Like Denver needs more attractions."

"It does. Ask the mayor. We compete for tourist dollars with places like Washington D.C., Portland, San Diego—"

"San Diego? We'll never be a San Diego. That zoo is world renowned." She fisted her hands. "Besides San Diego is beaches, we're mountains. There's a difference."

"That's not the point."

She slammed the list on her desk. "What's one more chimp, Charlie?"

His face turned red. "You know my role. I need to make sure our funding is secure. The money we generate must cover our expenses. There are other animals needing care and people to pay to take care of them, including you. Whether you want to accept the facts or not, we have enough chimps for a good attraction. With Sara's departure, we'll have the additional funds necessary to bring those white tigers here for a year and still have some left over." He crossed his arms. "Sara needs to go."

"Come on, Charlie, get off it. What is this, a game? See who has the fanciest, most exotic zoo in the country? If so, you're right. Sara doesn't fit here. And maybe neither do I." She tossed the list in the trash and clenched her fists.

His eyes opened like saucers.

She didn't think she acted that intimidating, until she heard someone clearing their throat behind her. Turning, she saw Gary standing in the doorway. His body took up the whole doorframe. She glanced back at Charlie. His mouth gaped open as if he were catching flies, and his eyes riveted—probably at how close Gary's head came to the top of the doorframe. If she hadn't been so angry, she would have laughed at the sight of the diminutive administrator.

"Ca-can we help you, sir?" Charlie stuttered.

"Sure." Gary slid his hands in his pockets. "I'm here to see about a chimp. Sara, I believe her name is if I overheard you right. I understand she's for sale. My source told me to talk to a Doctor Harper. That you?"

Charlie shook his head like a rattle. "No, no, but I'm the one you need to talk to. I'm Doctor Burrows." He held out his hand and approached Gary.

Gary took the outstretched palm and shook Burrow's hand once. "I'd like to see the chimp first, if that's okay. Maybe this young lady can escort me."

"Oh, oh absolutely." Charlie held up his hands and looked at her. "Doctor Harper, would you be so kind?"

She crossed her arms. "The chimp isn't for sale—" She glared at Charlie. "Yet."

"I understand." Gary extended his arm and leaned against the doorjamb. "Still, if you could show me around, I'd be much obliged." He threw her his come-on grin.

She rolled her eyes and released a feral growl. "I'm not sure I can manage."

"Of course you can." Charlie waved, trying to shush her. He looked at Gary. "Doctor Harper isn't keen on the idea of selling Sara. Now, what zoo did you say you were from?"

"Didn't. It's for a private sale, an acceptable one, I'm sure. I'll make it worth your while." He handed Charlie a card.

"This is highly irregular, Mr. Staunton." Charlie glanced at the card and squinted. "I'll keep you in mind for the auction."

"Auction?" Mira's voice rose. "What auction?"

Charlie's eyes widened. "Ah, it's how these things are handled, Miranda. Really." He held his palms up in front of his chest as if defending himself from a punch. "Well, I must go. Doctor Harper will show you the chimp."

He rushed out the door, right under Gary's outstretched arm.

Her eyes followed the administrator and stopped when he disappeared behind Gary.

Which left her looking at her other nemesis.

Oh God, she thought, unready to confront Gary yet. She still hadn't worked out the details of her plan.

She bit her lip and straightened to her full height of five feet seven, burying her fears. She would not be intimidated. "This way, Mister Staunton." She swept past him and out the door.

* * * * *

Gary followed, watching her hips sway in the form-fitting khakis. Until he'd seen her in them, he'd never realized how sexy a pair of pants could be.

"The ape house is over here," she said and pointed down a curved path.

She wouldn't look at him. He surmised she still nursed her anger. He chuckled. He hadn't seen this part of Mira before, at least not before last night. Fiery. And, God, passionate. He could still feel the heat in his arms. It impressed him, knowing she acted with ardor about her work too.

She stopped and swerved on him. "What's so funny?"

"Nothing." With the way she looked, he figured stupidity his best response.

She planted her fists on her hips. "So what are you now? My knight in shining-armor?"

"Huh?" Her caustic words caught him off guard.

"You. Romeo, or whatever name you're going by now."

Her pouting lips begged to be kissed. He tried to remember he couldn't afford another fumble. Clearing his throat, he focused on business. "I thought I'd come by to explain since Danielle told me you weren't talking to me."

"Oh." She sauntered toward him. "So in reparation you offer to buy my chimp."

"Well, I—"

"Look, last night was great, okay? Let's just put whatever happened behind us. Frankly, I have more important things to think about. Sara, for one."

"I understand."

"Yeah, well, Danielle thought you could help me, but don't think you need to rescue me, because you don't. I can take care of myself, and my chimps."

She turned and walked away. He hurried to catch up. "Maybe I hadn't thought about saving you. Burrows looked like he needed to be rescued more."

"Huh?" She stopped and stared at him.

"I thought you were going to deck him."

The corner of her mouth twitched. "The pompous ass." She smiled and the stiffness in her shoulders subsided. "I am worried about Sara, though. She'll have a tough time adjusting to another zoo. And if another zoo won't take her, well, I'm afraid a research lab will. She's unique. I'm afraid the change might kill her, much less any research the lab would perform. Apes have more emotions than we like to think."

"And you care about her." The emotion touched Gary. He ignored his better judgment and stroked her cheek with the back of his fingers. She closed her eyes and leaned her head into his palm.

He cleared his throat and pulled his hand back, shoving it in his pocket. "Are you going to show me Sara?"

She rubbed her neck and looked away. "You really want to see her?"

He nodded. "Guess I should know what I'm investing in."

She frowned. "Would you really buy her?"

"Maybe. If it'll get you to talk to me."

"Talk?" she squeaked.

"Yeah."

"Ah…"

She stiffened and licked her lips, which played hell with his concentration.

"Look, here's the deal." The expression in her hazel-green eyes hardened. "Help me figure out how to keep Sara here and I'll do this voice thing for you."

"But I need the voice in two weeks."

She held up her palm. "No Sara. No voice." She walked to the door of the ape house.

"How do I know you can do the job?"

She stopped, her hand on the knob, and turned to him. "Oh I can." Her breathy voice softened. "If you don't believe me, ask the male students who attend my lectures. They, for one, love me." She smiled seductively then sauntered into the building.

"Whew." He whistled, his body warming to the sensual sound. "Yeah, I bet they do."

A vision of her naked under his sheets flashed before him. This time, he lay naked beside her. Strengthening his resolve, he tried to crush his sexual urges, but worked at it. His male instinct impelled him to go for her in a more primeval way. His common sense told him he couldn't. He swallowed hard. He'd made some ground. He didn't need his baser drives getting in the way of his success.

Gritting his teeth, he walked to the door. "Think like a eunuch for once, bud." He stared at his lower body. "Otherwise we'll be sacked with no downs left." He grabbed onto the handle and opened the door, repeating the mantra, "Eunuch, eunuch, eunuch."

She'd bent over and her sweet-looking derriere stuck straight into the air. He remembered how his hands had molded around it. Groaning, he repeated in his mind, *Eunuch*? Then it hit him. How the hell would he know how a eunuch felt?

Mira knew he'd followed when she heard the door open. Why had she flirted outrageously with him? She wanted him as a witness for Danielle's prank, a reporter to Danielle about whatever wild thing she did each night. That was the sum total of what she expected. She didn't need his help doing wild things, especially the intimate ones that were going through her head. She picked up the broom that had fallen on the floor and put it away. Gary stepped behind her.

Straightening, she brushed off her hands and pulled out her keys. "She's in here." Unlocking the door, she walked through, into another world where she felt in control. A good thing, since being so close to Gary threw her off.

He followed and she closed the door behind him. The chimps went crazy, flying from tree limb to tree limb.

"You know I haven't been to the zoo in years." He scanned the trees. "Of course, I've never had this view before."

He stood within inches of her. She had to crane her neck to see his face. He stared like a small boy and she relished his look, enjoying the awe she saw in his eyes.

She cleared her throat. He was no boy, but a well-developed man. She studied the contours of his chin. His clean-shaven face sported a small scar underneath his strong, square jaw. His neck was thick, muscled. Had she pressed her lips against it?

"Do you play with them?" His deep, warm voice flowed over her.

"Huh?" She broke from her musings.

"Play. With the chimps." A grin tugged at the corners of his lips. Did he laugh at her? Did he realize she wanted him?

"Oh…" She pulled herself back to reality, realizing she couldn't afford to forget he'd become a means to an end. "We, ah, handle them if that's what you mean."

"But you don't play? Aren't you allowed?"

"Not really." She squirmed, trying not to think of whom she'd rather play with. "They are wild animals."

"Yeah, but they like people, right?"

"Sure." She shrugged. "Some of them do. The ones used to people come up to us all the time. Chimps aren't that different from humans. They know which people they like and which ones they don't. The folks they don't like, they stay away from."

"Like Dr. Burrows?" His brows shot up.

"Exactly."

He chuckled and looked upward again. "It's amazing how they move. Knew a tight end who used to move like that. Called him Monkey Jones."

"Ah." She wondered how tight his end felt and pretended to clear her throat again. "Well, chimps aren't so different from us."

"And yet they are." The gleam in Gary's eyes confused Mira. "The place doesn't look big from this side, does it?" He glanced at the ceiling.

She ignored the craving she thought she'd seen in his face. "No, which is why I'm afraid of moving Sara. Most other zoos don't have the room we do. If forced in something smaller, pulled away from her friends, Sara would feel locked up. Like a criminal. Assuming she gets to another zoo. No zoo may want her after they find out what problems she has. There's always the possibility of a research lab. She'd be cut on and studied there."

"Doesn't seem quite fair, does it?" His mouth slanted into a frown, his handsome face pensive.

"No, it doesn't." Warmth filled Mira, different from the strong sexual response she'd experienced being near him. In this light, he seemed almost human.

"So, what are her problems?"

Mira cleared her throat. "She, ah, has this unusual fascination with mating."

"That's bad?" He lifted a brow.

"Yes." She tried not to blush.

He chuckled. "What's so unusual about it?"

"She tries to mate with all the males."

He laughed then. "What a girl. Which one's Sara?"

Mira liked his lighthearted voice. She glanced at the trees. The chimps scattered as Sara dropped from a limb and rambled toward them.

Gary crouched and waggled his fingers at her. "Come here. It's okay. I won't hurt you."

Mira squatted next to him. "She must have heard her name."

"This is Sara?"

She nodded. The chimp moved closer and Mira opened her arms to hold her.

Instead, she jumped into Gary's embrace. "Hey, girl." He cradled her and stood. Sara rubbed his head and Gary tickled the chimp's belly.

Mira straightened. Absurdly, she felt rejected. Sara totally ignored her and now the chimp had Gary's full attention. She looked away, trying to convince herself she shouldn't care who Gary showed interest in. When she glanced back, Sara's lips puckered. Mira reached for the chimp. "Be careful, Gary. She might…"

Sara stuck out her tongue and licked his face then kissed him smack on the lips.

Gary pulled back but Sara had no intention of stopping. She smooched him on the neck. Isn't that where Mira wanted to be?

"Sara." Mira grasped the chimp around the waist and pulled her away. "No. Oh Gary, I'm sorry."

Sara stuck out her bottom lip and bared her teeth.

"At least she likes me." He wiped his neck.

"I said no." Mira stared at the chimp.

"Eek, eek." Sara shrieked and jumped away from her, right into Gary's arms.

"We need to go," she said.

Gary looked at the chimp, who now groomed his hair. "If you say so. She isn't dangerous, is she?"

"Well, obviously not to you. On the other hand, I think she feels I'm a threat."

"Are you?" His brow quirked up.

"Huh? Well, no, but…" She sighed. "She's never bared her teeth at me before. Now you see firsthand why Dr. Burrows wants to sell her."

"Because she doesn't like women?"

"No." Mira frowned. "She likes women. She just isn't herself around men. She gets aggressive."

"Aggressive?" He tried to balance Sara while she squirmed in his arms. "She seems friendly to me." Sara finagled her way around and lifted her rear in his face.

He held her from him, a look of revulsion in his face. "What's she doing?"

Mira bit her lip. "Trying to mate with you. When I said all males, I meant the human kind too. What do you think? She might be your type, you know." She covered her mouth but the sound escaped anyway. She laughed so hard her sides ached.

His brows shot up. "That funny, huh?"

She nodded, working to stop her snickering. "Oh…" She held her side. "I'm sorry. I should have explained in more depth."

"It's okay." He kept moving her rump away from him but Sara wouldn't have any of it and repositioned her rump toward him.

In his own defense, Gary held her at arms' length. "You know, I can think of another woman I'd rather mate with. Maybe if I kiss you, she'll get the hint."

Was he talking about her? She stopped laughing. "I…"

Gary dropped Sara and before Mira could stop him, he bent over and took her in his arms, planting his mouth onto hers.

His touch dazed her, causing her libido to fire and take control. A luscious heat shot through her. Her inner core trembled with heady anticipation. She curved her body into him and caressed the sinew everywhere her fingers touched. Warmth encircled her, holding her enamored, captive, as his embrace grew more intimate and heady. His arms molded her torso against his rock-solid body, his hands sliding lower against the cheeks of her derrière.

Need, want, laced her breathy sigh. Without thinking, she traced her tongue around his lips then plunged into his mouth, the desire to taste him overtaking her common sense.

He groaned, the sleek depth of his voice enticing her more.

"Ohhh," she sighed, leaving his mouth, lightly nipping his chin then down the side of his neck. The mixture of Gary's spicy aftershave and his own unique scent overtook her. Somewhere in her stupefied brain she thought she sounded like a purring kitten.

"Yeah, way to go, Tarzan."

The yell jarred her from her stupor. She pushed Gary away, appalled by her actions, and looked to where the voice came from. Two teenage boys stood outside the cage, smiling at the two of them.

"Oh God." She rubbed her head, wondering what she'd been thinking. Gary waved at the boys.

She stared. What a jerk. Did he think this funny? "So, now you're Tarzan."

That baby-come-love-me grin came back. "Only if you'll play Jane."

She wanted to pound him. "We need to leave."

Sara moaned and held onto his leg. He picked her up. "I'll carry her to the door then maybe we can slip out."

"All right." Mira swallowed, feeling like a class A dope and stomped away.

She opened the door and held the passage open for him. Before he could set Sara down, the chimp moaned in his ear. He gave her a strange look.

"Maybe I should leave you two lovers alone?" she said, a cutting edge to her voice.

He cleared his throat and patted Sara on the head. "Bye, sexy. See you again soon, okay?" He set her down and moved quickly through the entrance.

Mira slipped out and shut the door, crossing her arms. "You two look good together. Maybe I should have a key made for you?"

"Maybe. You jealous?"

"Don't be ridiculous." She marched away.

He caught her by the arm and turned her toward him. "Maybe I can make this misunderstanding up to you."

"How? By playing Tarzan to my Jane?"

"If that's what you want." He didn't smile now. Just stared at her, his eyes a deep sea blue. "Let me take you out, Mira. Show you something of the city."

"And what about my sister?"

"What about her?"

"A promise is a promise. I'm supposed to do wild things with her."

"Then do wild things with me instead." His head bent closer.

Isn't that what she wanted? Except he didn't make what she envisioned sound the same.

This was a business deal, not some romp in his bedroom. She reinforced the thought in her mind.

Stepping back, she took the space she needed to get her head together. "Yes. Exactly what I had in mind. I'll decide what wild thing we'll do each night, and you'll accompany me and report back to my sister in the morning."

"Huh?"

"Look, you doing this will keep Danielle's meddling away from me. And in the off times, we'll brainstorm. Try to find a solution to Sara's problem."

He crossed his arms. "And what about my work? I have an ad to do."

"I'll be reasonable and not take up all your time. You said Danielle's good. This is her idea. Let her handle most of the legwork."

"My clients will look for me."

"You want my voice, you save Sara." They stood toe to toe.

"And stick to you like glue." He paused. "I get to pick half of the wild things we do."

"Half?"

"Half." He bent closer. "You want to save the chimp. I've got the resources to do it."

She bit her lip, unsure she liked that idea, but did she have a choice? She swallowed. "Okay, half. Deal?" She thrust out her hand.

"Deal. We start tonight." He shook on it.

"Fine." She nodded, feeling better now that she had a companion in this. "And no funny stuff, Tarzan."

"Oh no, Jane." He leaned to within an inch of her neck, the response against her skin causing her synapses to fire all the way down to the vee between her legs. "The funny stuff is going to be the best part."

"Wait a minute..." she gasped, her sex drive threatening to take control again.

"Uh-uh." He touched his nose to hers, causing her breath to catch. "A deal's a deal. We shook on it. I'll pick you up at your place at six." His lips captured hers and lingered, making her want. With a mind of their own, her hands slid up his chest, savoring the feel of his powerfully built torso. He tightened his grasp on her, closing the space between them. The buds of her breasts peaked against his chest, the nubbin between the juncture of her legs throbbed.

He pulled her from him, his breathing labored. "Be there," he whispered the command. Turning, he breezed out the door before she could argue.

"Argh," she growled, regaining her breath. Each deal got her deeper into trouble. She touched her lips. They were still hot, pulsing with unfulfilled desire.

Do wild things with me instead, he'd said. Her body trembled. The simple words joined with his intense look, his heady voice, had penetrated her, probed her deepest sensual desires.

She rubbed her face, trying to squash her yearning. She knew she shouldn't want him. Her needy libido risked her ego big time. But did he really want her in return?

"Half." She'd promised. She always kept her word. Mira slapped her palm against her forehead. "Oh God," she moaned, wondering if this would be a good thing, or bad. "What if he insists his half be something…carnal?"

She squeezed her legs together, trying to halt the hammering of her feminine bud between them. Her logic rejected the idea as insane. Yet, deep within, she knew her body thrilled with the thought.

She shivered, half afraid, half eager for the coming onslaught, and rubbed her temple, the confusion overcoming her. "Oh lord," she gulped a gasp of air. "Now what did I get myself into?"

Unbidden, a smug self-satisfied look from her sister flitted into her mind. "Oh no you don't, Dani," she muttered to herself. She'd be damned if she'd let her little sister get her manipulative paws in her life, especially in her sex life.

With renewed determination, Mira stomped to the exit, slamming the door behind her. This was a fight she would win *her* way.

Chapter Five

ഇ

Gary hadn't known this kind of rush in years. Everything had come together. He had his voice. He'd get the exposure he needed. And he'd be spending time with Mira. What more could a guy ask for?

To have his old life back.

The thought stopped him, slammed common sense right into his gut. Behind him, a lion roared. He empathized with the animal. He wanted to roar too, angry at the cards life had dealt him.

All he ever wanted was to play football. The sweat, the blood, the thrill. He'd been a powerhouse, until the fluke of an accident took his knee and damaged then shriveled his left testicle. The world knew about his knee. Few knew about the other—his parents, the coach and the medical staff.

Well, and Darlene.

He thanked God all his injuries didn't make the news. Making his damage public would have crushed his will to live.

The doctors told him he could have a normal life—wife, kids, family. They didn't understand that a normal life for him meant playing ball and having full use of his physical abilities—including the reproductive ones. Yeah, everything worked fine, his one testicle was missing was all, which lessened his virility. More importantly, the scars and obvious missing equipment looked hideous. He wanted a woman to look on him with desire again, not sympathy. He refused to be a charity case.

He closed his eyes, wanting to forget the past, but thoughts continued to haunt him. He'd played touch ball with some local teenagers. He shouldn't have in the middle of the season, but what would it hurt?

A lot, he'd come to find out. Some construction crew had left for lunch and didn't mark their site well enough. One of the boys ran close to the hole and teetered on the side. He'd pulled the boy away and lost his balance, falling through the flimsy board the crew had used to cover the pit they'd dug. The opening hadn't been deep, only a few feet, but the steel rods they'd cemented into the bottom speared his groin and his knee.

After Darlene saw the damage firsthand, she bowed out. He didn't need to ask why. Her look had spelled everything out for him. Horror, then pity. He let her go and the image of her rejection had etched itself in his mind. He couldn't stand it happening again.

Yeah, he'd dated since, selective about who he took to bed. Only once did he indulge in a woman who didn't care she'd made love to an ex-NFL player. An older woman, she died of cancer months later. If she'd been healthy, he'd have considered something more permanent.

Except for her, he'd made sure his liaisons didn't last more than one night, keeping the mutual activity in the dark. It made things simpler and he'd never have to see the look of pity again.

So why did he come on to Mira? Yes, a liaison made a poor business decision—and a terrible personal one. He wouldn't get physical with her. He couldn't. He liked her too much. And he wanted to be around her.

Face it, Gary. You want her. Intimately. And the wanting tormented him.

It wasn't just sex. Not for him anyway. Sex he could get his fill of. But passion? He'd seen the fire in her. Felt it. He wanted to share every ounce of her ardor he could. More than anything, he missed the intensity of that emotion.

He grunted, sensing the deadness inside him. He'd had plenty of fervor when he played ball. Now the thrill had dissipated. Yeah, he did well at business but he didn't love it, not as he should. Being with Mira reminded him how much he longed for the exhilaration.

Perhaps he should stay away from her? Mira evoked yearnings again, hope of a life someone looked forward to everyday. A normal life filled with family and happiness.

His stomach churned, aching for the love he knew he'd never get. He wouldn't take the chance. If Mira ever pitied him, his ego would never be able to stand the blow.

His groin tightened with pain and desire. Every fiber in his body told him to love her while every gray cell in his thick skull told him to beg off. God, he wanted to take the risk. But if he did, would Mira give him the love and passion he desired, or cringe in revulsion at the sight of him?

He just didn't know, and he didn't like not knowing how she might feel.

Maybe the discovery was why he wanted to go through with this crazy idea. He could be close to her, get to know her innermost thoughts, experience her passion. They could be friends. It would kill him, being near her and not touch her the way he wanted. And if he decided not to tell her his darkest secret? Well, then, at least he could die in ecstasy.

He walked out the front gate.

"Hey, Tarzan." One of the kids at the ape house called to him. "You swing her off her feet yet?"

He smirked. "Not yet. I'm working on the vine part."

The boy laughed. "Well, let me know if you don't. We come here all the time to see her."

He shook his head, not surprised even young studs like him showed interest in Mira. "I'll keep you informed."

He rushed to his car, wondering what had happened to Mira to make her see herself as unattractive. What had Danielle said? Relationships with men were hard for her. Well, relationships with women were hard for him.

His mind churned. The business side had been set. In less than a month, they'd complete the ad. And afterward?

Mira would be free and so would he. Could he somehow work them through this?

He got into the car and started his Corvette. Could it be time to risk his heart?

Or maybe it was his soul?

He raced off, afraid. Where would fate lead him this time?

* * * * *

"Where could she be?" Danielle plugged Mira's number into the phone again and waited for the ring. She'd left work and no one answered at home. Mira's cell phone continued to ring.

Not good.

Mira had a date with Gary tonight. He'd called and said he'd arranged the whole thing. He'd be taking Mira out from now on too, until the deal she and Mira had played out.

That was good, very good.

Then he told her to stay out of the situation — totally.

That was *baaaaad*. Very *baaaaad*. She knew Mira better than he did. She feared the big galoot would run her off. But he'd insisted. Said he'd gotten too close to locking in Mira's voice for the ad and didn't want *her*, Mira's only sister, in the way. Thank God, he said he'd be gone all afternoon. It gave Danielle a chance to find her sister before she did something stupid.

The phone rang a third time. "Mira, where are you?" she mumbled. Frustrated, she hung up and dialed again.

Gary had been true to his word. She hadn't seen him once. He'd decided to run around and find sponsors for the chimp. He hoped to get enough funding to buy Sara and cover a year's worth of expenses at the zoo. Afterward, Mira could have an annual fund drive to support the chimp. Gary said he'd head up the drive. His lawyer, Jeff Worthington, would set it up as a nonprofit fund. That way, all the donations would be tax deductible—a big draw for most investors.

Gary thought he could do it. If he thought so, she believed him. When Gary set his mind to something, he became invincible. Besides, how much could a chimp cost?

She switched the receiver to her other ear as the phone rang again. She growled. The problem with this whole thing was their solution left her stuck in the office. Her piece of the "Save Sara" campaign included setting up all the work for the ad—the scheduling, the studio, the sound... The list went on. She'd finished some of the list, but she couldn't concentrate. She wanted her plans for Mira and Gary to work out. She wanted it bad. So what could be going on with her sister?

She let the phone ring. Focusing, she studied her calendar. Most things had fallen into place. With the tight deadline, they needed to be perfect. Still, there were several loose ends. Details that couldn't be tied up by the end of the day.

Which led to her other worry. Where had Mira gone? "God, I hope she didn't take off somewhere."

The answering system came on-line.

"Sheesh." She replaced the receiver and glared at the phone as if her frustration had been the dang thing's fault. Would her sister keep her date with Gary?

Mira was a woman of honor. She wouldn't break the deal they made, then again, anyone could be pushed. Mira had stretched her comfort zone to the edge and someone like Gary could unintentionally push her over her limit, forcing her to run and hide in geekland somewhere. Danielle picked up her pen and twirled it through her fingers, thinking. Gary did get her to commit to letting him escort her. Chalk another one to the good.

She sighed and tossed the pen across the desk, letting her head drop against the back of the chair. "Keep your fingers crossed, Danielle. She's not out of this yet."

But where could she be? "Maybe I can catch her at home." She glanced at her watch. *Five o'clock.* "Time to go." She grabbed her purse and reached for the keys.

The ringing phone stopped her. "Finally." She grabbed the receiver. "Mira?"

"Not likely," the male voice drawled, holding a hint of a chuckle. "Danielle?"

"Yeah." *Unfortunately,* she thought, and waited for the Fast Drive's promo man to announce himself. He always did.

"Hey, it's Sam Carter."

There it was. "No kidding?" She tried to feign surprise. Didn't the guy think she knew his voice by now?

He cleared his throat. "Did Gary tell you the ad's going national?"

"He told me." She cringed. The pompous Sam Carter had been the only drawback on this deal.

"I'm trying to get a hold of Gary. You know where he is?"

"Ah, he's out." She paused, trying to think. "Doing some PR."

"Damn."

"Is there anything I can help you with?" She batted her eyelashes and laid her finger against her cheek, imagining the women the man thought fell at his feet.

"No. But pass along a message for me, would you, sugar? Tell him we're gonna need the spot sooner."

"Sooner? You barely gave us enough time as it is." Her backbone straightened.

"Can't help it. Management wants it. You know how that goes. This is a great opportunity for Gary. Does he have the voice yet?"

"I'm working on it."

"You are? But I thought…"

"Well, you thought wrong," she interjected. "I'm getting the voice. She's perfect. You'll love her." She bit her lip, not wanting to carry the lie too far.

Sam paused. A sweet talker from way back, he didn't trust her, and she knew it. She had two long legs—and no short one in-between, therefore she had no brains to his way of thinking. It irritated her to no end. He spoke before she could toss out another barb.

"Tell Gary to call me. I want a status report. Got it?"

"Yeah, got it."

He hung up.

"Jerk." She dropped the phone back in the cradle. Sam Carter was her age and the most sexist creep she'd run into in ages. He came from Alabama. A good-looking guy with a great behind. He also had a keen awareness of his assets and used it to his advantage when he could. Danielle never bought into it. Besides, nowadays weren't male chauvinists burned at the stake?

She had to face reality. There were some of Gary's friends she didn't like, and in this business, there were more than normal.

She dialed Gary's cell. No answer. "God, now where is he?" What good were modern conveniences when people didn't use them? He could at least leave his phone on. She stared at the receiver. "What is this? 'Leave Danielle hanging in suspense and agony' day?"

Somehow, she had to find out what cooked. She needed to find Mira, and now she needed to find Gary. She hated to admit the fact but Sam Carter was right. His deal was Gary's biggest one yet. She didn't want to blow the contract for him.

Grabbing her keys, she headed for the door. By hook or crook, she would find Gary—and hoped Mira would be with him.

* * * * *

"Well, I never met a jock who liked hot tea."

Jojo handed Mira a cup of the brew and sat down. She'd gone over to her friend and neighbor's house, hoping to find some inspiration, or maybe it was fortitude?

Jojo's red locks bobbed from her shoulders. "He got embarrassed when I found him watching you get hennaed. Kinda like a big boy caught in the cookie jar. Danielle speaks nothing but praise about him. And, my God, who would have ever thought he'd have a cloth hanky?"

Mira had told her what had happened last night, at least what she remembered, and about the agreement she'd made with Gary. She left out the part about being naked in his bed. She couldn't be sure about that yet. "Why do I keep making these stupid deals?" She shook her head. "Thing is, they seem reasonable at the time."

Mira buried her forehead in her hand. She'd left work early, begging a headache. Her excuse wasn't a lie. Her head pounded with indecision. Should she go through with her deal with the virile man? Wasn't there another way?

She groaned. "Maybe Burrows is right. After what Sara did today, baring her teeth, well, she's never threatened me before. She could have bitten me." She rubbed her temple.

"Mira, trust your instincts. You know you're right about Sara." Jojo blew on the hot liquid. "Do you really think Danielle's boss is going to take advantage of you?"

She stared at her friend, afraid to answer.

Jojo chuckled and sipped the tea. "Maybe I'm reading this wrong. Perhaps you're hoping he will, that way you won't have to feel guilty about being seduced by a hunky jock like him?"

"No, no." Even as she denied the comment, the pang of truth hit her hard. "You getting professional on me?" A psychologist, Jojo specialized in sex therapy. She was a great therapist from what Mira could surmise. She closed one eye and studied her.

"No, just being a friend." Jojo took another sip.

Mira's headache pounded harder. She slapped the arm of the couch. "No. I will not be taken advantage of."

"Good girl. So even if he does put the moves on you, you'll tell him no."

"Absolutely." Mira jerked one quick nod with her chin.

Jojo quirked a brow and smirked. "So what wild ideas did you have in mind to do with him?"

"Well, I…" Mira had a hard time thinking of anything but sex when she was around Gary. She needed to come up with something that would take her mind off the thought. She snapped her fingers. "I know, Danielle never defined what 'wild' meant. How about a backpacking trip, going out *into* the wilds to study, er, something…?" She waved her hand haphazardly in the air.

"Something?" Jojo bit her lip. "And just what 'something' will you study?"

"Well, maybe elk. The bulls are fighting for dominance right now and—"

"Dominance? Oh yeah, I like that. Just what you wanted." Her friend burst out laughing. "Mira, you know they're fighting because it's their mating season. They're showing off for the females." Jojo waved her hand in front of her face as if she painted a picture. "I can see it now. You and that hunk observing the ancient symbol of fertility in action—*alone*—in the remote outdoors. The fresh air, you both sweating from the hike. Then a cool breeze hits and you want to strip some layers off. *Hmmm.*" She giggled. "And the atmosphere, it's heavy with the testosterone action of the elk and the champion bull calling to its mate. Who knows? Maybe you'll get to see the bull and doe go at it. My, all those pheromones in the air." She blew on her hot tea. "You know, Gary was a lineman. He's used to the head-butting stuff. How long do you think it would take before he starts putting what he sees into practice?"

A picture of her panting in the fallen leaves, letting Gary rip her clothes off and take her with reckless abandon formed in Mira's head. She gasped, her hormones flaring.

Growling, Mira squashed the ridiculous thought. "Funny," she said her voice thick with sarcasm. "Okay, maybe wolves. They can eat him if he gets too randy and suggests anything, uh, sexual."

Jojo waggled her brows. "Oh yeah. Wolves. The ultimate symbol for an alpha male, one who mates for life."

Mira groaned. "Fine. Forget the wilderness. We'll bungee jump. That should be symbolic enough for you, jumping without so much as looking first."

Jojo's smile took on a mischievous leer. "From the frying pan into the fire. Ooooh, that *will* be hot. And with all that macho expenditure, it's a sure bet that his testosterone will be up. Then afterward you two can bask in sexually heated glory."

"We will not. Besides, I'll be scared to death."

"And run right into Gary's open arms for safety. Typical mating behavior. Really, Mira, with a guy as sexy as that? How can you not take the opportunity? I mean, let's face it. The simple act of putting the words 'Gary' and 'wild' in to the same sentence can only lead to one thing."

"Errrr." Jojo was right. None of those normally intellectual stimulating activities would stay that way, not with Gary around. Things would get much too visceral. Frustrated, Mira sat back in the chair and banged her head against the headrest. "Then maybe I'll get lucky and my line will break and put me out of my misery. Is *that* wild enough for you?"

Jojo chuckled. "Nope. I can see him diving in headfirst to come after you. You'll be saved before you touch ground—and grateful." She wiggled her brows again. "Nothing like heavy physical expenditure to get one's blood going. And near-death experiences never fail to bring out the need to mate."

Mira inhaled a deep breath then sighed. "Fine," she snapped with defeat. "Then what do you suggest, oh wise one, to keep our animal instincts from taking over?"

Jojo shook her head. "What's wrong with letting them take over?" She put down her cup. "Mira, I think you're in denial."

Mira frowned. "You are getting professional on me."

Jojo chuckled. "Like you, I can hardly disown my training. You like him. What's holding you back?"

"I…" She put down her cup. "How'd you know I liked him?"

She laughed. "The mere fact you told me you initiated lip-lock with him clued me in."

"Oh." She grimaced. "Blame the drink…"

"No. It was more than the alcohol. The liquor only loosened you up enough to accept what you wanted. You ignored every other guy last night who'd made a pass at you until then. And believe me, there were plenty. It doesn't sound like he tried to engage, not exactly anyway. And, judging from the way he looked at you, I'm not sure he could help himself. He showed interest, a lot of it. He didn't show such intensity with anyone else."

Mira bit her lip. "I shouldn't be talking to someone who's an expert on sex."

"You make my qualifications sound like I have the ultimate in experience. I'm a sex therapist, not a sex goddess. Now, what's your problem?"

She sighed. "Brawny men. I can't date them. They give me hives."

"Sports guys."

"Yeah."

Jojo chewed her lip. "Well, he doesn't seem like the type to kiss a girl then abandon her."

"What do you mean?"

Jojo shrugged. "He didn't mind you throwing up on everything. Didn't kick you out of his apartment. He tried to make you tea." She chuckled. "I think his efforts were cute. Wish I had someone who would take care of me like that."

Mira shook her head. "I don't know, Jojo…"

"Look," her friend said, "what *this* doctor would suggest, Doctor Harper, is to face the dragon."

"I don't understand."

"Time to conquer your fear, my friend. Face the dragon, head on."

Mira flinched. "Kinda like Saint George, huh?"

"Exactly. Except in this case it's Saint Georgia — or Saint Miranda, however you'd like to put the phrase."

Mira frowned. "I don't know if I'm ready for sainthood."

Jojo leaned forward. "Then take things slow. Have some fun with the big guy. Find out what he's like. Then if you don't want to get physical, don't."

"Slow? We don't have time for that. Besides, how am I going to do some wild thing with him if we take whatever we do slow?"

"You, obviously, underestimate the use of slow." Jojo arched a brow.

The sexual connotation wasn't lost on her. "No," she said emphatically. "I'm not seducing him, slow or otherwise."

"Why not?"

"Because, I…"

"Look, Mira. In all seriousness, maybe what you should do is find out if you want to seduce him?"

"Huh?"

"You're interested in him. He's interested in you. See if there's some common ground."

"And what would you suggest?"

Jojo grabbed the phone book sitting on the coffee table. "Look, rummaging out in the woods isn't what Dani had in mind and you know it, so, how 'bout going to a place within civilization where you'd feel in control and he'd be off guard? You can get an idea about the real person that way and not let your imagination take over."

Mira raised a brow. "And, pray tell, oh angel of mercy and wise sexual advice, what place would fit my sister's insane criteria?"

Jojo winked at her. "Let Doctor Devereux show you the secrets of the wild in Denver. Trust me, not all the animals are in the zoo." Her smile overflowed with mischief. "After you see this, you might think the elks were the civilized ones."

* * * * *

Mira decided to wear a simple black dress, sophisticated, yet slinky. Sexy enough to do the job—she thought.

She sat in front of the vanity and touched the image of her made-up face in the mirror. "What are you doing?"

She pulled her fingertips away from the glass and shook her head. Jojo had been right. She wallowed in denial. Time to do something about her pitiful state. Tonight, she would risk her sequestered ego. She would find out if Gary Staunton, jock extraordinaire, actually had some interest in her. In the process, she hoped to release a wild part of her caged for too long.

Standing, she ran her hands across her bodice and down the length of the dress to straighten the folds. The movement reminded her of Gary's touch. Her body still hummed from his caresses, his lips upon hers.

She acted like Cinderella waiting for Prince Charming. A silly dream, she thought, but this time she couldn't help herself. Question was, would he be a prince or a toad? Her fingertips touched her lips. His kiss had devastated her. Even at "almost thirty", her body had never reacted to such an extreme.

A shiver ran through her, dread at what she thought might go on tonight, what might happen if she let her control get too lax.

Sex.

There. She'd thought it. The word. *Sex.* Would she let her guard down enough to do something with Gary she knew she'd enjoy? The image she'd been ignoring since she met him grew crystal clear. She wanted him in her bed—bad. Wanted to know every curve, every muscle of his body, to have his sweat-sleeked physique next to hers.

Her breasts tingled in remembrance of his closeness. The small nub between her thighs shot a delirious tension throughout her body. She gasped, the sensation overcoming her. Looking into the mirror again, she steeled herself. Could she go through with this?

She nodded. "It's a deal, Mira. One you're making for yourself. For once, you're going to make a man scream with pleasure. Let's just hope he does the same in return for you."

She rose and grabbed her purse. Going to the window, she looked out, not wanting to look back and rethink her plan. She still couldn't remember last night, but tonight, she intended to make a memory she wouldn't forget. She would know firsthand what it would be like to be naked and sated in Gary Staunton's arms.

She shivered again, but this time not from fear. No, her quivers came from anticipation.

* * * * *

Gary shut off his cell phone. He didn't want anything interrupting his date with Mira. He would romance her, get her on his side. They could be good friends. He hadn't done that in a long time, romanced a lady, because the women he'd dated were the type who made their purpose clear to him, the result being in his bed. Which had been fine with him, at least before Mira slammed into him and reopened that aching need to be touched by someone who cared.

Now he grew nervous. He could still turn on the charm, sure, but romance?

"Just like riding a bike..." he reassured himself, telling himself this would be easy. Besides, the eventual end he'd had with other women wouldn't happen with Mira. He'd decided he couldn't risk the close physical contact. No, a friendship with her was all he wanted. He could at least get some fulfillment from being with her.

He ran a hand through his hair. For once, he would enjoy himself without worrying about what the woman he dated thought about him. For that, he considered himself lucky.

Mira was smart, witty. Even when she tossed barbs at him, she stirred him. Mentally, physically. And when she relaxed around him...

He breathed deep, remembering her heady smell, the touch of her soft body in his arms. Those kind of thoughts made his below-the-belt friend restless.

He blanked her sexual charms out of his mind. He didn't want to think about them now he'd made the decision. Mira wasn't for him, not physically anyway. She deserved better. But he wanted as much of her caring and emotions he could get.

He turned onto her street and pulled into the drive. It took a few minutes for him to settle down. He wondered what risqué thing she had in mind and knew he would need the ultimate in control tonight to prevent expressing his full desire. But he could handle it. Couldn't be any worse than defending against some of the linemen he'd faced. He could do this.

More relaxed, he took a deep breath and stepped out, jogging up to the porch. Before he got the chance to knock, Mira opened the door. She wore a black dress that made the red one pale in comparison. The red dress had revealed more skin, yes, but this one molded against her well-formed curves in all the right places. Classy, innocent and seductive, all in the same package. "Whew." He exhaled through his pursed lips. No deep cleavage showed, just an enticing hint of skin. The view made him ache worse for her.

"Hello." Her voice sounded thick, sexy. He knew exactly what the guys in her lectures thought. She licked her lush lips.

What little calm he'd found, fled. She leaned against the doorjamb and his gaze dropped to the knee she lifted as she slid the top of her shoe up her calf. He savored the sight, from her spiky heels to her shapely legs, and higher. When he looked into her face, he swallowed. "Hi." The word tumbled from his mouth. This would be harder than he thought.

"I'm ready." She smiled and slung her purse over her shoulder.

"After you." He swept his arm open, hoping he didn't stutter.

She breezed past him, an I'm-up-to-something glimpse in her eyes he didn't like, and waltzed down the stairs, her hips swaying in the tight garment.

He rubbed his rough hand over his face, steeling his resolve. *This is a business deal*, he reminded himself. They could only be friends. Then a small gust of air swirled around her and lifted the edge of the hem. The movement didn't reveal much, but, good God, he'd touched those thighs. His imagination went crazy. The pounding in his veins skyrocketed, blowing his testosterone through the roof.

"Holy shit," he breathed through his clenched teeth, working to control the throbbing in his lower anatomy. The "save the chimp" team had executed a sneak play with their number one player, and he stood right in front of the main assault.

Swallowing, he put an iron grip on his reaction and hopped down the stairs after her, more afraid than he'd ever been facing an offensive line. Hell, he shook his head and amended his earlier thinking. This wouldn't be easy. In fact, this might be the hardest thing he's ever done.

* * * * *

Danielle arrived a few minutes too late. Gary had already pulled his Corvette out of the drive and she saw him turn at the stop sign.

"Damn." She parked and stepped out of her car. "I hope Mira went with him." She rushed to the door and knocked. After a minute, she knocked again. No answer.

She hurried over to Jojo's and rang the doorbell.

Their friend opened the door. Jojo had pinned up her hair and the 'do looked like Danielle had caught her before she got in a bath.

"Hey, Danielle," Jojo welcomed her. "Whassup?"

"Okay, did she go with him?"

Jojo lifted a brow and smiled. "Oh, you mean Mira? Yeah. They left a few minutes ago. Why?"

"Oh thank God." Danielle slapped her chest and leaned against the side of the house. "I thought she might try to skip town or something. Where'd they go?"

"I think you're getting a little overdramatic, don't you?"

"Jojo…" Danielle folded her hands together, begging. "I know my sister. She confides in you. She came over, right?"

Jojo crossed her arms and nodded.

"Tell all," Danielle pleaded.

"Why do you need to know?" Her brow quirked.

"I can't help it, Jojo, please?" She straightened. "I can't stand to wait and see what happens. Besides, I need to get a message to Gary. C'mon. Just this once. It's important."

Jojo frowned. "Danielle, you really should stay out of your sister's business. She's a big girl. One of these days, your meddling is going to get you into a whole mess of trouble."

"Jojo, you know she needs a lot of reinforcement. She's nervous about this." Danielle pushed out her bottom lip, looking as pathetic as possible. "You know how hard I've been working on setting them up."

Jojo raised a brow. "Did you ever hear the saying 'three's a crowd'?"

"Please?" Danielle used her I'm-absolutely-desperate look.

Jojo sighed. Her friend's reaction took a second, but Danielle could read the look of defeat when she saw it.

"I'm doing this for Mira, not you. We stick to the background."

"We?"

Jojo waved at her. "Yes, we. You don't think you're going to go after them alone, do you?"

"Why not?"

Jojo jammed her hands on her hips. "Because you aren't going into *that* place by yourself. Come in. It'll only take me a minute to change."

"Jojo…" She stepped inside. "Where are they going?"

Jojo smiled. "Danielle, there are certain benefits to being a sex therapist. One is that you find out where all the crazies go." She sauntered down the hall and shut her bedroom door.

"Ohhhh, boy," she mumbled. "Where did you send them?"

Chapter Six

ജ

Gary had asked where they were going, but Mira had been too nervous to tell him, afraid of what he might think. She opted to give him one direction at a time. Turn left here, right at the light. He questioned her more as the neighborhood grew worse, but she'd stuck to her guns. She would see this through, and so would he.

She pointed to a pink and mauve building, the paint on the exterior peeling off the sides. Gary pulled into the lot beside the bar and parked. "You want to go in here?" He arched his brows. The shock came through loud and clear in his voice.

If she could have bottled his look of horror, she would have. "Yep." She got out before he could ask her more.

The night had grown cool. The triple X sign flashed in her face, advertising the strip joint. She'd never been to a place like this. It was Ladies' Night. Male strippers from Las Vegas were supposed to be here. Except she only wanted to see one male strip tonight, and he wouldn't be on the stage.

Gary came behind her and rested his hand on the small of her back. "We don't have to go in, you know." He leaned close enough to whisper in her ear. "I could take you to a nice place in town. We could get something to eat."

His breath caressed her ear, her neck. Made Mira warm where it touched. He stood so close she could smell him, a combination of musk and the spicy aftershave he wore. Could she go through with this?

She inhaled a deep breath, determined to try. Leaning into him like a lover, she gazed into his blue-green eyes.

His mouth parted. "I'm sure I can find something else wild for us to do."

His rough, husky voice stoked her sexual fantasies. She licked her lips, knowing he probably had all kinds of wild ideas. But so did she. Well, at least this one. Mira questioned why she came here when she knew what result she wanted. *His bed.* Certainly sleeping with her sister's boss would be on the list of crazy things Danielle would accept. Only she didn't want her sister knowing that part. No, conquering Gary was a private mission, one to see if she could find a level of comfort with this very handsome, very sexy jock. A quest to see if she could get over her fear of athletic men. Their private time, if it happened, would be for just the two of them.

And what if he blabbed everything in the locker room? Then everyone would find out. His friends, his coworkers, even Danielle. Panic gripped her, made her afraid any interlude they'd have might go public. It'd happened before. She took several breaths to calm herself. Gary was a different person than the boy who had used her, Jojo advised. *Give him a chance.*

She studied him, his look one of concern, and she realized she wanted to take the plunge. Badly. She didn't like living sexually as if she existed in a cell, only allowed an intimate release with a select few. No wonder she'd never found someone who held her interest. She limited herself too much.

Time to find her freedom. Per Jojo, she needed to set the pace, take it slow at first, stay in control, and yet test her comfort boundaries. This meant she should stay on track with her plan.

Fortifying her resolve, she smiled at him. "No."

"No?" He looked confused.

Mira shook her head. "I need to do this." Although she couldn't tell him why. Besides, she also wanted some wild story Gary could take back to Danielle and she still didn't know what happened last night. She took a chance and blurted out exactly what she thought. "Dinner with an incredibly sexy guy wouldn't be wild enough for my sister."

"Incredibly sexy?" Gary chuckled and snuggled closer. "I didn't know you thought that."

She grew bolder and turned into his embrace, running a finger along his chin. "Didn't you? I can't imagine you would think otherwise after last night."

He frowned. "Mira, nothing happened. You know that, right?"

She gulped, wondering if he attempted to let her down easy. "Then how did I get half naked in your bed?" She rubbed her hands along his chest. "In fact, half overstates my level of undress…"

"You fell asleep on the couch. I put you to bed."

"Naked?" She batted her lashes.

"You said you were half naked." A corner of his full mouth lifted and he took her hands in his. "Look, why don't we go someplace where we can talk? I told you I'd tell you everything." His arms came around her waist and pulled her close. "You don't have to do this. If you're afraid of breaking the deal with Danielle, we can find something else."

"Talking doesn't sound very wild to me." Jojo was right. This had gotten him off guard. Would her plan work?

"I don't know. I can think of some pretty wild things," he whispered in her ear.

Her body shivered with anticipation and her mind went wild. The thought of him tackling her naked on a football field popped into her head. Did he know what he did to her? More importantly, did he mean to make her body heat this way?

"Ah, maybe not," she squeaked, not quite ready for sex — yet. She still worked to keep control, and keep her perspective. She wanted to find out more about him first, test him, see if he was the type of man her gut told her he might be. She licked her lips. "Have you been to one of these places before?"

He nodded. "Just the female version."

Something about his confession disappointed her and she slunk away.

He didn't let her. His arm wrapped tighter around her waist and led her back to him, holding her snug against his chest. "I don't particularly care for places like this, if that's what you want to know."

"Then why do you go?"

"I don't unless a client insists. As a kid, I guess it'd been curiosity, peer pressure. When you're part of a team, you do what the team does, to some extent anyway. Except some guys would take it too far. I never did."

He stared at her intensely, his look the essence of sincerity. She believed him. Then his expression changed, his gaze grew deeper, sensual, lighting a fire in her body again. His hand lifted, as if to touch her lips then dropped to his side, his look one of defeat. He backed away. "You certain about this?"

She swallowed and worked to get her desire in check. "Would you rather stay outside?"

"No," he said shortly. "I'm not leaving you in a rathole like this alone. It isn't safe."

She looked at him then at the building. Safe? It should be. Otherwise Jojo wouldn't have sent her there, would she? A crowd of ladies had lined up. She looked at Gary. He studied the front of the building and a frown settled on his face. He was out of his comfort zone. Isn't that what she wanted, to unbalance him? She swallowed. She'd made the deal with herself. She stood determined to see it through. "Maybe we should go inside."

He sighed. "Whatever you say." He pressed his hand on the small of her back again, guiding her into the line.

She bit her lip, questioning again the wisdom of her decision. Gary didn't look happy, and she didn't think his angst made a good prelude into his bedroom.

When Mira pulled him into her, Gary had almost let himself go. Almost. Thank God he came to his senses and stepped away when he did. Her closeness muddled his brain, made him stupid, made him believe he could have a relationship with her. God knows his body ached for it.

But he couldn't. He'd made up his mind. Still, he'd almost forgotten his plan and had escaped disaster by the skin of his teeth.

Calming, Gary studied her as she got into line, wondering what she thought. She'd come on to him, probably to convince him to go inside since she'd made it quite clear as part of their deal there would be no intimacy between them, at least no "funny stuff" as she'd put it. But if she wanted to stay away from the sexual stuff, why go here? He shrugged the thought off, figuring she'd never done something this goofy before. Not that going to a strip club was a bad thing. He guessed women were as curious as men sometimes. These days, a lot of women probably came to these shows at least once in their lifetime. But here? The place was a dive. Everything he'd heard about the bar was wild, even for him. There had to be better places to go. There were definitely better things to do. She wanted wild? How about making love to a half-sterile man on his balcony? Surely that would be wild enough for her. Except it would never happen. He squashed the thought. He wouldn't let it.

They inched closer to the door and the nearer they got, the more edgy he grew. There were all types of women in line, and a few men, he noticed, although some of the men seemed coupled to each other. Not that he cared, but it sure as hell wasn't for him. He'd known a few guys who swung that way, but only a few. Now, he seemed surrounded by them. It felt weird.

They reached the front where two large biker-types took the cover fee. He'd bet they were also the bouncers. One stood almost as tall as he, the other had about the same stocky build. The tall one looked him up and down then up again, slowly. Gary wanted to slug him. "Something wrong?" He glared at the man.

The guy growled and stepped in front of the entrance. "Yuh cain't com' in."

The bouncer had spaces where some teeth should be and Gary thought he could loosen a few more before his pal got the drop on him. "Why not?" He moved in front of Mira and clenched his fists, just in case.

She started to protest but the guy's partner cut her off. "Let 'em be, Georgio," the shorter one said. "I recognize this guy. Roller Staunton, right?"

Gary nodded, surprised someone would remember him. He heard Mira huff.

The shorter man punched "Georgio" in the arm. "He'd lay you flat before you knew what hit you, stupid. Get out of the way."

Georgio shot his friend a confused look.

"The guy's lost a few." The man pointed to his own head. "Name's Crowder, Bucky Crowder." He held out his hand. "Miss seeing you play. Used to love it when you sacked those guys. That's my favorite part."

"Yeah, I miss it too." He took Bucky's hand and shook it, relieved.

"Never thought I'd see you in some place like this." The guy squeezed one eye shut and stared at him. "Course, we regular guys never know what really goes on in that locker room."

For a brief minute, Gary thought about hitting both of them for the hell of it. "I'm escorting the lady here," he explained and pulled Mira from behind him. Her arms were crossed and she didn't look happy. "You going to let us in?"

"Sure." Bucky nodded. "It's okay, since you're escorting. We's gotta make sure nobody comes in who's gonna cause trouble. You understand."

"I understand." Gary nodded and handed the bouncer twenty bucks. "I don't intend to start anything, although I'll finish a fight if someone starts one with me." He glared at Georgio.

Bucky puckered his fat lips and nodded. "Yeah? That I would like to see."

The bouncer let them pass and Gary ushered Mira through the open door. As soon as they got in, she pulled him aside. "What was that about?"

"Male bonding?" he shrugged, hoping she'd let the incident pass.

No dice. Her face turned red. "Look, I've told you before I can take care of myself."

He stared at the top of her head, thinking the shorter of the two bouncers had at least five inches on her. Forget how much more they weighed. He decided not to irritate her any more than necessary. "Mira, you're supposed to have fun, not worry about guys like that. Forget it, okay?"

She came closer, her mouth set in a thin line. "They wouldn't have bothered me if I'd been here alone," she whispered.

"But you're not alone, remember?" He leaned close to her lips and resisted the strong urge to kiss them. "I'm with you, and wherever thou goest, I go." He straightened and towered over her, wanting to pat himself on the back for not touching her. "I can't help it they didn't like my looks."

She relaxed a bit and looked him up and down. "Oh I don't know. I think at least one of them did."

"Funny." He raised a brow.

She bit her lip, trying not to laugh. "Look, next time we have a problem, let me handle it, okay?"

"Sure, boss," he said, thinking with her spunk she would have given them a round for their money. He liked that.

"Good." She relaxed and turned to scan the room.

Gary studied the floor and didn't like what he saw. The place was loud, the bar scarred. Most of the tables had seen better days. Some chairs with missing legs were stacked in the corner. And the smell... Whew. Like one of the city's microbrews had dropped their dregs on the ground.

Yeah, he'd heard about this place and the bar lived up to everything said about it, and then some. Fights broke out almost every night. He didn't want Mira hurt. He hoped on Ladies Night, things wouldn't be so bad.

They walked past a small group of women. Smoke rose from their cigarettes and curled against the ceiling. The air grew thick with the smoldering residue and the show hadn't even started yet. He glanced to the side. Roped off in the middle of the room was the dance floor with two openings at either end.

"I can't believe I'm doing this," Mira said.

He came up behind her and rubbed her upper arms. "If it makes you feel any better, I can't believe I am either. I hope none of my clients are here. It'll ruin my reputation."

"Oh pooh. You're escorting me, remember?" She looked at the dance floor and pointed to a sign. "Although, it's Amateur Night. Maybe you'd rather be one of the dancers?" She glanced at him, a twinkle in her eye.

"Never in a million years." He spied a table near the exit and guided her to it. If they had to run, he wanted to make sure they got out quick.

Some of the women at the bar eyed him as he walked by. "Damn shame," he heard one gal say as she studied him from the corner of her eye. "Hate to see such a good-looking guy get that way."

He moved closer to Mira and she giggled. "Mmmm, I guess people are getting the wrong impression about you. They think you're—"

"Exactly." She didn't have to say the word. He wasn't gay. Far from it. If other guys wanted to be, that was their business, not his. He just didn't want to be associated with the thought. He had enough problems with his own image of his masculinity.

The rickety table had been the best of the bunch, away from the dance floor but close to the exit.

"This should do." He held a chair for her. "I want to be near the door in case the police raid the place."

Her eyebrow quirked upward as she sat. "You don't really think… This is legit, isn't it?"

"How would I know?" He shrugged and sat next to her.

Her face creased with worry.

"I'm sure it'll be fine. Who did you say told you about this place?"

She bit her lip. "Jojo. The woman who came up to you in the tent last night. She's, ah…well, a sex therapist."

Stunned, Gary paused a moment. "A sex therapist? And she recommended this place?"

Mira nodded. "I hope you're not mad."

"No. Just surprised." He shrugged. He couldn't imagine a professional sending anyone here. Then again, he wouldn't have guessed the redhead from last night was a sex therapist either. He waved for a waiter.

In seconds, a half-clad guy came up to them. "Oh my…" The man leaned into him. "Aren't we the big one? My name's Bobby and I'll be helping you tonight. What can I get you?" He waggled his brows.

Gary gritted his teeth. "Two waters and a menu."

"Anything you say, handsome." The waiter winked at him.

Gary groaned and looked around, noticing some of the other "guests". More than a quarter of them were men and they were together. Something told him this night could be more than they bargained for. What the hell kind of Ladies Night could it be when *this* many guys showed up? "Uh, Mira…"

The announcer cut him off. Lights flashed and some guy in a suit and tie jumped onto the dance area, whirling and shaking his butt as if he had red ants nipping at his gonads. The women screamed as the stripper removed his tie and ran the length between his legs. "I can't believe this." He buried his head in his hand and rubbed his forehead.

The waiter came back with the water and Gary ordered a beer. A tall one. He figured before this night finished, he'd need several. "Just keep them coming," he told the guy.

The waiter smiled and handed him the menus. "I'll keep whatever you want coming, honey." Then he walked away.

"God." He rolled his eyes and handed Mira a menu. She didn't even notice. Her eyes had glued themselves to the stage. "You want me to order a burger for you?" he asked.

"Sure." She nodded, her mouth gaping.

He couldn't watch. Didn't, until one loud woman's voice broke through the din. "Hit me, baby. Hit me hard." By the time he looked, the woman had a bill in her mouth and pranced up to the opening in the ropes. She must have been over sixty.

In one smooth move, the dancer swept her up, took the bill with his teeth, and swirled her around once while gyrating his hips against her. He couldn't believe what he'd seen. If some of the running backs he'd faced used those kind of moves, he'd never have been able to catch them.

"Did you see that?" Mira put a death grip on his arm. "She gave him a fifty-dollar bill!"

"Mmmm." He took a deep swig of the brew the waiter slipped in front of him. "Pretty damn smooth for fifty bucks. I would've thought he'd given her more for her money."

A woman would've.

Mira stared at him oddly then dropped her jaw again. The man onstage removed his shirt and threw his top to another aging grandmother who took flash pictures of his hairy chest. Gary swigged another gulp and closed his eyes. How the hell did he talk his way into this? He only needed a simple, sexy voice. *Mira's.*

That defined the problem. He could get a voice. But it wouldn't have been Mira's. Besides, he'd wanted to be near her. Talk to her. Be with her. That's why he made the deal. He wanted to be close to a normal woman, at least for some period of time without having to explain why.

The high-pitched screams drew his eyes back to the dancer. The man made some other kinky move. He would have thought the reaction impossible, but Mira's eyes opened further. How could he talk to her here? He'd never get the chance to explain what happened last night if they stayed. And he wanted her to know. He didn't want her to get any wrong ideas. It might mess up everything — the ad, his plans for a friendship. He couldn't let the mistake happen. He needed her too much, in too many ways. He clenched his teeth. He wouldn't fail. He couldn't afford to.

Another woman let loose an ear-shattering scream. He groaned then took another gulp when something landed on his head and draped itself over his eyes, blinding him. "Oh God, tell me this isn't happening." He removed the piece of cloth. It was the dancer's pants. "I think I'm going to be sick."

Mira laughed at him and he smiled. He liked seeing her happy. When she laughed, her whole face lit up. He wanted to see more of it.

Another whoop and she grew mesmerized again.

The waiter returned and he traded the pants for a pitcher of beer. The waiter seemed ecstatic about the slacks. Gary ordered burgers for them and refilled his glass.

"Mira…" He leaned near her ear. "Do we need to stay for the whole show or is one dance enough?"

Before she answered, the waiter returned. "You know," he said, "tonight is amateur night, in case you're interested." He threw him a kiss.

Gary about lost it. "Look, I'm not…"

The place erupted with women hooting before he finished his reply. He couldn't even hear himself. The waiter scooted off and Gary stared at the stage. The guy had removed a regular pair of briefs and pranced about with nothing on but a small flap covering what little there could be of his manhood. He stuck his moving butt into one of the elder ladies' face and the woman with the camera took a picture. If he hadn't known better, he'd have thought both of the women were having heart attacks.

"These ladies are crazy." He looked at Mira. She jumped up and down, yelling with them. And this was Danielle's timid sister?

He made a key decision. He'd get drunk, that's what he'd do. That way, he wouldn't know where he sat. He would do what Mira had done last night and pass out. Except he couldn't. His conscience would bother him. Mira needed someone to protect her in this insane asylum. Although, God pity him, a few beers wouldn't hurt.

"Oh my God." Mira reached over and put another death grip on his arm. "She's taking off her shirt too!"

Gary glanced at the stage. A woman of maybe twenty had bent backwards and lifted her shirt, laying a bill down between her naked breasts. "Jesus…" He rested his elbow on his knee and watched. The dancer picked her up and took the bill slowly with his mouth. With his mouth! What the hell? And he thought as a ballplayer you got the good stuff. He finished his second beer. This definitely got more interesting.

The music ended, thank God.

He turned to Mira. "Please have mercy and let's get out of here. I don't think I can handle any more. I'm beginning to think my grandmother is a sex maniac."

Mira bit her lip. "But not all the guys have danced yet. There's at least two more." She took his hand in hers and rubbed the backs of them with her thumbs. "Unless, of course, you want to volunteer."

He thought about her naked on his balcony again. He sipped his third beer. The brew gave him courage. "Look, if you really want, I'll do it. In private. I'll even figure out where to get one of those bikini things. Just get me out of here."

She laughed. The sound encouraged him. Would she agree?

"Please?" he asked. He wasn't beyond begging.

Then a frown spread across her face.

"Does the look on your face mean no?" he asked.

The music started again. She shook her head and mouthed something.

"What's wrong?" He had to lean closer to hear her.

"Trouble. With a capital D," she shouted and let go of his hand. She drummed her fingers against the table and looked over his head. "Hello, Danielle."

"Huh?" He turned just as Danielle and the redhead from last night stepped behind him. "Great." They were the last thing he needed. With Danielle here, they'd never get out. He finished off the suds in his glass and poured another one.

"I'm sorry, Mira," Jojo explained loudly. "But she insisted. Said she had something imperative she needed to tell Gary." She slapped Danielle on the arm.

"Ow." Danielle glared at Jojo. "I do," she insisted. "Can we join you?" Danielle stared at him, her face hopeful, as if he'd be the only one she'd have any luck with.

Screams filled the room again. "I can't hear what you're saying," Gary replied. "I've gone deaf."

Mira smirked. "Sit down, pest. We're leaving in a few minutes, anyway."

"Oh, but you can't leave yet. You haven't spent enough time togeth...er...here."

"We've spent more than enough." Gary looked at Danielle. "What do you have to tell me?"

"Ah, well, S..."

The women howled again and he couldn't hear a thing. Now all three women sat goo-goo-eyed over the new guy. Gary moved his chair closer to Mira and nursed his beer. This would be one hell of a long night.

The burgers had arrived, but Mira forgot about hers. Every so often, she glanced at Gary. Most of the time, he'd looked at her. Occasionally, he studied the dance floor, usually with some kind of smirk. More often, he sat nursing his beer. They were on their third pitcher. Danielle had seen they all gotten a glass. That was fine with Mira. She needed at least one drink to calm her nerves, give her a little of the courage she'd had last night.

Watching the male strippers had only made her think more of Gary and a bed. She let herself really look at him, the planes of his face, the thick cords of muscle in his neck. His arms too. How large and strong they were. And warm. She had grown hot in his embrace.

Then there was his chest. She'd experienced for herself how buff his pecs had been. Of course, she couldn't see his nude body now, but when he had stood in his boxers in front of her, every bone in her body had cried, "Yes, take me now."

She wanted to stop her denial. She wanted Gary, wanted to run her hands all over him, slowly, feel every nook, every turn of his powerful body.

Thinking about him made her hot.

She gulped the last drop of her beer for good measure and leaned over to put her hand on his arm. "You ready to leave?"

He lifted a brow. "Do you really have to ask?"

"Then let's go." She tugged his arm.

He nodded at Danielle and Jojo. "You think we can get them to go?"

"I don't know." She shrugged.

"Then we need to wait. I don't think they should be alone. I've been watching. Some of these guys aren't gay. A few of them have been hitting on the women at the bar. All these scum need is to find two tipsy women to take advantage of. Can't let that happen." He took another sip.

She smiled. "So now you're the knight in shining armor again. You do amaze me. Are you really a gentleman at heart?"

He leaned toward her. "It's not just heart, darlin', it's practice. Mom would kill me if I were otherwise."

Mira laughed, knowing how much of the beer he'd drunk, wondering if the alcohol would work to her advantage.

She lost all interest in what happened on the dance floor. Yeah, she'd watched, probably with more than a little interest, but she'd never seen anything like this before. Gary held much more fascination for her.

And not just his body, she realized. He was a real person, and nice. She'd met few men who truly were. Danielle described him as a big guy with an even bigger heart. Maybe her sister was right? Maybe Mira had been wrong about him.

Maybe she'd been wrong about a lot of guys.

Her stomach growled and she looked at the cold burger. Not very appealing.

Fortunately, the last man in the lineup danced. Except for the amateurs who wanted to try. They could leave soon. Maybe she'd take him up on his offer to strip for her, if he still wanted.

She looked at the stale burger. She'd like something decent to eat. "Gary…" She leaned toward him and ran her hand slowly up his arm. She wanted to be seductive for once, entice him to take her out on a "real" date.

But then the music stopped. He looked at her, confused. She backed away and cleared her throat. "I'm hungry and I don't want this. Can we…" She paused, not knowing how to say "Date me".

Gary downed the rest of his beer. "Eat? Sure. As long as it's not here. You don't mind, do you?"

"No." She smiled, relieved he couldn't tell she'd come on to him. "I'd rather be somewhere else." She didn't tell him the place she wanted was being half naked in his bedroom again. Perhaps they could start where they left off?

She picked up her purse and looked at her sister. "You guys coming?"

Danielle glanced at the stage then back at her. "Do we have to?"

"Yes," Mira insisted. Gary wouldn't leave if they didn't and she wanted to spend a lot of personal time with him. *Very* personal time. She was ready. The time was now or never.

"I can stay with her, amigos," Jojo said. "I want to see what this guy does."

An old acid rock tune came on and a tall, husky man sauntered onto the floor.

"Not again." Gary ran his hand over his face in disgust.

The amateur stripper rotated his hips and the bottle blonde at the bar whooped so loud Mira thought the rafters would come down.

The woman sitting next to the screamer got mad and cussed. She shoved the blonde too hard and the other woman fell off the barstool. The blonde responded by throwing beer in the other girl's face. Mira's jaw dropped, never having seen two women in a rumble.

Suddenly, the fun-loving crowd turned into a rowdy bunch. Beer and fists flew everywhere.

"Time to go, ladies." Gary stood, pulling Mira with him. Danielle and Jojo ran for the exit.

A chair broke against Gary's back. Mira gasped and looked behind him. A woman stood there smiling. "Come get me, big boy," she taunted.

Gary shrugged the fluke off and pushed Mira toward the door. "Let's go."

She didn't need any prodding. They rushed behind Jojo and her sister. In seconds, they were outside.

"Where's your car?" Gary asked Danielle.

"Around the corner," Danielle shouted over the din from the frenzied women filing out. "I couldn't park any closer."

"Get in mine." He pressed the button on his key chain to unlock the car then handed Mira the keys. "If I'm not back in a few minutes, take off."

"Where are you going?" she asked, afraid of what he might be thinking.

"Inside. Those old ladies were trapped."

My God, he is a knight. She couldn't argue with him. She grabbed the keys and followed Jojo and Danielle to the vehicle.

She bit her lip, her first thought that he *was* different. Her second thought? She didn't want him to get hurt.

Her mouth parted. The fact she cared what happened to him shocked her. Had she ever cared for a guy like that?

Gary rushed into the crowd, squeezing his way through the door. Once inside, he scanned the room. The older ladies huddled in a corner by the dance floor. He made his way to them. When he reached the group, he noticed the woman who had given the fifty bucks to the dancer held her head. "Are you all right?" he asked.

She nodded. "A bit wobbly though."

He picked her up and carried her in his arms. "Okay, ladies, stay between me and the wall and you'll be fine." He started to move. Thank God his grandmother look-alikes did as he asked.

As he turned to check on the ones straggling behind, a punch hit him across the jaw. Georgio, the bouncer, stood to the side of him, ready to fight. "Dammit," he said, and tried to maneuver away but Georgio blocked his path. He had to put the lady down or take a beating. Either way, the women were at risk. What a damned idiot. The jerk should be protecting these people.

Gary tried negotiation. "Hey, man, let me take care of these ladies. Then, if you want, we'll finish this outside."

"No dice," the bouncer growled.

From nowhere, Bobby, the waiter, appeared and engaged the creep. Landed a good one right in his gut. The pathway opened and Gary took off as fast as possible with five elderly women in tow.

He looked back to check on Bobby. As the shorter of the two men, the gay waiter landed a few good blows before Gary lost him in the craziness. He ushered the ladies outside. In the distance, sirens sounded and he wondered where Bucky, the other bouncer, had gone.

"Thank you, young man." The woman he held kissed his cheek.

"Be safe, ladies." He put her down and then the rest of them hugged him, planting more motherly kisses on his face. Well, he liked to think they were motherly. He couldn't be sure about the one with the camera.

He quickly shooed them on and rushed back inside to check on Bobby. Guilt motivated him big time. The guy saved him from a beating and allowed him to get the women out. The waiter deserved better than a thrashing by Georgio. When Gary rushed in, the bouncer was pounding that pretty face of Bobby's.

He rushed up to Georgio and tapped him on the shoulder. "Hey, you want me, you got me."

The bouncer turned. Gary'd been angry. He jacked Georgio's jaw with a right hook. Laid him flat. The bouncer moaned and tried to steady himself.

Gary looked at Bobby. The man's white teeth glared against his bloodied face.

Georgio pushed himself up on all fours.

"C'mon, Bob," Gary yelled before the bouncer could recover. "Let's get out of here." He turned for the exit.

Just in time to see the boys in blue rush in.

Chapter Seven

✂

"Omigod." Mira put her hand to her mouth. "Gary's stuck in there." She rushed out of the car toward the entrance.

A policeman stopped her. "Sorry, ma'am. You can't go in."

"But you don't understand. My date is in there. After he got us out, he went back in to help these older ladies and…"

The policeman pushed her back. "I said no. Don't make me arrest you too." He turned toward the door.

Just then, Gary showed in the entryway. He stopped when he saw the officer. Their waiter followed right behind him.

"He saved me." The battered Bobby scooted under Gary's arm and came to her, giving her a big hug. "I had been getting my…well, you-know-what beat and all of a sudden he appeared. Every manly piece of him." Bobby sighed. "I know he must belong to you, but tonight he's my hero. He beat that Georgio to a pulp."

She hugged him back, not knowing what else to do, and watched Gary run a hand over his face.

The policeman looked at Gary. "Sir, step outside."

Gary groaned as he took the few steps out of the door and held up his wrists.

The officer turned him around, pulling an arm with him, and clapped his cuffs on Gary. "Wait here," he instructed then hurried into the mess the barroom had become.

"Great." Gary rolled his eyes. Leaning against the wall, he peered at Mira.

Danielle and Jojo came up behind her. They were so loud she couldn't help but hear them. "But I didn't think something like this would happen," he heard Jojo argue.

"Why not?" Danielle spat. "This is horrible."

"You seemed to be enjoying the show well enough. We could have left earlier..." Jojo countered.

Mira let their voices fade into the background.

Bobby looked at her. "He does belong to you, doesn't he?"

She glanced at Gary. In that moment, Mira wanted to believe he did. "Yes," she mumbled and a spark came into Gary's eyes. She looked at Bobby. "Yes, he does."

Bobby glanced downward as Danielle's voice grew louder. Then Bobby shrugged and turned to her sister. "Ladies, ladies..." He gave them a group hug. "If you hadn't stayed, I'd have been meat for Georgio. Trust me on this, the man's an aaaannnnimal. I'm glad you were here."

They patted him on the back, reassuring him everything would be all right.

"Jesus, what a mess," Gary grumbled. Mira stood close enough to hear him, but the other two still calmed Bobby.

"Gary," she approached him, not knowing what to say, where to begin. "I'm sorry about this. I should have never brought us here. You did the right thing, though, getting those ladies out."

He raised a brow. "I'm not sure the cops will see my efforts that way. And this isn't your fault. You didn't know better. I did."

She pressed her lips together and came closer, her body within inches of his. "Maybe. But I know what you did, saving those ladies. You did the right thing." She ran a hand up his chest, suppressing her sexual fears. "You know, I've never known a guy like you. An athlete, that is, one who cares about someone else, something else besides his own ego."

He studied her. "Is that what it is with you?" he whispered. "The fact I used to play ball?"

She nodded. "Had a bad experience once."

She grew nervous because of what she let herself do, let herself feel. Would he make fun of her after all of this? "I've thought since then big guys like you, especially football players, were all the same." She wrapped her hand around his neck and leaned into him. Her pulse beat faster from her boldness. "Are you the same? Is the only thing you care about yourself and how the world looks at you?"

His Adam's apple moved up and down as he swallowed. She fingered it, intrigued with this man.

"I sure as hell hope not," he said, bending his neck so that his lips were within a breath of hers.

Captivated, she moved her fingers to his soft mouth.

He took a fingertip between his lips and caressed the ridged skin with his tongue.

Warmth bloomed within her, enveloping her in its heat. She moaned and moved her mouth to his, savoring the taste of him.

The girls argued behind her, but she ignored them, the rest of the world falling away as the urgency in Gary's response took over. Pressing his mouth to hers, he opened his lips and captured hers with an intensity she had never known. Need burst through her, the want to be with this man. Rising on her toes, she slid her arms around his neck and held him flush against her. He groaned and she felt his reaction in the hard pulsing of his manhood against her leg.

"Mira?" Danielle tapped her on the shoulder, breaking the magic moment. Couldn't Dani see she was busy? She looked up and caught the passion in his rich blue eyes. He swallowed and the look disappeared. Mira gritted her teeth and faced her little sister.

"I think we need to get Gary out of here." Worry lines showed on Danielle's face. "We can find someone to take the cuffs off."

"That's illegal," Mira said, getting her erratic breathing under control, working to think their situation through. "It's got to be."

"I have a lawyer," Gary responded after taking a deep breath. "Danielle, if you feel guilty, you can call him for me."

"Oh Gary. C'mon, let's go," Danielle urged.

"No," his deep voice demanded.

Mira wouldn't have argued with him, then again, Danielle wasn't Mira.

"Gary…" Her sister tugged at his upper arm.

Gary winced. "Watch the shoulder, sweetheart…"

"Sorry." Danielle backed away.

"Dani, go home," Mira said. "You've caused enough trouble for one night."

"Me?" Her sister put her hand to her chest. "But I—"

"But, nothing," Mira snapped, not able to hide the irritation in her voice. "If you'd helped me with Sara like I asked, instead of concocting this grand scheme, we wouldn't be in this predicament. But no, you had to meddle…"

"But—"

Mira held up her hand.

"Enough," Gary said then sagged against the building. "The last thing I want is for you two to be gnawing at each other. Now get out of here, all of you. Mira, take my car. I'll handle this."

"No." Mira's aggravation flared because of Danielle's interference but Gary's self-sacrificing had gone on long enough. She planted her hands on her hips. "Who do you think you are now? Batman? Are you going to call Commissioner Gordon to come release you?" She crossed her arms in front of her. "Do you really think I'd go and leave you handcuffed and stranded? I hope not, because at this point you should know me better. I do what I think is right and that certainly doesn't include abandoning you. After all, you are my escort."

"Stubbornness isn't always a good trait, Mira." He inched closer. "Please?"

"No." She pouted but she couldn't help the childish reaction. He'd been so nice about this and his selflessness made her feel funny.

"Even if being here means you might get in trouble?" Gary's brows drew together.

"Yes," she breathed.

He frowned. "Mira, you staying isn't going to help. I'll explain everything."

"Without witnesses?"

"Please?"

"No," she said softly. She would stand firm. Besides, the warm-fuzzy in her gut had taken over again. She let herself go with the feeling and leaned against his chest, listening to his strong heartbeat as the trio of Bobby, Jojo and Danielle argued again behind her.

Gary sighed and rested his chin on the top of her head. "Thanks."

"You're welcome." She wrapped her arms around him, the sense of something right, something shared encircling the two of them, something that didn't have anything to do with their sexual attraction. Content, Mira gazed at the door. The cops still pulled people out of the place but it looked as if things had slowed down.

"Last chance, Mira," Gary whispered in her ear. "I don't want you hurt. There's no need for you to go to the station. This may take a long time."

The intimacy in his tone bonded her to him. Before she could answer, some loud male voices sounded from around the building. Mira straightened as Georgio and Bucky strolled into sight.

Bucky caught sight of them and hurried over. "You okay, man?"

Georgio followed and Mira noticed the bouncer's mouth had been bloodied and swollen.

Gary sighed. "I will be if I can get these cuffs off." He glared at Georgio. "I can see you made it out okay."

The guy ducked his chin to his chest.

Bucky looked from Gary to Georgio and back again. "So, that's what happened." He punched Georgio in the arm. "I told you he'd lay you flat, you idiot. What did you do?"

Bobby saw them and jumped from one foot to another, as if he had to pee. Mira suspected he finally couldn't take the suspense anymore. "I'll tell you what he did," the waiter said. "He hit this guy while he carried an injured lady out. I slugged him and pulled him away for a while but this big boy came back and saw I had trouble. Georgio bruised me bad." He pointed to his messed up face.

Bucky's face screwed up like a prune as he studied Bobby's wounds. "You mean, you hit Georgio? He coulda kilt you."

Trembling, Bobby bit his lip and nodded. "I know."

Gary groaned and buried his head in the crook of Mira's neck. Her skin tingled and she realized she liked him there, the fact he let himself lean on her, at least for a smidgen of emotional support. He turned his head slightly and his steady breath caressed her skin. Heat fired from the sensation and radiated deep within her, stirring more than what she recognized as a hormonal response. She gasped, sure he didn't know how deeply his caring moved her.

A ranking officer came over. "I think we have everyone we're going to get tonight." He handed Bucky a piece of paper. "The city's tired of this place, fella. Tell the owner to call the station house in the morning. From this point on, this place is closed."

Bucky grabbed the paper. "Shit."

The officer turned and walked away.

"Wait a minute," Mira yelled after him. "You guys still have my friend cuffed."

The officer looked back and Gary turned around and lifted his hands as best he could.

The policeman came back. "Did you get the officer's name?" he asked.

"No." Gary shook his head.

The policeman went around the corner, shouting off some names.

"Don't worry, Roller," Bucky said, "I'll get you out of this."

Finally, the officer who had cuffed him came back. "I didn't forget about you," he said.

"I didn't think so," Gary retorted.

"You wanna tell me your story?"

"He's innocent," Bucky announced.

The policeman looked from Bucky to Gary to Georgio. "Just like that? Seems to me your man here," he pointed to Georgio, "accused this guy of starting the fight."

"Damn lie." Bucky stared at Georgio.

Georgio stuttered. "I...I musta been mistaken."

The officer snorted and adjusted his hat. "Yeah, fine."

Gary turned around. In seconds the policeman had the cuffs off. "Thanks." Gary rubbed his wrists.

The officer looked at him. "How much have you had to drink?"

Gary looked at Mira. "I'm not driving."

"Good." The policeman nodded and walked off.

"Oh thank God." Danielle made the sign of the cross over her chest. "Maybe I will have a job come tomorrow." She winced as she looked at Gary.

He glared. "You better be in early. You have a lot to do."

Bucky and Georgio walked off.

"I think it's time you went home," Mira said to Danielle.

"But I never did get to tell Gary..."

"Come on…" Jojo pulled Danielle away but then stopped and looked at Bobby. "Sweetheart, do you need a ride home?"

Bobby eased a hand around Jojo's elbow. "I could use some coffee. My treat. It's the least I can do for you ladies. Especially after your man saved me."

"Sounds good to me." Jojo winked at Mira and put an arm around Bobby, leading both him and Danielle away.

"Geez." Mira hugged herself, glad this scare had ended.

Gary put his arms around her. "You cold?"

"No." She shook her head and leaned against him, reveling in the strength and warmth emanating from him, a different warmth from the sensual heat of their earlier embrace. "I'm so sorry, Gary. Really. I didn't know the place was like this."

"I told you this isn't your fault. You just came here to experience something you never had before. You didn't start the fight so don't blame yourself. Besides, I knew what kind of place it was. That's why I didn't want you to go in there alone. I didn't mean to make you mad."

She smiled. "Thanks." She rose up on her toes and kissed him on the lips. Sensual heat still smoldering within her, the embers teasing her sexual desires. "You ready to go?" she murmured with a breathy voice.

"Very," he whispered. "You still hungry?"

She nodded. "How 'bout we go to your place? You can cook and I'll play doctor."

"Doctor?" One of his brows rose.

"Yep." She took his hand and walked him to the car, relishing the feel of his body next to hers. "I saw how you flinched when Dani touched your shoulder. I know the chair that woman broke across your back probably wasn't very comfy. Playing doctor is the least I can do." She held the passenger's side door open for him, hoping he would play along.

He held up her hand and kissed her palm. "I could take your offer a couple of ways, Mira. Be careful how you play this."

Would she be bold enough to make the move? Her nerves fired with anticipation. She fingered his collar then looked into his eyes. "One thing at a time, big guy. First food, then doctoring. Afterward, we'll see, okay?"

He paused a minute, staring at her. "Okay." He nodded and glanced at the open door. "You know, I'm not used to the lady being the gentleman."

"That's because you're not used to independent women." She smiled, more sure of herself. "Maybe you should be."

He leaned over and kissed her. "Maybe you're right."

He got into the car and she closed the door behind him, pausing a minute to catch her breath. Her heart raced. She guessed her rapid pulse came from a mixture of anxiety and the hormones her libido pumped through her system. Would she go through with this?

Could she?

She ran to the driver's side, a delicious ache building in her lower body.

* * * * *

Gary whipped up a quick omelet for her. Apparently, he could only cook breakfast but what he did make tasted great, especially with the white wine he served. She drank the liquid, needing a little bit more for strength.

They sat on his balcony and watched the stars mingle with the city lights. The view was beautiful.

And so was he, she thought. The angles of his face, the light sprinkling of hair that covered his chest, the hard, round muscles that seemed to cover his entire body.

And he was nice. That had been the kicker. The thing that drew her closer to him, the part of him that allowed her to take the risk. But this game wasn't over yet. She braced herself, knowing she would have to battle her inner ego.

She pushed her plate away. "I think it's time to look at your back."

"That isn't necessary." He shook his head.

"Yes, it is. It's part of the deal. You cook, I doctor. I am a doctor, you know. And I even know something about medicine."

He chuckled.

She backed away from the table. "Now, where's your Band-Aids and stuff?"

He pointed inside. "Bathroom."

She stood and left him alone on the balcony.

Gary watched her hips sway as she walked away. He wasn't drunk, but he wasn't sober either. Otherwise, he wouldn't be thinking what he thought.

And God, he certainly couldn't be thinking straight. Getting half naked around her was dangerous. Look at what they'd done already tonight. Making out, especially in front of Mira's sister. He sure as hell didn't want Danielle's meddling. So far, everything the girl touched in this deal with Mira had turned into a disaster.

Except getting Mira and him together. That hadn't bombed, not yet anyway, but if he didn't keep his head, it could. Good thing Danielle interrupted Mira's kiss when she did. Otherwise, he might have devoured her on the spot. It'd taken all his control not to touch Mira the way he wanted, and he wanted to touch her bad.

Mira excited him, but the emotion that hooked him was more than lust and he knew it. She was the one, the one he wanted to be with for life. He knew that when she first rammed into him. He didn't know how he knew, he just knew. It had been a curse of the Staunton males. It'd been the same for his father, his uncle, his grandfather, all going back to Great-granddaddy Will as far as he knew. Maybe the trait went back even further. At first, he'd denied it. Then he'd fought it, hoping the pattern didn't ring true. But sitting with her tonight, the moonlight glowing on her long hair, the laughter in her eyes, he knew.

And God, the realization scared him.

Part of the problem had been the drink, he realized. Alcohol had allowed him to drop his guard, punch holes in his rationalization that said he couldn't have her. The other part was loneliness. And he sure as hell had become sick and tired of being alone.

Perhaps now he didn't have to be.

"I'm back." She sauntered to the table and sat next to him, breaking his sober mood.

He looked away and stared at the moon.

"Earth to Gary. Are you with me?"

He wished to be. He needed a moment to mull over the thought. "I will be if you want me to." He looked at her and fingered her lips.

Her mouth parted and a slight blush rose on her cheeks. "Well, you, ah..." She licked her lips and pulled away. "You need to take your shirt off." Her voice grew hoarse.

"Right." Fear of failing with her gripped him. He steadied the ragged breathing his anxiety caused, his craving for her driving him onward. On one level, she wanted him. She'd already showed him that much tonight. Yet here she'd switched subjects. He thought she knew it too, and wondered if she'd changed her mind. Still, the shift didn't stop him from gazing into the green of her deep hazel eyes. He stood and faced her, opening each of his shirt buttons with anxiety and anticipation, working to have that shimmer of desire in her gaze once again.

She bit her bottom lip as her eyes traveled lower with each slow movement of his hands, the antiseptic shaking in her grasp. Her dark pupils widened, the green around her irises deepened. His shirt fell open and he watched with interest at the lust-filled stare she aimed at the vee the tucked ends of cloth made at his waist. This time when he brushed the side of her face with his fingers, her eyes locked on his, the want of sex rich within them.

Hopeful, he leaned toward her. The plastic antiseptic bottle eased from her hands and plopped on the hard red tile, forgotten. His pulse quickened as he neared. He kissed her, slowly, tenderly at first. Her lips trembled under his. She sighed then laid her body against him. He could feel her taut nipples through the thin fabric she wore, encouraging his pursuit. She pulled the shirttail from his belted pants and slipped her arms around his bare waist. The urge assailed him. *He had to have her. All of her.*

He needed her, would have her softness at least this night. His kiss changed. Harder, deeper. Demanding. Her tongue reached for his, seeking its own release, the interaction between them creating a dance all its own. She moaned and his body fired. Her hips rubbed against him, against his almost full erection. Her hand slid from his back to his stomach and fingered his waist beneath his belt.

"Doctor," he uttered between breaths, trying not to rush, wanting her to decide about this moment, needing her to want him for himself. "I don't think the pain is in there."

She licked her lips, her soft breath caressing him. "Are you sure?" Her voice sounded rough, uneven.

Was he? Any remnant of his pledge of abstinence fled. He stared a moment longer. "No," he said, with renewed confidence. "I'm not sure at all."

Chapter Eight

ఴ

A nervous flutter shook her as she slid her hands along the rough planes of his chest, a deeper sense of something happening here that she had no conscious awareness of.

But whatever it was, she wanted it, the stirring of this unknown emotion like nothing she'd ever experienced. Her hands trembled as she reached his shoulders. Swallowing, she slipped the shirt off.

She gasped, the sight, the feel, of his body taking her breath away. Never had she touched a man who moved her like this. She forced herself to focus, remembering her promise to tend his injury. "Maybe we should look at your back first."

"Chicken." He grinned, his heart-stopping smile shaking her resolve. She became lost. She stepped back, barely regaining her balance, and turned him around.

If anything could put a damper on the evening, the sight of his wound stopped her cold. "Oh Gary..." Parts of his bruised, scraped flesh rose from the swollen muscle underneath. "This looks awful."

He snorted. "Yeah, just what I wanted to hear."

She picked up the antiseptic. "I'm not sure how much I can do with this." Taking a cloth, she poured the liquid on it and dabbed his skin. She used the only thing he'd had, an old-fashioned type of cure-all that burned, but when she applied the antiseptic, Gary barely flinched. "Your nerves must be made of steel."

He glanced back at her, his hot gaze penetrating her ego-driven barriers. "Not all of them," he breathed, his full lips parted and inviting.

She paused, taken aback from the intensity in his deep, husky voice. And his eyes. They told so much more. His powerful look reached out and spoke to every hidden desire she'd had.

"Turn around," she ordered before her courage failed her, and moved his chin forward, struggling to keep control. "I can't see your back." When he did, she dabbed again and failed miserably to steady her breathing.

He chuckled softly, the low rumble deep, yet light. "I didn't realize cleaning my back would take this much effort."

"It doesn't." She sighed, reminding herself she would set the pace in this seduction, but afraid she would lose her sanity before she finished and her courage ran out.

"Really?"

"No. Why do you ask?" She inhaled a deep breath and concentrated on dabbing his wound, grateful she was almost finished. Conflicted by her angst and desire, she could barely focus on the task.

The shift in his body forced her to stop. When he turned, his piercing gaze locked on hers. "Then your heavy breathing must be from something else," he murmured and grasped her body, pulling her toward him.

Damn, she thought. Her pulse soared. She couldn't fight this feeling anymore, nor did she want to. She fell willingly against his powerful chest and into his welcoming arms.

He held her close as he sat down, guiding her legs to straddle him. His calloused palms slipped upward against her thighs, sparks of fire lighting her skin where they touched, rousing her feminine core in heated, delicious waves. He continued alongside her hips and up her back, his caress a gentle torture of sensual pleasure. "Tell me what you're thinking, Mira," he rasped and pulled her closer.

Her breath caught, her chest so heavy she could hardly inhale. Could she go through with this? She closed the small gap between them and whispered against his lips, encouraged by the raw desire she read in his eyes, an innate need that mated with her on some deeper level. "Maybe I can show you instead. Then I won't be so afraid."

She kissed him with every emotion she had. Passion poured out of her, of whatever the sensations were—fear, the pain…and love, she realized. God, she'd never felt this way. The powerful sense reached her toes, to the bottom of her soul, the emotions shocking, invigorating her.

Freeing her.

She ended the kiss and angled back in his arms laughing.

He arched his brows, concerned. "Are…are you okay?"

"Oh yeah." She offered him her sexiest smile.

His frowned. "Then why are you laughing?"

"Laughing?" She stopped to stare at him, appreciating the view of his half-naked, virile body. Without analyzing her actions, she fingered the light sprinkling of hair across his chest, the soft skin and the feel of his hard muscles underneath, the touch exciting her more.

He looked confused. "Yeah, ah…" His fingers massaged the small muscles in her back, leaning her closer to him. "Most women don't just break off a passionate kiss like that."

"They don't?" She enjoyed her first moments of sexual freedom. Shimmying nearer to him, she ran her hands up his taut abs and ribs then moved higher, enjoying the strong, steady rise and fall of his chest against her palms. "And just what do they do?" she murmured against his parted lips then teased them with her fingertips.

He looked even more perplexed. "They kiss you back. Harder." He smirked then whispered, "Or they slap you." His gaze narrowed, his seductive voice wavered. "Do you want to slap me, Mira?"

"God, no." She realized he was serious. She slid her breasts flush against him, taking his lips with hers. "It's just that…" she muttered between lingering pecks, "I did it."

"Did what?"

She licked her lips and eased back some to see his face. "Kissed you."

"But this isn't our first kiss."

"No." She wanted him to understand, unafraid that he might think poorly of her. Another first, she thought. "But it's the first time I kissed you and I didn't question myself. I actually let myself enjoy touching you.

"You didn't like it before?" He lifted her empty wine glass and sniffed. "You sure you didn't have something else in your drink?"

She giggled and slid off his legs, sitting on the rug covering the patio tile to put some distance between them so she could concentrate. "No, silly. I did enjoy this before, but..." She sighed. "It never felt so real. I hope you don't mind." She kicked off her shoe and slid her toe up his pant leg, encouraged by her newfound bravery.

He stared at her for a long moment, his eyes deep and unreadable. Then he nodded. "No, I don't mind. In fact, I think I know what you mean."

Her sexy legs showed almost to her hips. She was a vision. A temptress who had come into his life to test his moral fiber.

Her toe moved higher. He groaned.

Strike that. She was the devil's handmaiden, sent to torture him to eternity.

Yet when he looked at her, her nymphlike smile and sparkling eyes captured his heart. God, what had she done to him? His convictions shook to the core, made him think that perhaps they could have more than this one night. He quickly dismissed the absurd thought.

"You see..." she went on after licking her lips again, "I've *never* felt this way. With anyone. I've always been critical, about my body at least.

"Mira." Her foot slipped to his groin. With his solid erection, he had to work hard not to respond in kind, wanting to make certain she was emotionally ready for him. He didn't want her to think he was like every other man she'd dated, especially the bastard who hurt her. "Guys aren't as particular as you think."

She frowned and moved her foot to his crotch, her toes caressing his upright penis, touching the sensitive head underneath. "I don't know…"

He about came in his pants. Dropping to the carpet, he inched closer, craving her yet knowing she had to work through her anxieties first. "Trust me, okay?" He picked up a strand of her hair as he sat next to her and rolled the tress between his fingers. He couldn't help but touch her but the waiting tortured him. He bit the inside of his cheek to make sure he wasn't dead.

She lifted his fingers to her lips and kissed them. "You don't understand." She looked at his hand.

"Then make me." His voice grew hoarse, urgent.

He fought the hunger to take her, make love to her right there and show her how he treasured her beauty. Instead, he pulled his hand away.

She sighed and looked upward. "It was a long time ago. A guy I dated in high school." She looked at him. "A time I'd like to forget."

She snuggled up to him and ran her hand down his chest, causing his hardened shaft to quiver with need. He sucked in a breath, knowing she didn't realize how desperately he craved her. When she slipped her hand over the fly of his pants and squeezed his swollen shaft, he thought for sure he'd lose his mind. "Mira…" He put his hand over hers to stop her, wanting to tell her about himself first.

"Please, Gary…" Her eyes pleaded with him. "Just once I'd like to make love to a guy like you…and enjoy it."

Good God, he thought. What had happened to his plans to talk?

* * * * *

Mira could hardly believe she'd grown this bold. Maybe the crazy deal with Danielle spurred her on, or maybe the motivation had been him. She'd never been so daring, but, boy, did it feel good.

Empowering.

She touched her lips against his, timidly at first. In moments, his arms came around her, his mouth capturing hers. The passionate way he kissed stoked the fires burning within. She forgot where she was, forgot she was a plain-looking geeky scientist. Tonight, only the two of them existed and the driving, unquenchable need between them.

His kiss grew deeper, more intense with each touch. His tongue traced her mouth then plunged with vigor into her, broaching the barrier of her lips—and her soul, decimating any resistance that tempted her mind, any control she still possessed. His fingers slid up her arm to her neck, caressing the skin everywhere they touched. His arms closed around her and lowered her gently to the carpet. Then his hands slipped downward. When his palm caressed her breast, she gasped with keen pleasure.

"Mira..." he breathed raggedly between kisses, "I don't understand how a gorgeous woman could think so little of herself. You could have anyone you want. Anyone."

She pulled away and looked at him. His heady gaze, his taut, moonlit body enthralled her. "There's only one man I want tonight, Gary. That's you."

He stared at her a minute, a strange uncertain look in his eyes. "You're sure."

"Positive." She nodded.

He swallowed and pulled her close. "One night then. For both of us."

His kiss branded her soul. He slid his hand to her knee and slipped it under her dress. The cool night air clashed with his heated palm, the contrast rousing her hunger for him even more. She groaned, breathless, unable to think of anything but his caress, the longing for him churning lower within her. Slowly, he massaged her inner thigh, his fingers pinpoints of temptation as he moved higher. Reaching her waist, he slid down her hose. When he reached her lace panties, she lost the awareness of all else except his touch as he slipped his fingers inside her wet heat.

She knew only the sensation, the touch of him. He stroked her slick channel, rubbing the nub at the vee of her labia with his thumb. She moaned again and nipped his neck. The combination of the lingering scent of his aftershave and his own manly scent overwhelmed her senses. Compelled to touch him, she tongued the skin she caught between her teeth, the taste of him salty and sweet. She reached for the clasp on his belt, but he gently nudged her away, letting her hand fall lower.

She massaged him through his pants and he took his turn to groan. Burying his head in the cleavage of her dress, he sucked and nibbled her skin, causing her to arc against him so that he could reach for more.

The lust in her body blazed. She had to have him.

She reached for his buckle again but he stopped her. "Mira…" he uttered between breaths.

Didn't he want her? A bout of panic took her until a thought hit her. "I came prepared."

He looked at her, his eyes shaded. "So am I." He smiled. "You would have made a good boy scout."

She giggled and reached for him again. "Then why are you stopping me?"

"I'm not, not really. It's just I…" He sighed and traced her cheek with the back of his hand. "I want you to treasure this. I want you to experience everything you've never felt before. I want to give that to you." Then he kissed her and she knew she'd never known the depth of emotion that seared her with his kiss. "Trust me, Mira…" His hot whisper brushed her cheek. "I promise I won't hurt you. Not tonight."

She did as he asked, relinquishing the reins of seduction to him.

He pulled her close, nipping and tonguing her earlobe, stimulating her in ways she'd never dreamed. His hands skimmed over her, kneading her skin, the sensuously tensed muscles underneath. Her body flamed.

A breeze brushed her bare legs as his hand found its way to the panties again. This time Gary slipped his fingers over the top and pulled them down. Her lust sharpened, intensified as he sought and found again her feminine core. His palm covered and stroked her mons. When he thrust into her with his fingers, she squirmed with delight. The thought darted through her consciousness that she no longer set the pace. She knew she was on a ride she couldn't get off until he stopped it. Gary controlled the action now, and she accepted it. She'd done what he asked — let herself go and trust him.

Wanting to return the pleasure she felt, she ran her hands along the hard, rough planes of his torso, savoring the sensation of the tiny curls of hair covering it. She nibbled his neck, trailing kisses over him until she reached the nubs on his chest, laving them with her tongue. He sucked in a breath.

Pleased with herself, she reached for his back, careful to avoid the sore spots, and moved her hands lower, fingering the skin underneath his belt. "Gary, I want you."

He cradled himself between her legs and outlined her cheek with the pad of his thumb. "You'll have me, darling. As much of me as I can give. I promise you, tonight you'll find pleasure." He parted her mouth with his tongue and entered it. She shook from desire and anticipation.

"If my guess is right," he whispered against her, "you've never climaxed with a man, have you?"

She swallowed, her logical side not wanting to admit the fact, her body not caring her ego might be hurt.

She looked at him. His face reflected a mixture of want and some other emotion she couldn't name. "No," she murmured, not hearing her own words, her body thrumming with need.

"Then tonight will be a first," he said. "I promise."

He slid his hands along the sides of her body, lifting her dress as he did so. Instantly the dress disappeared, tossed somewhere in the darkness, her body too keyed up with desire to care where he'd thrown her clothing. For her, in this moment, there was only him.

His mouth dropped lower, to the tops of her breasts. She ran her hands through his tawny hair as his warm hands stroked her back, the fingers working the clasp of her bra.

The night air breezed over her bare skin. Within moments, the lace vanished and Gary put his warm mouth upon her nipples. His hands massaged the base of her breasts, pushing her tips higher. He sucked and pulled on one as another hand slipped lower, his fingers rubbing the nub of her womanhood and slipping into the wetness inside. She moaned louder, her body on fire, her mind only on the man loving her.

His kisses trailed to her waist, his tongue licking her, his mouth moving lower still.

Within a few slow, agonizing moments, his mouth replaced the fingers that had massaged her femininity, his hands running underneath her hips and pulling her mound up to meet him.

The intense sensation grew like wildfire within her, her body shaking with need. He laved and nipped her feminine bud, the center of her driving libido, and the labia underneath, plunging his tongue inside her until her release exploded, a white light behind her eyelids. The moan in her voice overpowered any other sound she could have heard.

Then darkness and mewling. Was that her? Gary's warm body covered her as he wrapped her in his arms. Unbidden, her ego-driven logic kicked in. She wanted to cry, confused and embarrassed from her fierce reaction.

"You're beautiful," he whispered and trailed kisses along her neck and cheek.

When she looked in his eyes, she knew he meant what he'd said. Her embarrassment fled. And something told her, she'd just been made love to for the very first time. "But what about you? I—"

He covered her lips with his finger. "I'm okay. But I wanted you to know." He looked at her strangely. "I'm not the man I once was."

She shook her head, not willing to accept his confession. "You're the man I want." She paused, not knowing how to say she didn't want this to end. "Take me, Gary. Please? Sweep me away and make love to me all night. Whatever, however you want to do it. I trust you. It's okay with me."

Biting her lower lip, she knew she meant everything she said. She didn't care who had control anymore. She only wanted to be loved by this incredible man.

He lifted her naked body as if a feather and carried her inside. In moments, they were in his bedroom and he paused at the edge of the bed. "I..." He swallowed. "You know I want you, don't you?" His voice was hoarse, deep, driven with need.

"Yes," she said and pulled his mouth to hers.

He laid her on the rumpled sheets and covered her with his body. Moonlight filtered through the windows and the open doorway, the only source of light in the dark room.

"You know, I never expected this," he whispered and nibbled her ear, his hands stirring her body again with its massaging rhythms. "I never thought this would happen."

"I know," she said, her breathing rough. "I never thought...I was your type. That you would want someone like me."

"Why would you think that?" He stared at her, deep and long. "Mira," he finally said, "you're more than I've ever hoped for, more than I've ever had."

He cradled her against him and kissed her deep and hard. Her pulse surged. "I can't believe this is happening," she mumbled against his ear.

"Believe it, sweetheart. I want you to remember every good thing about tonight." He lavished her neck with kisses as she lifted her hips to rub against him.

His body grew warm, the night cool, his erection more than ready to meet her. She savored everything about him, his scent, the sound of his breathing, the slight taste of salt on his skin, the feel of his body highlighted by the scant light. She did so not knowing if this would ever happen again. And, God, she realized she wanted it to.

She reached for the buckle on his belt and this time he didn't stop her. He moved so she could loosen the clasp and unzip his pants. Soon she had freed him through the opening she'd made, her hand moving up and down the length of him.

He groaned with pleasure and lifted his hips to slide his pants lower. His arm flexed as he slid it out from underneath her, his skin soft, his muscle like steel underneath. She heard a drawer open and shut. "I don't know if there's any good way to do this," he said against her hair, taking the foil packet and ripping it with his teeth.

She took it from him and moved him off her. "Let me," she said between breaths.

His pants clung to his hips, covering most of him, with the exception of his erection. His penis stood tall and proud. He sat back on his heels, his legs astride hers on the bed sheets, his broad shoulders highlighted by the moonlight. He was like a god, and she would make love to him.

Even the thought made her shake with anticipation. She'd become absolutely insane, and she loved it. She slid far enough from underneath him so that she could sit up. Bending over, she kissed the tip of his penis, licking and teething slightly on the skin of the head. He released a low growl, and she felt the pulse in his manhood quicken.

"Mira," he pleaded.

She smiled and looked up at his shadowed face then eased the condom over him. "Gary, I've never been with someone like you either. Come to me. Make love to me."

He sighed and kicked off his shoes, shifting her toward the other side of the bed and lifting the sheet to cover her. He turned and sat at the edge of the bed, removing the rest of his clothing. She rubbed and teased his back until he covered himself with the sheet and slid underneath. In moments, he lay beside her, his body next to hers. His fingers found the inner warmth of her vaginal wall again, one of them easing inside and massaging an erotic spot she never knew she had. She gasped, raking his powerfully built arms with her fingers as the sensation pushed her higher toward ecstasy and sweet oblivion.

When she thought she couldn't take another second, he plunged into her, rocking her with the rhythm of the ages. Her own groans seemed distant in her ear. She leaned into him, grasping onto him like a ship in a tempest.

Her tempest.

The sensations drove her to an almost wicked pinnacle, a height she'd never thought she'd reach. The sense invigorated her, fired her spirit. She fed on the feelings, rode it to the very top. She came fast and furious, riding high. When her rapid breathing eased, she found an innate satisfaction feeling the pleasure rise in Gary. She sensed him tense with his release. Then his arms tightened around her shoulders, holding her like a valued treasure, his deep voice rumbling softly in her ear. "God, Mira," he rasped.

She swallowed as the realization dawned on her. She'd just made love to a jock. "Gary?"

He pulled back slightly, his face unreadable in the shadows. His breathing had grown erratic, shallow. The pad of his thumb brushed her lips. "Mira, I...I need you tonight. Stay with me. Please."

She nodded, sure that the tears that threatened to fall would betray her conflicting emotions. "Yes," she mumbled, not able to say anything else, feeling the depth of him in more than an intimate, physical way. Something more than sex had happened tonight and she found it hard to name.

One thing she knew, though. Gary did what he had promised. Tonight had been a first. She'd climaxed with the man, not once, but twice. She'd been made love to in the most exquisite way.

A tear traced its way down her cheek. She didn't know how to feel. What had she been afraid of all these years?

He brushed the moisture off with his forefinger. "Why are you crying?"

She fingered his face. His brow wrinkled with concern. She smiled. "Thank you."

"Huh?" He cuddled her closely.

She bit her lip, afraid to say more, but knowing the man who had given her this gift deserved to understand. She touched his lips. "Don't worry. They're tears of joy. You were right. About this. I've never felt this way. I probably never will again." She paused. "We promised one night. I know you must have all kinds of women waiting in the wings…"

He covered her lips with his finger. "Don't be so sure about that, darling. Besides…" He kissed her. "You're the only one I want to be with."

"Really?" She wrapped her arms around his neck.

"Really." He nodded.

"Then make love to me, again, Gary. Let's make love all night until we drop 'cause I know I must be dreaming. And…" She breathed against his lips. "I don't want to wake up."

Then she kissed him with every emotion she had, knowing he would be by her side in the morning.

* * * * *

Mira had fallen asleep. Too keyed up to follow, Gary had lain awake. He lifted his head to glance at the clock. The wee hours of the morning ticked by, but too much went on in his head to let him sleep. Mira had expected one night of lust, but that isn't what they'd had, well, not exactly anyway. More than that, their union launched a fiery, hot passion. They'd made love, and he knew he'd never experienced the like before.

He was afraid he would never be loved like that again.

His gut churned. How could he have let this happen? For sanity's sake it probably would have been better never to know what her sweet body tasted like. Surely, now he'd be tortured for life.

He pushed away an errant strand of hair from her face so he could see her better. Before he lost her, he wanted to enjoy every moment he could.

She stirred and snuggled her head against his chest. He loved the feel of her. She was so beautiful. Wrapping her in his arms, he treasured the touch of her gentle breaths against him. Life should be like this between a man and a woman. Close, satisfying, complete.

He sighed, wondering what she would expect in the morning, and confused about what he could give. What kind of schmuck dropped a woman after what they'd done tonight? Not one he'd be proud on being. What would he do?

He kissed her brow. They had shared intimate secrets only the two of them would know. Small, erotic things communicated with a touch, or a smile. Her body had told him more than what she probably wanted but he'd been damn glad it did. She was lonely, like him. And she'd been hurt pretty deep. He could only wonder why.

Of course, he still had his little secret. Even being slightly intoxicated, he took care not to let her get too close to his damaged testis. Hopefully she would never find out. But how would he sneak out of bed in the morning without her knowing?

A pain began in his groin and ended in his gut. Mira stirred his dreams. Thoughts from his former life rushed into his head. A good woman to sleep next to, marriage, a family like his mom and pop had. But Mira deserved better than half a man. This would be a one-night stand. A great one. Just leave it at that.

But it became damn hard to convince himself.

He took a deep breath and kissed her softly.

She shifted and her eyes fluttered open. "Hi," she murmured, the sound of her raspy voice heady.

"Go back to sleep." He touched her forehead with his lips. "I didn't mean to wake you."

"It's all right." She smiled. "I don't need to be at work until ten tomorrow."

"You work on Saturday?"

"Just small stuff." She frowned. "And then there's Sara. I need to check on her."

He half smiled. He admired her loyalty. "I thought maybe you'd want to catch up on some shuteye. Besides, I have some calls to make to get help for the chimp. Then we could go somewhere, do something within the bounds of your agreement with Danielle." He cleared his throat. "I didn't think you'd want to include everything we did tonight in your deal."

"I don't." She fingered his face. "Actually, I'd like tonight to be only for us, if you don't mind." She bit her lip. "I'd rather Danielle not know. Or anyone else for that matter."

He lifted her fingers to his lips. "Yeah, I'd rather they didn't either. Danielle already gets way too much info on my personal life and then bugs me about it."

"You too?" Mira giggled.

Her laughter made him grin. "I didn't know, you know, about..." He didn't know how to ask about her feelings, why she gave herself to him tonight. What she thought. In the past, he'd had plenty of women who had thrown themselves at him. He still did. And he knew exactly what they were after. They wanted a round in the bedsheets. But Mira wasn't the type. So why did she do it? "I thought you two talked about everything."

"Almost," she admitted. "It's just... Well, I haven't dated a guy like you in years."

"A guy like me?"

She nodded. "Yeah. A sportsman."

"A football player."

"A nice football player. I..." She pulled away, a frown marring her face. "I've never really met a jock who'd cared about someone besides himself. You do and it confuses me. All the jocks I've known would have never gone back into a bar to help a bunch of old ladies. There would have been nothing for them to gain by doing that."

"So some asshole ballplayer hurt you."

She nodded. "Yeah. I'd gone out with a few in high school. They were way too hormonal." The tip of her finger caressed his lip and she swallowed. "When I met you, I assumed you'd be the same. But you're not." She huffed. "I guess I have a pretty stereotypical view, don't I?"

"I'd say so." He didn't like the idea she'd been hurt.

"Look, Gary, I...I know we said one night. But I actually think I like you." She ran her hand through her hair. "You don't know how much that scares me. I usually date these really intelligent men, guys I have something in common with. I mean, you and I have nothing in common, but..."

"But you like me anyway."

She paused. "Yes."

"Why? Because you think I'm not as smart as you?" That thought bothered him somewhat.

"No, that's not it. I..."

He squeezed the bridge of his nose. "Mira, did it ever occur to you it might take at least a smidgen of brains to play football?"

She opened her mouth to answer but her bottom lip simply bobbed.

"Do you know anything about the game?"

The corner of her mouth quirked. "No, and no to your other question too. The egos on most of the guys I've met were higher than their IQs." She winced. "Sorry."

"Okay. That does it." He leaned close to her parted lips, tickled he could show her something he knew a lot about. "I get to choose what we do for the rest of the weekend."

"What?" she squeaked.

"You're going to see football from the inside out. Meet the guys involved. See how they really are. Learn the game. That'll be wild for you."

"Do I have to?"

"Yes," he demanded. "You're going to get this stupid idea about jocks out of your head then maybe you can ease up and let yourself meet someone you'd have an interest in."

Her breasts rose and she took a deep breath, shifting closer to him, her leg sliding over his as she turned into him. "Maybe I already have."

Her hand slid around his neck and she pulled him into her. Her mouth, her body, warmed and invited a response from him. His pulse quickened, the feel of her next to him driving him wild. "God, Mira, you don't know what you're saying."

"Yes, I do." Her eyes searched his face, looking for some understanding. "Gary, if you say no, I'll understand…"

"Say no to what," he mumbled, his tired body on fire again, his mind dulled by the warring of his stale logic of why he couldn't have her when his burning desire was to keep her in his bed. He nipped at her neck.

"To my proposition."

He stopped kissing her and looked into her face. She bit her lip again. Not a good sign.

"What if we pretend to be lovers?" she said. "Just for the length of my prison sentence with Danielle?" Her eyes widened and her breathing grew shallow. "Judging by your reaction…" She fingered his stiff penis. "I think you like me too."

"I do." He nodded.

"Besides, I…think…you could show me more about wild than I'd ever find on my own." She screwed up her face in the cutest way.

He almost laughed, she looked so funny, but the thought of loving her for more than one night sobered him. "I'm not sure I could pretend, Mira." He brushed his thumb against her temple then bent over and kissed her cheek, caressing the soft skin with his tongue. "Mira," he whispered against her, "it's been a long time since I had a steady lover."

"Me too." Her erratic breathing flowed over him. She leaned into his side and ran her hands up his chest, teasing his earlobe with her teeth. "Then let's not pretend," she murmured. "It'll only be a few weeks." She pulled back to look at him. "Say yes, Gary. Please? I think I'm going to need the feel of you in me for a long time to come."

He wanted to fight, his mind tried to pull back and regroup, but his libido went wild. She grasped his shaft and stroked him, letting her thumb massage the underside of the head. His member pulsed and stiffened in moments. "Mira," he groaned.

"Please, Gary. Love me." She paused. "Love me for just a few weeks. Maybe…we both need this."

Maybe she was right.

He steadied his breathing and looked at her. "Only for as long as you want. And promise me we'll stay friends afterward. No matter what."

A distant look breezed across her eyes before she smiled. "I promise."

"Good," he said and rolled her underneath him. "Then we have a deal."

"Deal," she said offering her hand to shake on it.

He took her palm and shook it once. Laughing, he held her close and rolled across the bed. "You want wild?" He arched his brow as he caged her with his body. "Then, honey, that's what you're going to get."

He captured her lips between his and fingered her labia, her wetness coating his fingers. She was ready for him and the realization made him yearn for her even more. He slid the full length of his erection inside her warm depths, marveling at the intensity of the pleasure, wondering at what point he had gone completely insane.

* * * * *

Dawn hadn't come, but more light from outside now filled the room. Mira settled into Gary's chest and listened to his even, quiet breathing. He slept and Mira could only imagine his exhaustion. He hadn't fallen asleep when she did. He'd said he just wanted to lie there and watch her. Now as she looked at him, she knew what he meant. His chin held a hint of a bruise along his stubbled jaw and she wanted to remember every scar, every turn of muscle in his body. She would never forget tonight.

She ran her fingertips through the curly, soft hairs covering his chest that made a vee down his abs. They'd made love again, and he had done everything he could to pleasure her. "Gary," she mumbled, feeling a completeness she'd never known. In some ways, she wanted to cry, tortured by what she thought. No, he wasn't the nerdy, scientific brain trust she always imagined herself being with, but then again, she'd never experienced a man like him. She couldn't define how she felt. She only knew she wanted more. Her selfish side asked that of him, and he'd already given more passion, more sexual fulfillment than she had ever had, with the promise of more. Still, would a few weeks be enough?

She let her hand brush lower, wanting to touch him without awaking him, wanting to keep the memory of this night alive. Tonight had been something very special to her. Based on what he'd said, she believed he felt the same.

She reached lower, softly touching his manhood, her cheeks growing flushed at the thought of the pleasure he had brought her. She didn't want to lose this. She ran her hand lower, cradling him, fingering his testicles. She caressed a large swell on one side, but on the other...

She felt again. There was only one? She looked at his face, curious about what had happened. He still slept, thank God. Maybe he didn't want her to know? She wondered if the injury had been part of the accident he'd had, or if something else had happened. Danielle hadn't mentioned anything like this, then again, why would Gary tell her sister? In fact, why would he even care about the flaw? Women still went goo-goo over him. And he was potent as hell.

No, his big thing was he couldn't play ball anymore. It had become clear to her that he still loved the game, still itched to be on the line. *Sack those quarterbacks...*

She wanted him to sack her again. Her breasts tingled just thinking about the act. My God, she giggled softly, she'd turned into a sex maniac overnight. She trailed a finger along his square chin.

Gazing at his face, she wondered what he really thought about the two of them. Was she a quick roll between the sheets for him? Somehow, she didn't think so, but not knowing drove her nuts. Then again, not knowing could be a good thing. She had her job, her profession, everything that held importance to her. She didn't see how he could fit into the world she had built. Nor, how she could fit into his.

They had promised each other a couple of weeks. Sighing, she figured she would leave thoughts of having something more with him alone. She wasn't his type. Why push an unworkable arrangement?

She let her hand rest over his injured area and studied him for the longest time. She never wanted to forget this, never wanted to forget the feel of him next to her.

She didn't want to let him go.

Aching with the realization, she finally closed her eyes, letting her head rest against him. He'd said he wanted to stay friends afterward. Is that what ex-lovers did? She realized she didn't have a clue, her limited social skills being what they were.

She kissed Gary's flesh, thankful for the night, her last thought a prayer, hoping this really wasn't a dream.

Chapter Nine

❧

Light seeped through the window and stabbed Gary in the eye. He groaned, a tad of a headache beating in his brain, his chin aching. He moved his jaw to loosen it. How much had he drunk last night, anyway? Not that much, he remembered, and attributed the pain to the beating he'd taken.

A pain he had forgotten when he made love.

Mira slept next to him and he felt her even breathing on his skin. He placed a gentle kiss on her brow. She stirred next to him. What they shared last night had been incredible. Yeah, he'd made love to several women, but coupling had never been like this. He kissed her, wondering what he would do with her. Then he realized her hand rested on his injury. My God? Did she know?

Breathe, he thought and steadied himself as he gently pulled her hand away. Mentally he went over the moments from last night. He couldn't think of any time she could have known. He'd protected himself, taking over the lovemaking, sending her body rocketing higher each time.

And God, did that feel good.

He'd become whole again. For the first time since the accident, he felt like a man. That had to have been what made him agree to her wild proposal, spending the next several weeks as lovers. What else could have made him agree to such a scheme?

He frowned, not knowing what to do. How could he keep up the deception? Did she already know about his withered scrotum?

Probably not, he guessed, but he'd find out when she woke up. She might ask him about his missing part, but the real test would be how she looked at him.

He studied her, wanting her again, memorizing the curves of her body. He hoped she'd just snuggled next to him in her sleep. He didn't want to lose her—not yet. Maybe this time he'd be lucky.

But odds had it that he wouldn't be lucky again.

He didn't know what to do. He wanted her, but he couldn't have her. Yet, they were supposed to be lovers, if only for a few weeks. So how would he pull this off?

He brushed a loose strand of hair from her face. The light from the windows highlighted the auburn shades in her dark brown hair. She looked like an angel in her sleep and he knew he would never get enough of her.

But one taste had been too much. Now that he knew how well her body fit with his, how could he give her up after such a short time? His libido kicked in again, the heat in his loins boiling. He knew he'd have to at some point. Mira deserved more than the crippled man he'd become. Somehow, he had to convince her she deserved the best.

And he had less than a month to complete the task.

He feathered another kiss on her brow, determined now he had his goal set. Mira moaned in her sleep and threw her leg over his hips. Swallowing, he wondered how he would get out of bed without waking her, without her noticing his deformity.

Kissing her fingertips, he lifted the arm she'd slung around him and eased out from under her. Perhaps he could dress before she noticed.

Ringggg.

"Damn phone…" he muttered as Mira's eyes flew open. He turned his back to her and sat on the edge of the bed, covering his lap with a pillow. "Hello?" he bit out.

"Gary, it's Sam Carter. Sorry to bother you so early, but I wanted to make sure I got a hold of you. Did Danielle give you my message?"

"What message?"

"That we need the spot sooner. Danielle assured me you could do it but I wanted to hear from you."

"We can do it." He'd find a way. Why hadn't Danielle told him?

"Did you find the voice talent?" Sam asked.

Gary looked behind him at Mira. "Yeah, I did."

"Great," Sam replied, and asked when they could meet.

Mira raised her brows and rubbed her hands along his waist. "Who is it?" she murmured in a husky morning voice as she slipped her head under his arm and laid it on the pillow.

"My client," he mouthed back and stroked her hair. She smiled and snuggled her cheek against him.

Sam's conversation brought his attention back to the phone. "Sounds good," he said.

Mira ran her hand down his abs.

"It shouldn't take much more than that." Gary watched her, his heart racing as Sam kept talking.

Her hand slipped lower, under the pillow. He panicked and grasped her fingers before they groped too far. "Hey, Sam. Let me get back to you." Not waiting for an answer, he hung up.

She looked at him and pouted, her bottom lip jutting out like a child's.

"You hungry?" he asked, realizing he'd hung up on his most important client.

"Yeah, but not for food…" She tried to move the pillow off his lap.

Thank God—she didn't know. She'd almost succeeded in freeing the pillow before he stopped her by pulling her head to his, kissing her thoroughly before he let her go. God, he wished she could continue, but daylight intruded. He couldn't take that chance. "I'll let you have the bathroom first if you want."

She frowned and pulled away. "I'd rather have you. Do you need to go to work?"

He nodded, as good of an excuse as any. Besides, he needed some time to work on Mira's problem with the chimp.

"All right." She squished the features of her face together. "But don't look."

"Why?" He laughed. She looked funny with her face puckered.

"Because…" She sat and covered herself with the sheet. "I'm not ready for you to see me nude in the stark daylight. I'm sure I don't have the body of the other ladies you've been with." She grimaced. "I…don't know if you're going to like it."

"Mira…" He inched closer to her. "I've touched almost every part of you and I like your body just fine. Don't cage yourself. You have a great body, and I'd like to see it." He ran his hand along her face. "And I still haven't seen the tattoo up close and personal. I'd like that very much."

The irises of her eyes darkened with desire.

"You have a lot more to offer a man than you think," he whispered between parted lips. "You're beautiful…"

Their lips met.

"Intelligent…"

She kissed him back.

"Witty…"

She darted her tongue into his mouth.

She went for the pillow and he pulled away again. "Don't belittle yourself."

She swallowed and sat back, her face twisted in confusion. He acted aloof but he couldn't do anything about it. He was naked and vulnerable.

For a moment she didn't speak. "I'll try not to, in the meantime..." She lifted her hand and twirled her forefinger in a circle. "Turn around."

He smirked and looked at the wall to give her privacy, a commodity he understood only too well. When he heard her feet hit the ground running, he glanced back to see the tattoo on her backside. His body immediately reacted. Looking down, he saw the pillow had a large lump in it. He shifted to get his wayward manhood in a more favorable position then rose to find a pair of boxers.

A knock sounded at the front door. "What the hell..." he grumbled, rummaging through his drawer. Didn't people realize it was an early Saturday morning? He found a silk pair of boxers he'd gotten some years ago and quickly put them on.

The knock sounded again, louder this time. Who the hell could that be?

* * * * *

Mira shut the bathroom door and looked at herself in the mirror. Her cheeks were flushed. She bit her lip. "You finally broke down and did it, didn't you? You made love to the man." She pretended to yell yes without making a sound and gave herself two-thumbs-up in the mirror. She had accomplished her goal. She had overcome her fear of making love to a jock. She didn't know where this would go from here. "But one step at a time." She nodded firmly.

For once feeling good about a sexual relationship, she strutted out of the bathroom, hoping to find her clothes.

And stepped in full view of a tall, slender blonde arguing with Gary from the doorway.

"Whoa, Gary." The blonde pushed her way through the front door that he tried to close.

Mira heard him groan and he spat out a few words as she dashed for the bathroom to grab a towel.

When Mira turned around, the young woman stood in front of her.

"Hey, like the tat," she said. "Romeo, huh?" She smirked and glanced at Gary.

"It's hennaed," Mira answered as she wrapped the towel around her and studied the willowy woman. She was gorgeous, just the type she imagined Gary would go for. Wouldn't you know that a sex goddess would show up? And right when she felt good about herself, right when she believed she topped the world. God, why did this have to happen?

Mira frowned, wondering how many times the two of them had been intimate. She shook her head, not wanting to ask, trying not to question herself. Gary had committed himself to her, even if it stopped with end of the deal.

"Cool," the stranger said, after a brief pause. She stuck out her hand. "Hi, I'm Nicole."

"Mira, I'm sorry." Gary walked over and towered over the blonde. "Some people are pests." He glared at the woman's head.

Mira looked between him and the woman. Finally recovered from her shock, Mira took the woman's offered palm and said, "Mira Harper. I'm…ah, a friend of Gary's."

"Obviously." She beamed and looked at Gary. "Well, well, well." Nicole crossed her arms. "Guess you'll need to bring Mira by sometime." The woman's baby blues gave Mira a look from under a pair of perfect brows that said trouble. "I'm sure everyone will want to meet her." Nicole smirked.

"It isn't like that," Gary insisted. "I mean…" He grimaced as he looked at Nicole then her. Did she catch a hint of fear in his eyes?

Mira's shoulders dropped. She should have known. This probably was his real girlfriend. Maybe something happened between the two of them and Nicole came by to make up, but she didn't think Gary would lie to her…did she?

No, maybe he thought the relationship had ended. But now, he'd want Nicole back. And here Mira was, naked, mucking up the works. "That's right." Mira lifted her chin, refusing to feel bad for what she'd done. "It isn't what you're thinking. Gary and I aren't even friends really. We're just business partners working on a very specific deal. Trust me, he's all yours."

She lifted her chin and walked out of the bathroom, forcing the other woman to back up.

"Mira, you don't understand…" Gary followed behind her as she walked toward the bedroom, trying not to cry. "She's my sister."

Mira swerved, coming face-to-face with Gary's naked chest. His arms came around her and she struggled to control her relief, holding herself back from indulging in the urge to cover his skin with kisses. "Your sister?" She studied his face.

He nodded and ran his thumb along her cheek. "My youngest sister, the pest."

Ducking her head under Gary's arm, she took a peek at Nicole. The younger woman stood there with her hands on her hips, grinning. When she saw Mira, she waggled her fingers in greeting.

Mira winced and wiggled her fingers in return. Straightening, she looked at him. "Oh."

He chuckled.

Then he kissed her, his embrace holding her tight, his tongue pushing through her parted lips. She groaned.

"Well, I'll, ah, go," Nicole said and Mira heard her walk toward the door. "By the way, I'll tell Mom and Dad you'll bring Mira by. How does this afternoon sound?"

He pulled away. "Nic…" Gary's voice threatened.

Mira heard Nicole giggle as she closed the door.

Gary sighed and ran his hand through his hair. Mira wanted to apologize, feeling like she'd messed something up, although she couldn't think what it could have been.

"I'm sorry," Gary said again. "Nicole isn't the first person in the family I would have wanted you to meet."

"Would you have wanted me to meet any of them?" Mira swallowed. *Where did that come from?* Geez, she'd gotten brazen in her old age. But she wanted to know. Did Gary think more of her beyond the crazy scheme she'd evolved?

He sighed and ran a hand through his hair. "Maybe." He nodded. "I told you I want to be friends, no matter what happens between us."

She licked her lips. He was serious. Did he expect their sexual interludes to continue?

He smiled and ran his thumb over her mouth. "In the meantime, we've got some time to be lovers."

Well, maybe not. Not after the deal was over anyway.

He pulled her to him, holding her flush against his nearly naked body. Heat spiraled inside her.

And he kissed her again.

She sighed. Okay, so maybe afterward they'd be friends, but she had almost a month of this to go. How lucky could a girl be?

* * * * *

"Okay, Mira, where are you?" Danielle punched the numbers on her office phone hoping like hell her sister would answer. Gary had called Danielle in to work. An emergency session, he'd said. She needed to know how much of an emergency the situation really was. After the nightclub fiasco, what happened? Danielle shouldn't have insisted they stay, but for God's sake, things were going so well. What else could have gone wrong?

Regardless, Gary had been upset. She just wanted to make sure exactly why.

Which meant she needed to talk to Mira—fast. But her sister wasn't at home and she wasn't at work. Surely, Mira couldn't be with Gary. He had told her he'd dropped Mira off at home. "Oh Mira, tell me you didn't blow it. Tell me you didn't run off into geekland somewhere." She picked up a pencil and tapped the end on the desk. Gary was on his way and it would only be minutes until he got there. She tried the phone again, this time calling Mira's cell. At some point, she had to answer.

The ringing stopped and a moan answered. "Oooo."

"Mira? Thank, God. Are you all right?"

"Hmmm."

"Girl, I've been trying to find you all morning. Where have you been?"

"Ah…"

Danielle clicked her tongue in frustration. "Okay, never mind. Just promise me you're not running away from anything. Last time you went into deep introversion, you ended up staying at all-night chess games. Now look, I've only got minutes. Gary's on his way in and he's upset. What else happened last night?"

"Oooo."

"Mira?" Danielle pulled the receiver away and stared at it. She'd been in so much of a panic, she didn't even notice. This wasn't her sister's voice. She brought the earpiece back to her head. "Look, who are you and where's my sister?"

"Mmmm."

"You dog, tell me where she is right now. What have you done with her?"

The line went dead. Before she could redial, Gary's deep voice sounded at her doorway.

Oh shit. She looked up. "Hi, Gary." She forced a smile. He didn't look happy.

"Come into my office," he said and stomped off.

She ran after him. "Gary, wait a minute. I think Mira's been kidnapped."

He stopped and she ran right into him, busting her nose.

"What are you talking about?" He turned. "I just lef— I talked to her a little while ago. She's fine."

"Then who's answering her cell phone?" she asked, trying to ease the ache in her nasal appendage by squeezing the muscles in her face.

"I don't know but I think she lost it at the zoo."

Lost it at the zoo? Ha, on purpose, more likely. No wonder. Things started to make sense. But then who answered the phone?

He looked at her funny. "What's wrong with your nose?"

"Nothing." She smiled and straightened. "I'm fine."

"Good." He grimaced then swerved and entered his office.

She wiggled her nose to make sure it worked okay and followed. "So, what's the emergency?" she asked. He stood behind his desk so she plopped in a chair in front of it.

One of his brows rose, accentuating his frown. "Sam Carter called me this morning."

"Oh shit." She smacked the palm of her hand against her head. "I forgot to tell you."

"Yeah." He nodded. "You have some work to do. I expect it done today." He leaned on the desk. "Which is why I wanted you in the office. The script still needs to be finalized and the studio scheduled."

"Got the studio," she clipped. "Took care of that right away, Boss. But you always finalize the copy. You want me to do it?"

"Yeah." He nodded. "I'll review it when you're finished."

What he said floored her. She never got to do that. "Why?"

"Because I have other things to do."

"Other…things?" She sat on the edge of the chair, hopeful. "What could be more important than this ad?"

"None of your business." He scowled and straightened some papers on his desk that were fine where they were to begin with.

"Okay." She shrugged. "But I need to check on Mira first. I haven't talked to her this morning and I'm worried about her."

"I told you she got home just fine," he growled. "Danielle, don't you think you should stay out of your sister's life? You've got your own life to mess up."

"Gee, thanks a lot, Boss. And here I thought you were my friend. Just trying to help."

"I am your friend, Dani, which is why I'm telling you to back off," he said. "She's an intelligent woman. Let her live her own life. She'll be fine."

"She will?" Danielle questioned. "If that's the case, then what else happened last night? This surly mood you're in certainly couldn't be because of Sam, although he always sure as hell irritates me."

He sighed and ran a hand through his hair. Danielle had never seen him so stressed. "Look, I'm still in pain, that's all, okay? Besides, per your and your sister's agreement, I'm still witnessing Mira's crazy pranks." He leaned on the desk. "You know if you'd call the deal off, she'd forget this mess and we could actually get some work done."

Didn't he want to spend some time with Mira? As irritated as Gary was, she thought she might have to give in—almost. "Why should I? She's finally getting out for once in her life."

"You call last night going out?"

He was upset. If Danielle didn't know him any better, she might be nervous. The big lug didn't know when he became intimidating. She pushed another button. "So, what did you do after you left the bar?"

"I…" He grimaced. "Look, I have some calls to make. I have some ideas to help Sara and I want to get them in motion. Then

---

I'm picking your sister up so you're on your own." His scowl deepened.

"Good." Danielle smiled and nodded. "And what wild thing are you guys planning for tonight?"

"Look, you only need to know we're going to do something. I won't break Mira's trust and tell you. Besides, I don't want you showing up, is that clear?"

"Ooookay." She pinched her lips together, wondering what went through his brilliant head. Gary had imagination. What could he have planned?

His cell phone rang.

"Hello?" Gary pressed the receive button and shoved the phone between his shoulder and ear.

The sound of the caller reverberated in the room. Danielle heard the moaning from where she sat. Wasn't that the same voice that answered Mira's cell phone this morning?

"Look…" Gary sighed. "Get some help. You obviously need it." He ended the call and fell into his seat. "The last thing I need is some juvenile prank caller."

"Ah, Gary? Is that the same girl who's been bothering you?"

He nodded and rubbed a hand down his face.

Danielle eased the phone away from him. "Let me take care of it. I'll be right back."

"What are you going to do?" he asked, a tinge of fear showing on his face.

"Trust me," she said and stood.

"The last time I trusted you I almost had my head handed to me."

She winced, looking at the shadow of a bruise on the side of his face. "I promise it won't be anything bad."

"Right."

She didn't let him say more and hurried to her office. The call gave her a great idea — and an excellent excuse. She wanted Gary and Mira to have uninterrupted time together. They didn't need that creep, Sam Carter, calling them and ruining their day. Besides, by giving her the script, Gary officially put her in charge. The jerk would have to deal with her.

And, somehow, she would find this prank caller and Mira's phone. Who the heck was it?

She pulled out her cell phone, the same type Gary used. He'd never notice. Dropping his in her purse, she carried hers to his office and laid it on the desk. He sat gazing out the window and she wondered what could have him so bothered.

"Here you go." She slid the cell closer to him.

"Danielle." He looked over his shoulder at her. "What happened to Mira to make her so unsure of herself?"

He asked about Mira? A good sign, she thought, but Mira wasn't out of the woods yet. She shrugged, feeling the pain she sometimes felt when she looked at her sister. "Honestly, Gary, I don't know. Maybe if you ask her you'll have better luck finding out."

He nodded and stared out the window again. "Maybe I will."

Chapter Ten

ജ

Mira patted Sara's head as she sat with her in the chimp cage, wondering what kind of pickle she'd gotten herself into now. Why were things always messed up when they initially went so well? It formed the bedrock of her sex life. Bad enough Gary's sister had barged in that morning seeing Mira revealed in all her glory, but then his mother called shortly after, asking about his new girlfriend and wanting him to bring her by this afternoon.

What a mess. To Gary's credit, he made excuses, but his mother wouldn't relent. Mira gave in, only to help Gary get out of hot water. But now she didn't know what to do. What did you say to the parents of a short-term lover?

She wondered how many girlfriends he'd actually introduced to them. Something inside her hoped not many. "Cut the jealousy, Mira. This is temporary, remember?" But something inside niggled at her, wishing she hadn't placed a limit on their affections. Regardless, she didn't intend to break the deal. She'd shocked herself too much already by even proposing it. Gary was a great guy. He'd make some lucky girl a great husband someday.

It just wouldn't be her.

And why not? She shook her head to lose the absurd thought. Gary and she had found something good in the bedroom, but that would be as far as their liaison went. She knew what to look for now. She could find the sexual attributes she loved about him someplace else, right? Other than sex, the two of them had nothing else in common. Which meant that after the next few weeks were up, her era of wildness would be over. For good. She wouldn't sign up for something this insane again.

Yet for some reason, the thought troubled her, and she had the devil of a time figuring out why.

She watched a few of the chimps jump from tree to tree, chatting it up with each other. Other than the physical limits of the cage, they did pretty much what they wanted. Maybe their freedom showed her what she lacked. The last few days she'd lived by her own set of values, but for years she'd lived in self-imposed seclusion, running by rules set by her family. Well, ever since that incident so long ago.

God, what a mess that had been. Her father finding her and Sean McAfee half naked in the woods, led to them by a friend Sean had posted behind some bushes with a telephoto lens, one who'd suddenly developed a guilty conscious when her father had come looking for her. But how could she have known that Sean had made a bet to see if he could go all the way with her? Apparently, he had planned to pass the pictures around to the whole football squad. Thank God, her dad had ruined the camera. When she'd confronted Sean later, he'd tried to explain it as a matter of "honor".

"Honor my ass." She'd been such a virgin she hadn't even known what he was doing to her. She just knew it felt good.

"Stupid, stupid, stupid."

She'd never been so embarrassed in her life. She had to wonder what would have happened if her dad hadn't found her.

Guilt overwhelmed her again, knowing she'd let her father down. Soon afterward, her dad died in a car accident. She'd made a promise never to do something to disappoint him again.

She prayed she hadn't.

She ran her hand through her hair, wondering what the promise meant anymore. Her dad had still loved her. He'd told her as much, but he'd also set some pretty stringent limits on what she'd been allowed to do, giving her a real strong lecture about boys and sex.

God, had it been fifteen years?

She'd focused solely on her studies afterward. Okay, so maybe she was a geek, but the transformation hadn't been entirely her fault. She'd trapped herself with these thoughts of pleasing her dad, living down the embarrassment of long ago. Yeah, she lived in a cage, but a self-imposed one. Maybe she should take the time to let herself out.

She bit her lip. She had to face facts. Sean McAfee had made her a smarter woman with little to no real damage. Why should she keep herself trapped now? Why couldn't she have a relationship with anyone she wanted? She liked Gary. A lot. What harm could there be in dating him? She was a grown woman. She had good judgment. Besides, something felt right between Gary and her. Why shouldn't she take the time to find out what that right thing could be?

Probably because he did the deal out of compassion.

Another blow she had to accept. She wasn't some sleek chick. He insisted it didn't matter but she knew she didn't have the body a jock would go for. She clicked her tongue, frustrated with her confusion. "In no time, Mira, all this craziness will be over. Stop torturing yourself. Why do you have to overanalyze everything?"

Yet how could she deny the pleasure Gary had given her? She still yearned for him.

After the deal ended, Gary would get on with his own life. He'd indicated as much. She'd already thought the possibilities through. They'd have to come up with some excuse for his parents as to why they broke things off. With his sister embroiled in the deal, that could be tough. But what could Mira say? "Oh, I only keep boyfriends a week or more, especially those of the jock variety. Standard policy." Somehow, she didn't think his savvy younger sister would buy the excuse.

And what about his older sisters? He'd said he had three. Laurie, Courtney and Jessica. If they were anything like Nicole, she was headed into a heap of trouble. Thank God, Danielle didn't know anything about what happened. Pairing Nicole and her sister would make things a thousand times worse.

What a mess. And all because of this crazy deal with Dani, a deal made in desperation to save Sara. What had she done to herself?

The chimp sidled up to her. "It's all right, girl," Mira said to Sara, knowing the chimp's safety had been the primary impetus for her actions. Mira's love life could wait. The old girl fidgeted and Mira swore the dear worried about its future. "You're going to be all right," she said. "Gary's making sure of it." Mira's confidence had risen about the outcome with Sara. In fact, her confidence about everything had grown since she'd been with Gary.

She knew part of it came from Gary's attention and sweet praise but she vacillated over what had happened. Gary liked her. At least, she thought he did. He said she was beautiful, or could it have been a line? Something said between lovers to enhance the moment? And still, how did she feel about him?

Her head hurt with conflicting emotions. "I don't know, Sara. He's very nice but he and I are in different leagues. Besides, I always imagined having someone like Dad. Someone who'd be interested in finding the next cure for cancer or something."

"How about a cure for loneliness? He sounds like he's doing a pretty good job at that."

She hadn't heard Candy come in.

The student zookeeper smiled. "Is Sara our new broken hearts counselor? If so, maybe she could help me." The other woman sat next to them. "Hey, maybe we could start a column, like a new Ann Landers. The press could bring in enough revenue to save her. Wouldn't that be a kick? I wonder what Doctor Death would think about *that*."

Mira chuckled. "She'd do as well as anybody else. What do you think, Sara?" She tickled her belly.

"Ooooh, ooooh, eeeh," the chimp answered. Mira wondered sometimes if the old girl understood her.

"By the way," Candy said. "Your sister called. I told her you wouldn't be in until ten, but she insisted because she couldn't get you at home or on the cell. Per orders, I'm letting you know you need to call her back. She was pushier than usual."

Mira glanced upward. "Thank you, God." Hiding that phone had probably been the best thing she'd done in a long time. She looked at Candy. "I appreciate the heads-up. Thanks."

"No prob. So, what's the reason she couldn't get you at home or on your cell?" The gleam brightened in Candy's eye.

"None of your business," Mira replied, trying to keep her secret.

Candy chuckled. "That's what I thought. If that sexy voice from the other day landed you, I say good for you. You deserve it."

Mira acted nonchalant but it obviously didn't work. She sighed. "Candy, what if you met a great guy but thought he couldn't be the guy for you?"

"And why *isn't* he the guy for you?" The other woman studied her.

"Maybe because he's from a different world? One I don't understand at all. I'm a scientist. He's a pro athlete—or was. What do we have in common?"

"A jock, huh?" Candy snorted. "Look, Doc, give yourself a chance. You spend too much time thinking and not enough time living. Be like Nike—just do it. You might find you like him more than a little, and for good reason. Besides, then you can find out what he really thinks of you."

Mira grimaced. "You sound like Danielle."

Candy laughed. "Maybe because we've talked a lot about you. Doc, I have a lot of respect for you. If not for you, this place wouldn't be what it is today. But you have planned everything in your life and have never experienced the joy of letting yourself go. Just let it happen with this guy. If it works, great. If not, then don't sweat it. Nobody's judging you except you. Cut it out."

Mira thought for a minute. "You know, for a student, you're pretty smart."

Candy grinned. "Not as smart as you, just more experienced in the man department."

"Just go for it, huh? Cut loose and be wild."

Candy nodded. "Yep. In fact, I'll tell you what. You let yourself live a little, and if I'm right about this, you'll help me study for my comps this spring."

"You up for your comprehensives already?"

Candy nodded.

Mira grinned. "And what if you're wrong?"

Candy grimaced. "I'll take your place cleaning the cages on the weekend."

Mira laughed.

"Ah, excuse me."

She recognized Gary's warm voice and turned to see him outside the cage bars holding a red rose in his hand.

He smiled at her. "There's a gorgeous brunette I'm supposed to pick up. That wouldn't happen to be you, Doctor Harper, would it?"

"It is the same guy," Candy murmured as Sara oooo'd.

Mira nodded.

"Oh," Candy said.

Mira thought the other woman might be drooling.

"Definitely go for it." Candy glanced first at him then back at her. "No question. Someone who looks like him and a rose to boot. You go, girl."

Mira laughed and set Sara down. "Okay, you've got a deal." She stuck out her hand and they shook on it. Mira figured one more deal couldn't get her in any more trouble.

She left the cage and Gary met her on the other side.

"What's that all about?" he asked.

"Oh nothing." She smiled.

"You ready?" He slid his arm around her waist.

"I'm sure I need to change. I must smell like the animals."

He leaned toward her and buried his head in her neck. "You smell fine to me, Doctor Harper. But if you insist, I'll take you home first."

"Are you sure you want to do this?" she asked, getting nervous. "I mean, don't you think your parents will ask more questions?"

"Like what?" Half a grin showed on his face.

"Like how long we've been dating, you know, stuff like that. What if one of your sisters asks how I feel about you?"

He looked at her with that unreadable gaze—deep, penetrating. "Tell her the truth." He brushed his thumb over her lips then bent down and kissed her.

She melted into him. His body seemed so right next to hers. Should she go for it?

"I need a bath," she whispered. "Care to share one with me before we go?" After all, her bathroom had no windows. She could keep it dark and he wouldn't be able to see her well.

He answered with a groan.

* * * * *

Gary sat on the couch in Mira's living room, listening to the running water, sorely tempted to jump into the shower with her and say to hell with it. Take the chance. Maybe Mira wouldn't care. He'd almost given in, but fear held him back. Fear that once she knew his secret she would make excuses not to be with him anymore. He wouldn't risk that. He had a mission now. Somehow, he would show Mira how incredible she was and get her to believe it. And he would enjoy doing it. He just needed to get creative.

Just how creative, he couldn't be sure.

But first they had to see his parents then he needed to find an excuse to get out of there quickly. Just his bad luck Nicole showed up this morning, wanting to talk about her latest tiff. Nicole was a bit on the wild side but basically a good kid. He wondered what she'd done now to make his parents upset. He bet it hadn't been as wild as finding a naked woman in her brother's apartment. Would Nicole use the information to blackmail him? He wouldn't put the effort past her.

He ran a hand over his face, looking for an excuse he'd give his mom if she asked how close Mira and he had gotten. He didn't believe in telling lies, especially to his parents. So what would he say?

The water stopped and he looked at the closed bedroom door, wondering what Mira thought about all this. He hadn't really had time to ask her, not about his parents, and especially not about last night. He'd experienced the most incredible night of his life and the only thing he knew so far is she might like him.

Might. She'd said that.

Hope bubbled up again and he squashed it fast before he ended up doing something he'd be sorry for. He wanted no more regrets in his life. He'd had enough failed episodes.

He rubbed his knee and listened to Mira's footfalls as she scurried around in her room. Her small house looked quaint, an early twentieth century model that populated some of the older sections of town. He wondered what her bedroom looked like, if it had as many frills as her living room. If things went right, perhaps later he'd find out.

Or should he? He still stewed over pursuing the relationship. He had no intention of continuing their sexual interlude, at least after the specified time had ended, but he worked hard to justify stopping it early. Morally, to lead her on was a crappy thing to do. But she wanted him. Would her desire be enough to keep them going?

Mira exited the bedroom, dressed in a belted, trim pair of slacks and a black blouse that showed some of her cleavage. He steadied himself, remembering how phenomenal her breasts had been in his hands, his mouth…

"Wow." He swallowed and stood, hoping he didn't make too much of an idiot of himself. "You look incredible."

She smiled. "Thanks, lover." And took his arm. "Well, I'm ready when you are."

Then he remembered. He still hadn't come up with an excuse for his mom.

* * * * *

"Shoot." Danielle still hadn't gotten the verbiage for the ad quite right. She'd missed something and she had a hard time putting her finger on it. "What is it?"

She'd created a great concept for the ad. A hockey player gets distracted by a sexy voice and is hit in the head by a hockey stick. It was funny. Still, the piece needed something more.

She reviewed the setup and still didn't have another idea. Frustrated, she tossed her pen against the paper and put her feet up on the desk. She had a hard time thinking. Probably because her interest lay in what was happening with Mira. Did her play at matchmaking work? Between Gary's surliness and Mira's secrecy, she couldn't tell.

Gary's cell phone rang, interrupting her thoughts. "Oh joy." The pig-headed Sam Carter had to be calling her again. How many times had it been now? She picked it up and answered, "Hello?"

"Ooooh." The voice.

"Now look, lady. The man's tired of your harassment and has asked me to deal with you. You won't get him anymore, got it? You need some help."

"Mmmmmm."

The girl sounded even more determined. Did the woman harass her now? "Look, cut it out. You understand?"

"Ahhhh…"

"Give it up. Neither of us is interested and if you keep it up you'll have the law on you. You know I can find you with this thing. And the FBI has some high-powered tracking device. Give it up, for both our sakes. You'll be better for it. Oh…" She remembered one thing. "And if you are a kid, talk to your parents, or if not them, your school counselor, somebody who can get you some help. *Ciao*, darlin'. Have a better life."

She hit the button to end the call. "Some people will go to any lengths." The gal had to have known Gary. "But then why did she start bothering me?"

She shrugged then picked up the pen and started scratching her head with the blunt tip. Some people were *really* out there.

Sighing, she read the ad again. The script would have to do. Penciling in a few minor changes, she got ready to leave, not knowing what she'd do today now that Mira was with her boss. Gary's phone rang again.

"Hello?"

The voice moaned. This time she seemed in pain.

"Do you need help? Hello? Hello?" The phone went dead and for a second she stared at the receiver. Should she call 9-1-1?

The phone rang again and she answered more quickly this time. "Look, lady…"

"Lady?"

Not the woman, but Sam Carter.

"Well, I've been called a lot of things, but lady was never one of them. Danielle, is Gary around?"

"Gary? Ah…" She paused a moment, the sudden switch putting her in a state of confusion. She needed her head together to talk to Sam. "No. He isn't."

"This is his cell phone, isn't it? Or did I call you by mistake."

"Oh no, dear." She sat back and made herself comfortable. "It's mine."

For a moment, silence reigned on the other end. "Then why does my phone say it's Gary's number?"

Darn, she'd forgotten you could look that up. "Don't know." Heck, coy could be her middle name. "Is there something I can do for you?"

She heard a long sigh through the receiver. "Have him call me when he can."

"Will do." She nodded briskly. "*Ciao.*" Then pressed the end button. "No prob, butthead," she said to herself, shaking off her irritation. Gary had put her in charge. Sam would have to deal with her, even if it killed her. But his call did give her an idea. She could locate the strange caller with the phone. She went to the menu and scrolled through the previous calls. "There you are, you crazy chick."

When she looked closer, she recognized her old number, the phone she'd given Mira. Her sister had been the other voice? But how?

Then it clicked. "You lost your phone, did you, my clever sister? Yeah, I bet." She hit dial recall. When the familiar voice answered, Danielle could hear the voices of other chimps. "Hello, Sara," she said, her creative mind churning, "do I have a deal for you."

She smiled at herself, quite pleased she'd figured out at least one of her sister's secrets and thrilled at the new twist to the ad she had drilling in her brain. "This might work."

Chapter Eleven

ಐ

Nicole arched a brow. "And how did you and my brother meet?"

Mira grimaced. In the short time between the morning and the afternoon, Gary's mom had somehow organized a family cookout in their backyard. Amazing. Mira wondered what miracle Gary's mother had conjured up to meet the almost impossible task of getting everyone together. A husband of one of the elder sisters had been the only person missing.

Then there were Gary's siblings to deal with. They reminded her of wild lionesses on the prowl. They had roamed around for some time before she and Gary arrived. She figured they were eager to devour fresh meat. Up to now, she'd done an admirable job of avoiding them. Wouldn't you know Nicole would be the one to corner her away from the crowd? Mira glanced around, trying to find an escape. "Through my sister." She stalled, wanting to catch Gary's eye but his dad and one of the siblings' husbands kept his attention.

"Harper." Nicole tapped her well-manicured finger against her chin and Mira thought she could see the younger woman's brain-wired circuits lighting up. "You're Danielle's sister?"

Well, she made the connection. Mira was raw bait. She tried to dispel the thought and nodded, noticing Gary was still preoccupied.

"Oh." Nicole smiled mischievously. "That explains it." She leaned toward Mira and whispered. "It's about time we got to know you. Danielle is practically like family anyway. I'm glad Gary's finally interested in someone. Maybe we should have invited her and your mother."

"Oh, I don't think so," Mira protested, afraid. The combination would have been all she needed. Her mother and Danielle together? She'd be surprised if they didn't bring the preacher. Sheesh. The further away she could keep those two from this debacle the better.

"And what are you whispering about?" Laurie, the eldest, sauntered up. Just her luck. The lionesses closed in.

"Nicole, don't monopolize Mira's time. We all want to know her," Courtney, the second eldest, said as she and Jessica came from behind. Now, the whole pride gathered. Oh God— trapped! *Yum, yum.* She could feel them licking their chops.

"I am not monopolizing her time," Nicole protested, "just getting information." She smiled like a Cheshire cat, one with really big claws. "She's Danielle's sister."

"Gary's assistant? Really? Well, maybe we should have invited Danielle," Jessica exclaimed and suddenly the girls began chitchatting about Danielle and Gary's work.

Sweat gathered around Mira's neck. Would they go for the jugular? She looked for Gary again but this time he had disappeared. Now what would she do?

She spied the grill. Food could be a good excuse. She turned to slip away but Jessica put a hand on her arm and stopped her.

"So..." Jessica pulled the hand away and ran her finger around the tip of the glass she held. "How long have you and Gary been dating?"

Oh here it comes. She could feel the teeth marks now. She squirmed. "Well, ah..."

"Long enough." Nicole nodded briskly then winked at her.

A reprieve? *Whew.* "It's been a little while," Mira said. Her smile weakened.

"Well, it's been a while since Gary brought anyone around," Laurie interjected. "You two must be close."

"Oh they are," Nicole stated emphatically.

Mira winced, feeling a proverbial nip on her backside.

"And," Jessica said, "exactly what do you think about Gar—"

Oh God, not now, she thought. *What am I going to say?*

Then she felt a hand on her back.

"You know, girls, one-on-one would be fairer." Mira turned to see Gary standing behind her. "Or at least you could play in zones. All of you at the same time are uneven odds."

Laurie clicked her tongue. "Oh Gary, really. We were only talking."

"Well, time's up. We gotta go."

"We do?" Mira shook off her gripping fear. She'd almost been asked the big question. The one she couldn't even answer for herself. How did she feel about Gary?

Gary stared at her. "Yes."

What could she be thinking? The further away from here the better. "Oh, of course we do." He gave her a way out. "I'll get my purse."

She hurried into the house, looking for where she put her pocketbook and the light jacket she'd brought but hadn't needed.

Gary's mother, Beth, walked out of the kitchen. "You going so soon?" She put down the pitcher of lemonade she'd carried and wiped her hands on her blue jeans.

Mira nodded. "We had something already arranged. We're working to get funding for Sara, the chimp I told you about." Gary's mother had actually been interested.

"I hope it works out." Beth frowned. "And here I hoped to show you some of Gary's awards. You know, they aren't all in football."

Mira grabbed her jacket and purse. "Oh, I'm sure Gary was quite the athlete. Perhaps we can do it another time?" Mira needed a way out.

"How about dinner this week? I'd love to have you and we'd have more time to talk. I could show you his academic awards as well. You know he was valedictorian of his high school class." She smiled.

"He was?" She'd never realized. How jaded had she become?

"Oh yes." She nodded. "So, dinner, Wednesday?"

Mira bit her lip. "Sure, I'd love to."

Gary came through the back door. "You ready?"

"Yes, I'll be there in a minute," Mira said.

He kissed her on the cheek and nodded. "I'll go get the car. Meet you out front." He turned to his mother and kissed her goodbye.

"Oh Gary," his mother said, "how about bringing Mira to dinner on Wednesday?"

He stopped and looked from his mother to Mira. A brow on his face rose.

Mira cringed. What did he think?

"Wednesday's fine with me," he said with a smirk.

Oh God. She'd have to go through the charade again? Did he want to be with her? Mira looked at Beth, thinking this couldn't get any worse. But hey, it was a free meal. She shrugged. "I guess we're on. Thanks so much for lunch. I had fun." Even if she did have to fend off the lionesses.

"I'm glad we could meet you." Gary's mom hugged her. "Take care of my boy."

"Oh, I'm trying." She risked a glance at him. He laughed. Did this mean he hadn't been upset?

His mom walked them to the door and after another hug and a kiss on the cheek, his mom allowed them to leave.

Gary opened the car door. When she sat down, she let out a huge breath and rubbed her temples. Her head throbbed, but she had survived.

Gary hopped in the other side. "It wasn't that bad, was it?"

She smiled. "No, I guess not. But I feel bad deceiving your parents."

His smile disappeared and the look of want in his eyes deepened. His fingers brushed against her hair then her cheek. "I didn't lie about anything I said about you."

"I didn't either," she whispered against the sensual lips he brought toward her.

Then he kissed her. For a moment, time stopped, need and belonging consuming her.

When he backed away, panting, he cleared his throat. "We better go."

"Yeah," she breathed. "Gary…" She wanted to get the dinner thing cleared up front. "I didn't mean to rope us into another visit with your parents."

He huffed. "I'm surprised dinner is the only thing you got roped into." He looked at her, smiling again. "It's all right. Mom's a good cook." He kissed her again and her body flooded with the warmest feeling. She felt…weird. Foreign and good at the same time. Right. What could this sensation be? She watched Gary pull out of the drive, and wondered, did he feel this too?

* * * * *

Danielle walked to Sara's cage, having to prove what she thought to herself one more time. She couldn't afford to be wrong, especially after the goof-ups that had already occurred. She'd finished what she needed to do at the office. Now came the time for truth. She dialed Mira's number. Sure enough, a phone rang from somewhere in the cage and Sara hurried over and pulled it out of the tree. The chimp deftly flipped the phone open and the familiar "oooh'ing" started. Ha. Better than she expected. If Sara could do this for the commercial, it would be the bomb. She could see the spot now—tough hockey player hears the voice and turns toward it, ignoring the game. The puck bangs him in the head, he sees stars, and turns to Sara all goo-goo eyed in love. Then she could make the association with all the other products out there. "Ever been blinded by love?" she mumbled. "Then go with the product you can trust in any state." Perfect. She took a pen from her purse and scribbled the script on a scratch piece of paper. It would be a hysterical commercial. The salary Sara earned would be plenty to keep her at the zoo, especially with the annual fund drive that Gary worked out. A flawless plan.

Well, except she'd have to get Mira to buy into it.

And the client…

Maybe the zoo.

Would the studio make space for a chimp? What else did she need?

She listed off the items required and realized she'd have to face Sam Carter about it. Yuck.

"All right, Dani. Get a grip. He's a man, and what man haven't you been able to seduce if you needed?"

Well, Gary was one, but she made an exception for him. He had become like an older brother who stood around making sure she didn't get into trouble. And right now, he occupied himself with her sister. He wouldn't be around to interfere. What could be more perfect?

* * * * *

Later that afternoon they finished with the business of saving Sara. Gary had taken Mira to a lawyer friend of his and they began the process of building a trust for the chimp. He'd also had some ideas for a fundraiser and a banker he'd had in mind to do the job, plus he had some friends and acquaintances on the zoo board. Gee, what more could a girl ask for?

Mira rubbed her chin, wondering why she'd been so sullen. Everything had worked out for the chimp. And Gary had been impressive. His wit, his contacts, and his sheer business sense brought them success. Everywhere he went, he inspired confidence. She wondered if his size had something to do with it or if he had acquired the ability from playing ball. The fact he had been able to pull everything together so quickly said something.

As he drove along the city streets, she looked at him from the corner of her eye. Today, she'd seen him from a different perspective and she liked what she saw. He wasn't only big, gorgeous and nice, he had a good head for business. She appreciated his skills, especially now. She wondered if he knew how perfect he was.

She crossed her arms, disgusted. Of course he did. He had to know how he appealed to any normal, red-blooded woman. If anything, the way he looked at them with that come-on look made putty out of any woman. But why did he do that to her? He treated her like a lover wherever they went. Why?

Because he needed her right now, and she needed him. The reason had been the only answer she could fathom. They had a mutually beneficial arrangement. And their playacting was fun, so why try to make more of it? It would be over quick enough. Enjoy it.

She huffed, bringing his attention to her.

"What's wrong?" he asked.

"Nothing." She tried to smile.

He raised his brows. "It doesn't sound like nothing. You sure?"

She nodded, not wanting to let him know what she thought. She didn't want their relationship to end anytime soon. She wanted something more but had a hard time figuring out what. Or maybe she had a hard time accepting what her gut told her she needed—she needed him. She pasted on a smile. "Sure."

"Okay." He shrugged and she looked away. Gary wouldn't tell her where they were going, but fair was fair. He'd picked tonight's wild evening. He'd insisted. Mira decided, since she hadn't revealed their destination the other night, she couldn't complain. Except now, the lack of information made her nervous. What she had picked out hadn't been much fun for him. How would this be for her?

Gary drove into a local park. Miniature football players covered the grassy areas. He parked and one little guy ran in front of them on the field.

"He's so cute." Mira pointed at the boy who wore a complete set of gear and couldn't be any more than three feet high.

"Peewee league," Gary said, biting his bottom lip to keep the corners of his mouth from turning upward.

"Did you start that young?" she asked, running her finger along the dimple in his cheek.

"Yeah." He nodded. "It was the most fun thing I'd ever done." He looked at her. "Until I grew up." His come-on grin appeared. "Then it became the second most fun thing I'd ever done."

She stifled a laugh. "Well, I think you're still pretty good with at least one of them." She couldn't help herself. She leaned toward him and planted her mouth on his.

"Thanks," he whispered as she pulled away a bit.

"Hey, coach." A sharp rap sounded at Gary's window. A tall, skinny, dark-headed kid shot Gary a toothless grin. A smaller tow-headed boy with freckles stood behind him. "Hey, is she your girlfriend?" The boys giggled.

"Coach?" Mira asked.

"Yep," Gary answered and rolled down the window, nodding his head at the boys. "This is Miss Mira."

"Hi," they both said, almost in unison, hanging their heads shyly.

"You guys run on," Gary said. "I'll be there in a second."

The boys walked off.

"You're the coach," she reiterated, stunned a single guy like him would spend time with these small boys.

"Well, assistant coach, actually. I don't have enough time to be the number one coach." A dimple deepened in his face. "I said you'd meet some real football players." His beaming grew infectious.

"They're boys," she said.

He nodded. "I don't know a guy who plays ball who isn't, except for Sally. She's our quarterback."

Mira laughed. "You're kidding. You have a girl?"

"Yep." He nodded. "She's pretty good too."

Mira giggled. "And we're going to..."

"Watch." Gary shrugged. "Actually, I'm going to coach the defense, and honey, you're going to be their number one cheerleader."

"Oh my God," Mira said, raising a brow. "Now I know you have the wrong sister."

Gary laughed and bent toward her. "Uh-uh. You're the one I want." Then he kissed her and any thought of protest fled.

Laughter rang outside the car and Mira looked to see a whole slew of short football players standing on the field in front of them.

She didn't think she'd ever stop blushing.

* * * * *

Danielle couldn't have been more pleased. She'd come back to the office and made the necessary calls. Luckily, she even able to contact the studio management. Everything was set. Now all she had to do was drop the news on Sam Carter. His sexy voice would be a chimp. She crossed her fingers, hoping the jerk would like the idea.

She put in a call to his office. He wouldn't be there on a Saturday, which gave her an out by leaving a message. She certainly didn't want to talk to the creep.

Danielle put her feet up on her desk as the phone rang. Once. Twice. She waited for the machine to answer.

"Hello?" It was Sam.

"Oh shit." Her feet made a loud whack as they hit the floor. "I mean, ah…"

"Danielle?" Sam answered. "Is that you?"

"Uh, yeah, uh." She tried to think. "Sorry about that. I caught my finger in the drawer." She looked at her perfectly fine hand. "And it smarts like the dickens. Look…" She sat straight, trying to focus. "I had an idea, a new twist to the script. I, uh, thought you might like to hear it."

"Did Gary approve of the change?"

She frowned. "Gary put me in charge of the final edits." She heard silence.

"I see," he said finally.

"Well, ah, what if—instead of a real woman we use a chimp, ah, instead?"

"A chimp?" She heard the skepticism in his voice. "Danielle, what are you telling me? Couldn't you get the voice?"

"Oh no." She swallowed hard. "That's not it. It's…a small change."

"Do you know how hard it is to work with animals?"

His caustic reply steeled her, putting her confidence back on track. "Of course I do." Not that she really did. That was Mira's bag. "Look, how about we meet? I could be at your office in a few minutes."

He sighed. "I'm not in my office. On weekends, I have the office phone forwarded to my home."

"My, we have an exciting life, don't we?" she said, and then cringed. She'd almost been able to hold back the scathing remark.

He cleared his throat. "Look, if you really want, we can meet for dinner."

She looked at her watch—5:30. Where had the time flown? She'd spent the better part of the day in the office and she could always think of something else better to do with her weekend. Spending time with Sam wouldn't be one of them.

She crossed her fingers. "You know, I didn't mean to bother you. I only wanted to leave a message. How about I come to your office on Monday?"

"You've already bothered me, Danielle. Besides, this is too important. Why don't you meet me at Maggiano's at 6:00? It won't take me long to get there."

"Fine." She gritted her teeth. "I'll see you there. *Ciao*." She hung up and stared at the phone. "Sis, you better appreciate the sacrifices I'm making for you."

She gathered her purse and stomped out.

* * * * *

Mira had bought Gary dinner—a first. She'd insisted since he had already done so much for her with Sara. She could tell he didn't like it but she didn't care. She had fun. The football game had been awesome and she wouldn't have believed she could have enjoyed herself so much. The boys, on both sides, had a hard time concentrating. Every time they lined up they would look at the little cheerleader girls instead of the ball. Man, did they start early.

"So, it's still your turn. What crazy thing did you have in mind for tonight?" she asked. With the excitement of the day, she didn't know if she could take any more. Her comfort zone had been more than stretched—it'd been broken.

"I thought your place sounded good."

She cringed. Her place? What if Danielle showed up? Or, God forbid, her mother. "I...don't know, Gary. Danielle is pretty unpredictable. She could show up at any time. Once she came over at 3:03 in the morning, just because she'd been excited about a guy she met. I could have killed her."

"3:03? You're sure?" He chuckled.

She clicked her tongue. "Yes...okay, so I'm a nerd and I'm anal-retentive."

He pulled over to the side of the street, bent over, and kissed her. "A good-looking one, for sure." He ran his hands along the side of her arms and her breathing hitched.

"Gary…" She leaned against him, liking this lover stuff. She wanted to say let's do this all the time, but couldn't, too afraid she had put too much of her heart into this. Instead, she nipped his neck, enjoying the moment. What had Candy said? Just do it. So she did. She kissed his neck again.

"I got another idea, then," Gary mumbled between the pecks he planted on her hair and ear. He pulled her chin to him and tasted her lips, leaving her wanting. When he broke away, he straightened and drove off.

"Where are we going?" she asked.

He flashed her that drop-dead gorgeous grin. "You'll see."

Chapter Twelve

∽

Gary pulled into a bed and breakfast. A large Victorian home stood in the middle of the property and smaller cottages were out back. Their little bungalow sat the furthest away, near a well-manicured garden. The patch still had some mums and yellow snapdragons flowering in it.

Gary led her along the stone walkway to the door. She swallowed, suddenly uncertain of herself. "Are you sure you want to do this?"

"Yeah." He nodded. "I've been curious to see the place but it isn't a hotel a guy goes to by himself, if you know what I mean."

She nodded. She knew exactly what he meant. The place looked as if built for lovers. And isn't that what they pretended to be?

"Come on." He lifted her in his arms and carried her through the open door of their cottage. When he'd stepped inside, he kicked the door shut. "You know, I've always wanted to do this."

She grew uncomfortable. The day had stretched her to the breaking point, and here he acted as if they were married or something. "Gary, you can put me down."

"Why?" He smiled. "I kinda like carrying you." He walked over to the bed and sat, placing her in his lap.

The way he looked, his rich blue-green eyes alight with laughter, his hair windblown from the trip, the grin on his face asking for more. How could she refuse? "So." She nibbled at his lower lip. "What did you have in mind?"

He groaned and laid her sideways on the bed, covering her with his body. He lifted her arms above her head. "I'll show you." He kissed her lips, returning her passion. His hands reached for her breasts, massaging them through the fabric of her shirt.

Her body heated. How quickly he could make her believe, in this act, this intimate moment between a man and a woman, they were meant for each other. But she fantasized again. She couldn't think of a reason why he would want her, not for the long run anyway.

Let yourself enjoy this, Mira. Just do it. She remembered what Candy said, but when Gary slid his hands underneath her shirt, she could only think of him.

He trailed kisses along her neck then nibbled her earlobe. "Have you ever been skinny-dipping?" he whispered between nips.

She pulled away. "Swim naked?" She'd never done such a thing in her life.

Gary laughed. "I'll take your response as a no." He planted a quick kiss on her lips. "It's almost dark. There's a creek near here with a small hot spring. It's secluded. The desk clerk thought we would be alone."

She frowned. "What could have made him tell you such a thing?"

He winked at her. "This is their honeymoon suite. I signed us in as Mister and Missus. His imagination did the rest." He closed the gap between them and suckled her lips. "We're already pretend lovers, Mira," he whispered against her. "What could be wilder than acting like we're more?" The color in his eyes deepened and he traced her mouth with the tip of a finger. "Besides, I still want to see that tattoo up close."

Before she could answer, he penetrated her parted lips with his tongue and his arms encircled her as if they would consume her. She let him. She wanted to. She was his, at least for tonight. She wanted to believe it could be forever. She moaned as he slipped her blouse upward, his fingers massaging the bare skin underneath.

Before her brain went totally fuzzy, she allowed herself one rational thought. Did he realize he played with her heart?

* * * * *

Danielle drummed her fingers against the table. Her watch read after six. Sam was late. She should have figured and planned accordingly. Maggiano's hadn't been far so she'd come early to get the advantage, insisting the maître d' tuck her in a table in the corner by a window. She wanted to see when Sam arrived to know when to stop practicing her pitch and arm herself for the upcoming battle.

She sipped the remaining drops in her glass of the expensive wine she'd poured. She'd requested a whole bottle, confident a little *vino* would loosen up Mr. Wonderful. When it did, her quick wit and charm would act like a rapier to his objections, slicing his concerns to pieces. He would love the idea.

Besides, she needed a little moral support. For whatever reason, Sam always got her off balance, and he surely knew it.

She glanced at her watch then out the window again. What kept him? She poured another glass, for fortitude she reminded herself and looked at her notes again. She had them memorized by now, but one couldn't be too careful.

A large group passed by the window and she watched them. They were in pairs, lovers, she assumed, and she wondered why she sat there wasting time. She took another sip of wine and her stomach growled. She was starving. She'd been so busy today she'd missed lunch. Grabbing a breadstick, she spoke to it. "Sam, you're going to want it—bad. Trust me." Then shoved it in her mouth.

"Sorry I'm late."

Danielle almost spat out the whole bite on her plate. She glanced up, her cheeks full of breadstuff, the end of the stick bobbing in her mouth. Sam. All six-two of him. His black hair was slightly damp and his blue eyes were alight with humor. She couldn't help but note how his polo shirt clung to him, highlighting the ripped muscles he'd become so fond of bragging about. He put his hands on his hips and his biceps bulged out from under the sleeves. She gulped, then choked on the breadstick.

"You okay?" He pounded her back.

"I'm fine," she squeaked, afraid he would pull her out of the booth and give her the Heimlich maneuver. She pointed to the seat across from her and tried to say more but her voice came out garbled. Oh yeah, this would impress the man.

He studied her face. Apparently satisfied she wouldn't die, he nodded then sat across from her and poured himself some wine. "Good vintage." He glanced at the bottle then shot her a smug look. "You sure Gary is willing to pay for this?"

She nodded, still catching her breath. She sure as hell wouldn't tell him this would come out of her pocket. Gary didn't need to know a thing.

He chuckled and gave her the funniest look. She should have schmoozed him by now, instead, he laughed at her while she made an idiot of herself.

Remember your charm, she reminded herself as he and his snotty look planted themselves across the table.

"So, what's the plan?" he asked.

Her breath returning, she looked at him. "What took you so long?"

He sat back and a black brow shot upward. "Business. I apologized, didn't I?"

She grunted. Business, her foot. She'd bet some woman got him detoured.

Don't get off track, she reminded herself. "Yes, you did." She cleared her throat and went into some of the details, forcing herself not to think about what may have kept him and why it bothered her so much.

When she finished, she downed her second glass and Sam poured her and himself another round. He signaled for the waiter and they ordered.

After the waiter left, he looked at her, his face unreadable. "And where do you propose we get a trained chimp?"

"Got one." She jerked her chin in a firm nod.

"You do?"

She relished his surprised look. "Absolutely."

"Who?" he asked. "From where?"

She picked up her glass and took a drink. Putting her elbows on the table, she leaned toward him. "Let's say it's my job." She let the cleavage from her low-cut blouse show, smiling when she knew the view wasn't lost on him. "You tell me if you want her, and I'll get the chimp."

Sam's subtly roving eyes found their way to her face. He studied her a few minutes, frowning. "I don't like being uninformed of the talent sources. I have the final say."

She sat back. *I have him*, she thought. "Tell me if you like the idea then we'll talk turkey."

Before he could answer, Gary's cell phone rang. Ignoring it, she smiled at Sam. "Well?"

The phone rang again.

Sam sneered. "Maybe you better answer that." He pointed to her purse where the sound came from.

She cleared her throat and rummaged through her pocketbook. "Why didn't I turn this damn thing off?" she muttered, wondering who it could be. She couldn't really explain anything to the caller, not with Sam sitting across from her. She forced a smile and pulled the phone out. "Hello?"

"Is…Gary there?"

"Nope," she replied. "Try later."

"Danielle?"

She almost hung up but the question stopped her. "Yeah?" This could be important.

"It's Nicole. Gary's sister."

"Nikki? How are you?"

"Fine." She giggled. "God, I can't believe Gary is finally dating, and with your sister no less. You know I found them both naked in his apartment?"

"Naked?" Danielle shouted. "Wha—" She stopped herself and looked at Sam. His attention targeted her and this conversation. "Ah, just a friend." She covered the receiver with her hand.

Sam's look grew dark. "Danielle, it's one of those calls where I can hear the other end from over here. You mean to tell me Gary's been ignoring me because he's busy seducing your sister?" His voice rose as he spoke.

"It's…it's not exactly what it seems. I'm sure it isn't." She waved her hand in front of him, trying to calm him down. "You see, I made this deal with Mira, my sister? Anyway, we made it to get you the voice and…"

"Danielle…" Nicole's voice came through the phone. "Who's there with you? You mean to tell me them having sex is part of some deal they made?"

"No, no, not exactly." Danielle tried to console her. Sam rose and threw his napkin on the table. "Let me call you back," she replied and slammed the phone off. "Sam." She ran after him, catching him when he got outside. She grabbed his arm to stop him. "Please, listen. It isn't what it seems."

His eyes flashed as he took a deep breath and looked at her. "Danielle, Gary isn't the only one with a lot riding on this deal. I sold him. It'll be my neck if it gets screwed. This is the biggest thing we've done yet. If the deal blows, I blow with it. Now, you have one chance to sell me. Then I'm pulling the account."

"Oh God no," she begged. "Sam, please." It dawned on her that maybe this time her meddling may have cost her. "Sam…" She bit her lip. "If you want to know the truth—

"You're damn right I do."

He stepped within inches of her, towering over her with a look that said he would throttle her with another wrong word. She gulped. "Gary doesn't know anything about this. It's my idea. My fault."

His gaze softened a bit and he shook his head. "What did you do this time?"

She steeled herself, not letting the barb affect her. "Look, I'm trying to help everyone involved, including you. My sister wants to save this chimp. Gary can help her. Mira had the sexy voice we needed for the ad, so pairing them together to help each other seemed perfect. Look, Gary's a great businessman. He wouldn't do anything to screw this up. Nicole has to be wrong about them. Mira would have told me if something happened."

He took a deep breath. "Doesn't your sister work at the zoo?"

She nodded.

"And it's the zoo chimp she wants to save that you're proposing we use."

She nodded again. "Good guess. If we use the chimp for the ad, it'll bring in enough revenue to help take care of her. That way the zoo won't sell her."

He ran a hand through his hair and looked away, quiet for a long moment before he gazed at her again. "When can I see the chimp?"

My God, the man did have a soul, albeit a small one. "I probably can't arrange it until Monday."

"I'll wait." He nodded. "Call me."

"Yes." She released a squeal of delight and jumped on him, wrapping her arms around his neck. "Sam, you're all heart. Thanks." She laid a big one on his lips.

He almost choked and grasped her waist. "You're welcome." His arms came around her and he placed a longer, deeper kiss on her mouth. She went into some weird trance before he broke it off.

He set her down but still held her. And he smiled. "You owe me, Danielle. And I'm going to make sure you pay. You're not out of the woods yet. I still need to approve of this chimp thing and part of it is going to depend on the chimp. I still might pull the ad. You tell Gary. And I mean everything. If I don't hear from him on Monday, you guys are through."

She bobbed her head, thinking the strange, floating feeling she got after kissing him had to be because she'd drunk too much wine on an empty stomach. "Whatever you want." She struggled to breathe.

He brushed her cheek with his thumb and released a low chuckle. Then he let her go. "I'll remember your promise — and hold you to it." He walked away, blending into the crowd.

"Omigod." She slapped herself. "I kissed the man. Yuck." She snapped her fingers. "But it got me what I wanted." Whistling, she went back into the restaurant, thinking that the whole thing turned out fairly well, considering. Her stomach growled again. She smiled as she passed the maître d' who had held the door, watching them. Time to eat.

* * * * *

Only a sliver of blue remained in the sky when they headed for the small pool with towels and a large blanket in hand. The creek hadn't been far but Mira wished it had been. A romantic night like this begged for the fantasies flittering through her head.

The cool night air made her shiver and Gary's arms came around to warm her.

"How about a fire?" He pointed to a small pit, used, probably, several times before by the many honeymoon couples staying at the inn. She nodded, worried that in the firelight Gary would see her whole body. How would she compare to the skimpy women he'd dated? She braced herself, hoping looks didn't matter to him.

Gary added a few logs to the pit from a pile stacked to the side and lit the fire. After nursing the embers, he stood and pulled off his shirt. Mira gulped. The glow of the flames bronzed his taut, sinewy muscles, making his sleek and powerful body even more enticing. On the female side, her body could hardly compare.

Gary spread the blanket and sat down on a corner. "You ready to take a dip?"

"I guess." She drew the words out.

He chuckled. "Good." He rubbed his hand across his chin. "But I want to see your tattoo first. Come here."

"Ah, Gary, I don't think—"

"A deal's a deal, Mira. My turn to choose." He stood and pulled her toward the blanket. "Don't get cold feet on me now." He sat down and took her with him.

"Gary, I…"

He hushed her with a kiss. "We're lovers, right?" His eyes grew dark and unreadable.

She wondered what he thought. "Gary…" She slid her hand down the hard planes of his chest. "I know this is part of the deal, but really, I don't have a body like I'm sure you're used to."

He frowned. "And what kind of body is that?"

"You know." She hesitated. "Like Danielle's. Sleek."

He laid her down and hushed her again, this time with a deeper kiss. "Every time you talk yourself down, I'll kiss you. Mira, let me be the judge of what I like and what I don't."

She swallowed. "But right now is just pretend."

"Yeah." He nodded and when he spoke, his voice grew rough. "But both of us want this." He brushed her cheek with his fingers. "Let's make the best of it." He half smiled. "Now you're supposed to be doing something wild. I suggest you get started."

"But what about you?"

His smile grew but darkness remained in his gaze. "I'm here to watch, remember?" He unbuttoned her blouse. When he'd exposed her bra, he kissed the fleshy parts of her breasts.

She moaned, remembering her mantra—*just do it.* "God, Gary, you don't know what you do to me."

He chuckled. "I'm glad you like it."

"You don't understand." She lifted his chin and looked into his face. "I meant it the other day when I said I'd never felt like this. No one has ever taken the time to show me how to enjoy myself. Not about…" She swallowed. "Sex."

He didn't respond at first, just studied her. She teetered on the edge, wondering what he thought. *Just do it,* she reminded herself.

"Mira, I understand. For me, I…" He tenderly touched her lips with his. "I'm remembering how to enjoy making love."

His breath caressed her mouth, and even in the act of speaking, he embraced her. His gentleness would be enough for now. She leaned into him and kissed him, her hands exploring the taut form of his chest then moving to his back to bring him closer. Her eyes closed as she treasured this moment, the cool night air breezing against her skin as he removed her blouse and her lace bra.

"You're beautiful," he whispered into her ear, nipping at her earlobe. She strengthened her resolve when he loosened her belt and slipped her pants over the tops of her hips. "Move for me, Mira." The rhythm of her heart beat faster. *Just do it.* She licked her lips and shifted so he could disrobe her. She sat there, naked except for her panties, him looking at her as if he could devour her in one bite.

Mira couldn't deny the fiery want in his eyes. A slow grin spread over his face, the one she couldn't resist. "It's time," he said.

"Time for what?" She bit her lip.

"I want to see it, Mira." He bent forward and laved her breast, taking her nipple in his mouth and raking his teeth gently over the bud. "The tattoo. Turn over."

She gasped briefly. *Just do it.* She bit her lip and turned, separating her knees and kneeling slightly then crouching on all fours. His hands slid down her back then his fingers slipped into the top of the lace underwear, slowly pulling them down. She held her breath, not able to stand the torture. She wanted him. Every small caress from his fingertips made her burn hotter. The underwear fell to her knees. Her breath hitched. He fingered the tattoo and she looked back at him, her breathing heavy with a mixture of anxiety and expectation.

He bent over and kissed the tat, gathering part of the skin tenderly with his teeth and tonguing it briefly, causing waves of sexual pleasure to spill over her. "I like it," he said, his voice thick, his breath hot against her. He placed soft lips against the spot again. "I like it a lot."

He kneeled between her parted legs, settling behind her. His hands massaged her buttocks then lowered, his target her inner thighs. His fingers teased the tender skin. Her legs tingled, a burning itch for more. Her need for him spiraled upward, emanating from his touch to her quivering mound. Instinct drove her, made her move to press the soft folds of her labia together. But she couldn't finish the task with her legs spread, not completely, and she whimpered with unrequited need.

Gary must have understood. His fingers plunged into her sex, heightening her desire, her craving for his touch. "You're wet," he taunted, his voice husky and lust-ridden.

She moaned as he wrapped his other arm around her. Warmth radiated from his abdomen to her bottom, heating the tensed glutes. She mewed when he lifted her to her knees and pulled her against him, his chest muscles flexing against her back as he gathered her close. He chuckled softly in her ear then nipped her lobe as he teased a nipple with his free hand.

"Oh God," she rasped as his teeth raked sensuously across her neck.

"You like?" he taunted, his breath caressing her. She could only nod.

"I'm going to take you, Mira. Like this."

A shiver of anticipation took her. She heard his pants zipper open, felt the cool night against her sex as his fingers left her. He penetrated her, fast and hard. She was ready. "Oh," she moaned, his fingers replaying what they had done within her channel on her clitoris.

"God, Mira," Gary uttered hoarsely, tension in him building.

Mira could feel his pleasure in the warm breath he brushed against her skin. Her passion rose in slow, aching moments. When she finally peaked, she shuddered and her arms gave way. But Gary's firm grasp prevented her from falling. He held her fully against him, not letting her go. Seconds later, he quaked with his release, grasping her tightly, his breath heavy against her skin.

She turned her head to kiss his jaw. "Is this how lovers do it?"

One corner of his mouth rose. "Yeah." He panted. "Yeah." He turned her enough so he could fully kiss her on the mouth, then withdrew his staff from her, turning her around and sitting her in front of him. He still wore his pants and only his satisfied member showed through the zippered opening. He studied her, looking her up, down, as if he wanted to memorize every part of her. "You're beautiful," he said after moments of silence. "Mira, from all of this, promise me you'll never again think otherwise."

She didn't know what to say. From the look of him, he really did believe what he said. How many times did he have to show her until she accepted it? In one way, she hoped a lot.

"Okay." She swallowed.

"Good." He brushed his thumb across her lips. "You ready for a swim?"

She laughed. "Sure." She headed for the pool, for once not worried about her nakedness but stopped at the edge of the water when he didn't follow and turned to face him.

He stared at her, a somber look on his face.

"You coming?" she asked.

"After you." He waved her on. "I'm just the witness, remember?"

Laughing again, she jumped in and dipped her head under the water. "Come on. The water feels great." She swam in the shallow pool.

He nodded. "Let me watch you a few minutes."

"Fine." She smiled. "But you don't know what you're missing." She wiggled her brows then headed for the small falls feeding the pool.

Gary forced a grin in return, fighting the melancholy seeping inside him, knowing he couldn't keep her from finding someone better. Although the sun had set, the firelight glistened on Mira's water-sleeked skin. Gary pulled his boxers over his hardening penis, hoping she wouldn't notice and prayed he'd accomplished his goal. Made Mira see how attractive she was. He thought he had. And it wouldn't be long before some other guy noticed and benefited from her new outlook on life.

The thought of another man touching her the way he had depressed him. Tamping down the pain, he swallowed, pleased, yet saddened with the turn of events, suppressing the regret leaving her would bring. But he'd determined he had to. Soon. He had already taken too many risks.

Gary rubbed his hand over his chin, the foreseen loss of her affection stabbing him. He'd hoped convincing her would take longer, but he didn't know how to get around his issue much longer. She'd almost stripped him in the cabin. If not for his quick reaction, she would have had him butt-naked. Then his secret would be out. She would know.

And he would see that look of pity from her that would destroy him.

Gary shook his head. He'd kept them from making love then, yet he'd promised her something wilder. He'd fulfilled his promise. Now maybe she would think more of herself, at least enough to let her find some guy worthy of her brains and beauty.

Yet Gary knew, if he had been the guy he once was, he'd have guaranteed that the man would be him.

Gritting his teeth, he determined to enjoy what he could and watched as Mira glided through the water, appreciating the view.

"Oooh, this feels *sooooo* risqué." She giggled, a seductive look gleaming in her eyes, then pulled herself onto a boulder jutting out of the falls. Resting on her cute derriere, she let the water drizzle on her skin. "The water's really warm." Closing her eyes, she arched her back, letting droplets fall into her open mouth and thrum against her breasts. Her nipples pebbled.

Gary grabbed himself, hoping to allay the blood gushing into his penis. "Damn," he cursed under his breath, unable to prevent the rock-hard state. His stiff rod flailed against the thin fabric of his boxers, begging for release.

"Are you sure you don't want to join me?"

Her sultry voice was more than he could take. He gulped, his throat parched. He forced a smile on his face that looked more relaxed than he felt. "Maybe I will." The tempo of his breathing escalated. He almost ripped off the rest of his clothes until his brain kicked in. This close to the firelight, she'd see him.

Instead, he turned and tore off every stitch of clothing but his boxers then quickly jumped in and swam toward her, reaching her in a few short strokes.

"Hey, no fair," she said and pouted when he stood and leaned his chest against the rock, exposing the trunk of his body. She slipped into the waist-deep water to stand next to him. "These have to go." She eased her thumbs into his waistband and tugged the garment down, running her hands down his water-slicked rump. His erection popped through the surface of the water. Gary gulped, hoping she couldn't detect anything else in the dark pool.

"Mmmm," she purred and nestled her body into his, her mons tight against his erection. "God, Gary, I love the way your body feels against mine."

"I know what you mean," he said, his voice roughened with heightened passion. He took her head in his hands, stroking his fingers through her wet hair and rubbing his thumbs over her cheeks. "I want you, Mira."

The impish gleam in her eyes deepened into fierce desire. "Then take me, Gary. Tonight, I'm yours to keep."

He stared at her, yearning to divulge the depth of his need. Instead, he kissed her, probed the depth of her mouth with his tongue, wanting to capture these last moments with her and never forget.

She moaned and kissed him back, moving her lips across his chin, his neck—and lower.

Her fingertips stroked his chest, led the way for the erotic pecks that followed. When her touch reached his nipples, she took each one in turn with her mouth and suckled.

Then her nails grazed against him, easing slowly down his sides causing his skin to erupt with want where she passed. Carnal tension built in his groin as her mouth glided down his torso, chasing away all doubts. Only the thoughts of her in his arms, of possessing her desire this night, remained.

He dropped his hands to her arms, caressing them, wanting her to know his pleasure. When her touch reached the sensitive skin around his manhood, his breath hitched, the anticipation of what she might do teasing him.

When she placed her mouth on his sensitive tip, he about came. "God, Mira, I need you. Can't hold…"

"I know." She licked the top. "I want you to." She sucked his shaft, raking her teeth gently over him.

He exploded, not able to hold himself back.

Gary leaned on her shoulders and gripped them, losing control. Empowered from his unspoken response, Mira grasped his rear cheeks and held him in place while she squeezed his rod with her mouth, her tongue caressing the underside. Then Mira felt him pulse one last time, tasted the salty emanation that came from his body, letting it fill her cheek. She swallowed what she could, the rest dripping from her mouth, and giggled, intrigued with the unusual taste.

Breathless and unsteady, Gary eyed her, his gaze heavy with a combination of astonishment and satisfaction. "God, woman."

"You like?" Mira raised a brow.

"Oh yeah." He chuckled. "Just surprised me is all." Sliding into the water, he leaned against the rock and pulled her close. "Give me a minute to catch my breath."

She laughed and rested her head on his chest. "Too wild for you?"

"Hell, no." He grinned back. "Although I would definitely put this in the 'wild' category. You're an expert."

"After one time? Well, I'm a quick study." She laughed. "And I'm glad it meets your criteria." She snuggled against him, reveled in the warmth of his body.

His hands slid against her. "You'd never done that before?"

"Oh no." She peeked up at him, watched the firelight dance over his strong features. He excited her like no other man. "Never really felt comfortable doing it before." Her voice grew husky. "I experimented. You're my first."

A corner of his lips quirked upward. "I see. Well, I'm glad I was your lab rat."

She giggled again and turned into him, taking his nipple in her mouth again. "Well, to keep you fully informed, there's a lot with you I've never done with anyone else."

"Like?" His brow rose.

"Being naked in the water, this feeling of freedom and rightness, losing control and gaining it. I didn't know I could affect a man like that, especially one like you."

He grimaced. "Mira, you could affect any man like that."

"You think?" She smirked and arched an impish brow.

"I know so." He pulled her upward to meet his lips. "Although I'm not sure I want to share." Mira groaned when his mouth captured hers.

When his lips released hers, she gazed into the depths of his blue eyes. "You might not have to," she said, and kissed him, rubbing her hands over his broad shoulders and down his sinewy back to his taut glutes, for once plunging headlong, taking the first move to get what she wanted. Gary moaned against her neck, causing shivers of desire on her skin. His penis throbbed against her leg, telling her without words that he wanted her to. "So, lover," she whispered with heady abandon in his ear, "what other wild thing would you like to do tonight?"

He pulled back to see her face and touched his forehead to hers, lust and mischief glinting in his eyes. "Well, Doctor, that depends on you. How much experimentation would you like to do?"

She shrugged, her smile plastered to her face. "Show me," was all she said.

And he did.

* * * * *

"In here, Joe." Candy Thompson inched the door of the cage open then mumbled to herself. *I finally land a date with the cute intern and what does he want to see? The ape that bit me.*

The zoo had closed, but she kept the keys. On the weekends, she became queen of the apes. She'd simply told security when they passed them she needed to check on a few things she'd forgotten earlier. Still, she kept the lights minimal so they wouldn't disturb the sleeping animals, which meant she and her date were feeling their way through some of the entrances. She heard him bump into something else before he stood behind her. She pointed to the Rhesus monkey.

"So that's Anthony," his baritone voice rumbled as he peeked in behind her. They could see him in the moonlight. Anthony released a yell, waking the whole cage. The monkeys screamed and scurried about. Afraid they would wake the others, she hurried Joe out. She worried about waking the apes. They weren't nice the next day if they hadn't slept well.

She heard a low moan from one of the other cages. It sounded like Sara. Other than minimal cleaning and feeding of the chimps, she hadn't looked in on her. Mira had said to leave them alone. Maybe she was hurt?

"Come on," she told Joe then closed and locked the door. "Just one more stop, okay? I have to check on Sara." She strolled over to the chimp's cage, Joe right behind her.

"Sara?" A hint of humor sounded in his voice. His arms slid around her and brought her close. "Who's Sara?"

She ran her hands up his arms and encircled his neck. "A chimp with a little problem. I'll be right back." He kissed her before he let her go and she took a couple of deep breaths to steady herself. Oh yeah, he's hot. She wiggled her brows at him and he chuckled.

She hurried, exercising caution when she opened the door. The monkeys had settled down and she really hoped no one else would awaken. Sara sat in the tree, looking lost. "Poor baby," she murmured and walked over to pick her up. "You're lonely, aren't you?"

The door creaked behind her and Joe tiptoed in.

"You shouldn't be in here," she whispered to him.

"Hey, I got lonely too," he said and winked at her. "Why can't I come in?"

She frowned and put Sara on the tree. "This is Sara."

"Nice to meet you." He bowed stiffly and Candy giggled. They'd probably had one too many beers.

Sara "ah'd" and waved at him.

"Hey, she likes me." Joe straightened.

Candy snorted. "She likes all guys. That's part of her problem. She tries to mate with anything that's male, even human guys."

"You're kiddin'." Joe's brow shot up.

"No, I'm not." She pushed him to the door.

He grabbed her, running his hands very intimately over her backside. "How 'bout we show her the difference."

"Slow down, cowboy." She shoved him away. "We aren't there yet. Besides, we need to get out of here. If I get caught, it'll be my job and my career."

"After you, princess." He bowed again.

She giggled and walked out. He followed behind her.

"I got the door," he said and pulled it shut, distracting her by laying a big one on her neck.

"Oh yeah." She giggled again and let his hands wander wherever they wanted while they were in the dark.

* * * * *

It took a while, but the noise moved away. Sara moaned again. Where had everyone gone? Not even the voice she liked answered on her friend's box. She went to the door and leaned her head against it. A wind blew through. She looked at the exit. Was it open? When she first arrived, she used to get out all the time. Then they changed things. "Oooh." She slid a finger underneath. It moved. "Eeek." She screamed then quieted. No one should hear her. She rushed back to the tree and picked up the box from inside. She would find her voice herself. And when she did, she wouldn't leave.

Going back to the door, she opened it the rest of the way and went out. The keeper's voice could still be heard. They were somewhere inside, but it was okay. Sara could wait.

Chapter Thirteen

** හ**

The morning sun peeked through the window shade of the cabin. Mira stretched against Gary's back, more sexually sated than she'd ever been in her life. She reveled in the discoveries she'd made, the power she'd found over Gary, the seduction. A give and take of hunger and satisfaction. He didn't do anything she didn't want to try. The experience exhilarated her. And she loved teasing him, making him lose control. He'd done the same to her. Heightened with longing, together they soared into sensual bliss, their bodies moving in concert, instinctively knowing what each other's deepest sexual desires were. She'd never felt the like and, she surmised, neither had he.

Gary had cherished her. Loved her. And she returned the act with everything she had.

Rubbing against his boxer shorts, she slid an arm around his taut torso. He'd insisted he needed the underwear, afraid he couldn't make his "little friend" go to sleep if he didn't. What a guy. She could barely believe this had happened to her. That a guy like Gary could care for her. But after the incredible lovemaking last night, she had to. Why else would he act this way? He found her attractive. And he was considerate. How lucky could she get?

She grimaced, wondering if she should she ask him about afterward, when the deal ended. Or should she wait and hope he said something to her? What happened if they broke this off? Would they wish each other a good life and shake hands? Boy, she just didn't know. All these sensations, these emotions, were new to her. She didn't know what to do with them. The only thing she knew for sure was she didn't want to give him up.

Unlike other guys she'd dated, he made her feel good about herself.

Gary stirred beside her and turned into her embrace. His lashes fluttered open and he grinned. "Mornin'."

She kissed the corners of his mouth. "Back at you. Hungry?"

"Almost." He pulled her closer. "I want to hold you for a while first," he said, breathing the words into her hair. He kissed her temple then trailed small pecks against her skin until he reached her lips. She relished the way his mouth met hers.

"Mmmm." She brushed her thumb against his lips when he'd finished. "I have to say, I do like the way you taste."

He chuckled. "Good. Because I want you to have more."

He kissed her again, deeper this time. Now she knew what it was to be loved, how could she do without it?

She fingered the soft, curly hairs on his chest then moved her hand lower, slipping her fingers into his boxers. He stiffened and moved her hand and pulled away. "You know, thinking about it, breakfast sounds like a good idea. Besides, I need to contact Danielle and see what she's done. Sam Carter called, the promo man for this national commercial. They want the spot sooner."

"But..." She reached for him. He jumped out of bed before she could catch him. She didn't want this to end, not yet. "If you'll need my voice sooner, does that mean that the length of my deal with Danielle is shortened?"

He stopped amid sliding a leg into his pants. His eyes darkened again, tinged with sadness. "I don't know." He finished pulling on his pants.

She sat up and covered herself with the sheet, confused with the drastic change in his demeanor. "And what about our agreement?"

He didn't look at her at first, but when he did, seriousness clouded about him and made her cold. "That'll end too."

He turned his back and slipped on his shirt.

Her chest felt heavy, weighed down with betrayal. What had she been thinking? Mira knew this was temporary, yet she let herself be lulled into believing so much more. She wanted to cry but bit her lip instead. It had been the deal. He'd certainly fulfilled his part. Mira couldn't complain. She wouldn't, couldn't, let him know how he'd gotten to her, how he had reached her heart.

* * * * *

Candy arrived a little late. It was one of those days where she needed the large espresso she sipped on. She still walked in a fog. Joe had been fun and kooky. She liked him. Would he ask her out again?

She did her chores, checking on Anthony to see if he was all right. That monkey was something else. He seemed fine and she continued her rounds. When she got to the chimp cage, she checked on Sara, just in case. The old girl had acted pretty weird last night, at least for her. She hadn't approached Joe at all. The chimps jumped from limb to limb as she went inside the cage. She scanned the interior. Where had Sara gone?

Candy checked the tree where she had seen her the night before. No Sara. She scanned the cage again. "Oh God," she muttered. "She's gone."

* * * * *

Gary didn't know what happened. Instead of getting something to eat, Mira insisted he take her home. She said she had some things to do and urged him to finish the work he'd said needed to be done. He really blew it this time, but what else could he do? When she'd fingered his underwear, common sense slammed into him. He couldn't let her see him in the daylight. She would know his secret, and God, he couldn't stand seeing her shocked face and the disgust that would follow. It would break him. Hurt him too bad…because he loved her.

Good Lord, when did that happen?

When he pulled into her drive, he faced her. He needed to say something but didn't know what. "Mira, I…"

"It's been great," she said. "Thanks for your help. I certainly know what to look for in a guy from now on."

"Mira, wait a minute."

"No. You wait. You're right. Our deal's over as far as I'm concerned. You'll finish with my voice this week. There's no use in drawing this out. It was fun." She swallowed and her eyes were shiny. "Interesting. Leave it alone."

"What about our friendship?"

She stopped in the process of opening the door. She wouldn't look at him. "I don't know."

"Mira, I'm an idiot."

"Yes, you are." She crossed her arms. "And you know I like intelligent men."

He ignored the jibe. "Don't shut me out, please?"

She bit her lip and a tear in the corner of her eye threatened to fall. "Call me when you need me." She rushed from the car.

Gary banged on the steering wheel when she got inside, knowing he'd lost the best thing he'd ever had.

* * * * *

Mira dropped her purse on the table. Closing the door, she let the tears fall. She should have anticipated something like this, but didn't. What did she expect? Life never worked out for her the way it did others. Wildness wasn't part of her repertoire. Every time she tried to let go, she got hurt. She should have known better.

The rationale didn't console her. Gary had gotten her to trust. In their short time together, she'd fallen in love with him. Unfortunately, she'd assumed he felt the same. Bad postulation on her part. He had never said anything of the sort to her. But what led her to the conclusion had been what he did. She simply read too much into it.

Grabbing a tissue from the box on the table, she dabbed at her eyes. He couldn't be faulted for her broken heart. The blame lay with her. She'd had the wild ideas. She'd been the one who decided to go for it.

The phone rang. She sniffed once before she answered.

"Mira?"

"Yes?"

"It's Candy. I, ah, have some bad news."

She straightened. Wasn't a broken heart enough devastation for one day? "What is it?"

"It's Sara." Candy paused. "She's gone."

"Gone? What do you mean she's gone?"

"She's not in the cage. I don't know where she went." Candy sobbed. "I've looked all over the zoo. Even in some of the carnivore cages, to make sure, you know?"

"What did the guards say?"

"They haven't seen anything unusual, but they're looking." Candy's breath hitched between sniffs.

"Okay, Candy. Be calm. Did you call Dr. Burrows?"

"No," she blubbered.

"Damn." Now what had the jackass done? Had he sold Sara behind her back? "Look, Candy. Stay at the cages and don't do anything. I'll be right there."

She hung up and dug in her purse for the keys to her car. Burrows had to be behind her disappearance. Who else would do something this underhanded?

Her phone rang again. "I don't have time for this." She lifted the receiver. "Hello?"

"Mira, it's me."

"Danielle, look, I'm busy. I need to get to the zoo." Besides, Danielle was the last person she wanted to talk to right now.

"But this is important. I really screwed up this time and I'm afraid I screwed you too. Gary's gonna kill me and—"

"Danielle." Mira rolled her eyes. Right now she didn't give a flipping tahooty about Gary or anything associated with him. "Is this supposed to surprise me? Look, I need to go. Sara's missing and we need to find her. I hope Dr. Death Burrows hasn't sold her behind my back. Talk to me later, okay? Bye."

She hung up and rushed out the door.

"Mira, wait—" The line went dead. Danielle stared at the receiver. If Burrows sold Sara, her butt would really be in a sling. Now what? She'd left messages at Gary's place and on her cell that he unknowingly carried. He hadn't returned any of them. She only had so much time. Sam would be calling and he'd fire them if she hadn't told Gary by the time he called.

She dialed Gary's number. She needed to let him know what a mess she'd made of everything. Only Gary could fix this now.

It rang. Once, twice, four times. Damn. Where did everyone go when you needed them? She tapped her finger against her cheek. "Well, there's only one thing to do."

She stiffened, preparing herself for the worst, then picked up her phone and dialed Sam's.

* * * * *

Gary drove around for at least an hour before he settled things in his mind. What the hell had he been doing? Mira had every right to be upset. Yeah, he'd met his end of the bargain, but he gave and took a lot more than the deal called for. So did she. But one fact stood out above the others.

He loved her.

He'd never loved another woman. Not even Darlene Woods. With Darlene, marriage had been the next step in their relationship. No steps existed with Mira. She just took and gave, regardless of tomorrow. Now things were clear, he had a mission. Maybe he couldn't tell Mira everything. But, somehow, he needed to get her back.

* * * * *

Mira rummaged through the official files on the animals. Nothing in any of them indicated Sara's sale. "They must be in his office," she said to Candy. "Can we get in?"

Candy grimaced. "I don't think so. Look, Mira, maybe I ought to…"

Mira waved her hand to shush her. "Candy, let's stay focused. If we can find where he sold her, maybe we can get her back. He couldn't have finalized all the paperwork yet. It still hasn't been voted on by the board."

"Maybe he didn't sell her," Candy said.

Mira scowled. "If he didn't, she would be here."

Candy looked even sicker. "Maybe not. Mira, sit down, please?"

Mira's curiosity piqued. She sat. "Spit it out, Candy."

The girl swallowed. "Well, see, last night. I had a date. You know the guy who bandaged my hand at the hospital?"

Mira nodded.

"Well, he called me and we went out."

Mira frowned. "Get to the point. What does your date have to do with Sara?"

Candy folded her hands in front of her. "He wanted to see Anthony."

"What?" Mira leaned forward in the chair.

"Yeah." She shrugged. "So I brought him here."

"In the middle of the night?" Mira's voice rose. She could feel her temperature rising.

Candy nodded. "Yeah. Sara was moaning, a lot. I thought I'd better check on her while I was here. We haven't spent much time with her and I thought maybe she hurt herself. So I went in. Joe followed."

"Joe." Mira grabbed the armrests so she wouldn't throttle her aide.

"Yeah. I didn't think he would, but he did. Sara didn't want to have a thing to do with him. Just sat in my arms and moped. When we left, he closed the door. I forgot I'd had problems with the lock again. You know that latch?"

"I know the one." Mira buried her head in her hands. A royal headache had developed behind her eyeballs. She stood. "You're telling me Sara got out, right?"

Candy grimaced and nodded. "I think so."

"Call the police. And get animal control. We need to report this." She walked to her office door and yanked it open. "I hope the night was worth your job."

"Mira?" Candy cringed.

Mira stopped and looked at her young assistant.

"Who's going to call Burrows?"

"I will." Mira huffed. "I hope you've learned from your mistake, Candy. Having fun is one thing but you need to take your responsibilities seriously."

"You're...you're not going to tell him I let her loose?"

She rubbed her aching temple. "We're not sure you did yet, are we? I'll tell him the latch broke and needs to be fixed. The miser should have had the lock replaced a long time ago."

"Thank you, Dr. Harper. You know, I really want to be like you when I grow up."

"Don't patronize me, Candy. Just promise me you'll never do anything this stupid again."

Candy crossed her heart with her forefinger. "Promise."

Mira shook her head and walked out, wondering if she shouldn't take her own advice about doing something stupid. When would she learn not to mess with athletic men?

* * * * *

Gary pounded on Mira's door again. No answer. Where did she go? He couldn't have been gone more than an hour. He peered into the front room window. No sign of life. Would Danielle know where she went?

"You know, a big, tall guy like you looks funny knocking so hard on a door to an empty house."

Gary glanced up and saw Mira's neighbor staring at him. She stood on her front porch, a hand shading her eyes from the sun.

"She left a while ago," Jojo said.

"Do you know where?"

She walked over. "Probably where she always goes when she's upset. The zoo. Her work is her refuge."

"Thanks." He stepped off the porch. "I knew she didn't have to work. Guess I don't think of people going in to a job unless they have to."

Jojo laughed. "Didn't you feel that way about football? It was a job, wasn't it?"

"Yeah, I guess." He huffed. "But it was more play than work."

She nodded. "I know what you mean. Why don't you come over for a while? Give her some time to cool off. We can talk about it."

"Talk about what?" Gary eyed her.

"Your fight, silly. Aren't you here to make up? With her, you may need some extra ammunition." Jojo walked toward her home.

Gary stood there a minute and debated his options. Except he hadn't many. Jojo was right. He needed as much ammo he could get. "Wait." he called, running after her. When he reached her he asked, "You're a sex therapist, right?"

"Right," she answered.

"Then what I tell you should be in strict confidence?"

She turned to him, confused. "Yeah, if you want my professional help. But I thought we'd just talk. Mira has her own issues."

He sighed. "Yeah, and so do I. I don't want to talk about Mira, not exactly. I want to talk about myself." He swallowed. "I'll pay for it. I sure as hell need it. I don't want to lose Mira. And I've already botched things up enough as it is."

She frowned and took him by his elbow, leading him to her house. "Okay. For Mira's honey, I'll make an exception about after hours. Besides, maybe we do need to talk." She smiled at him as she took him through the front door. "I understand that you like tea?"

* * * * *

"Look, Dr. Harper, I didn't sell Sara, okay? How could you accuse me of such bunk? It still hasn't gone to the board for a vote." Doctor Burrows sat in a chair in front of her desk as Mira paced.

"Just checking, Charlie." Mira rubbed her aching temple. "Then it has to be the lock. It needs to be replaced, pronto."

"Why? Look, Miranda, I know you didn't drag me down here for nothing. What is going on?" Charlie adjusted the glasses sitting on top of his beaked nose and peered through them at her with his beady eyes.

She stopped and studied at him. "Sara's gone."

"What?" For such a short man, he almost hit the ceiling. Mira would have laughed if the situation hadn't been serious. "How long has she been missing?"

She paused, wanting to say the right thing. "Candy noticed her absence when she got here this morning. She's probably been gone all night."

"Then...then...she could be anywhere," he stuttered. His face turned crimson.

"We've already alerted everyone." Mira rubbed her shoulder. "Except the media, of course. The fewer people who know the better. I'm going back out now. We've sectioned off the area. I thought you could man the radio. Hopefully, she didn't go far."

"Just-just wait right there, Doctor." Charlie shook a nervous finger at her. "I'm the administrator. How dare you take these actions without consulting me? And what are you thinking, telling me what to do?"

"Charlie, this couldn't wait," Mira protested. "Besides, it's standard procedure and somebody needs to man the radio. You're our fearless leader. It should be you coordinating everything."

"The procedures are for the carnivores."

"They're for anything, Charlie. And if you want to mince words with the SOPs then fine. Do it later. We have a chimp to find."

"Doctor Harper." The tension in his voice rose. "I'll have your job for this. It's your fault Sara's missing."

"My fault?" She walked over and eyeballed the worm back into the chair. "I'm not the one too cheap to fix the lock. Explain that to the board."

She swerved and walked down the hall. He ran after her but she kept going. "You probably sold her yourself," he yelled. "Or-or better yet. You've hidden her."

She stopped when she reached the end of the hallway. "Say your prayers, Charlie," she said and grabbed the doorknob. "Your days as administrator are numbered."

She jerked the door open and walked out, determined to do the one thing she did well — take care of the apes, including Sara when she found her.

She stomped over to the ape house. Where could that little minx be? She pulled out the walkie-talkie and signaled Candy, who had the same hand-unit. "You see anything? Over."

"Nada. Over," Candy replied.

"Damn." From a distance, she could see Danielle running toward her. "Double damn," she muttered. "Keep looking," she told Candy and signed off.

"Mira," Danielle panted as she reached her, breathless from the run. "Did you find her?"

"No, not yet."

"I'm sorry." Danielle squinted then turned her back to Mira and ran a hand through her hair.

"Okay, Danielle. What's so important you need to bother me now?"

Danielle looked at her and wrung her hands. "I need to find Gary. I thought you guys were together."

"We were. We aren't now." Mira walked toward the next designated section for her search.

"Do you know where he is?" Danielle ran after her.

"No. And I don't care. I don't care if I ever see him again."

"Oh God. What happened?"

Mira stopped. "Nothing, so drop it. I have more important things to do. Leave me alone, Danielle, unless you want to search for Sara."

Danielle hurried behind her. "Your nothing doesn't include sleeping with Gary, does it?"

"No." Mira knew her sharp answer would cause Danielle to make further comments.

"Strange. That isn't what Nicole told me."

Mira stopped short and Danielle rammed into her. "Later, Danielle, okay?"

"Okay," she relented. "But there's one thing you should know."

"What?" Mira stopped, realizing she needed to let Danielle get this out before she could continue her search.

Danielle bit the inside of her cheek and crossed her arms. "We were fired."

Chapter Fourteen

ഏ

"Fired? What do you mean, 'fired'?" Mira asked.

"The big ad, Mira. The spot we needed to use your voice for." Danielle crossed her arms. "While Gary and you were off having your lover's quarrel, Sam Carter pulled the ad."

Mira was almost afraid to ask. "Why?"

The question had been all the impetus Danielle needed. "Because Sam thought Gary ignored him so that he could seduce you and —"

"That's ridiculous," Mira cut in. "Gary and I, well, we..." She stopped when she saw Gary round the corner of the sidewalk.

"He thought Gary lost interest in his business," Danielle continued. "Sam's red neck is on the line, so he pulled it, but —"

"But what?" Gary had stood behind Danielle in a way her sister couldn't see him. If Gary hadn't been so upset, Mira would have laughed at the look of surprise on Danielle's face.

Gary shook his head and strode around Dani. "Tell me later." He approached Mira. "We need to talk," he said.

"I have nothing to say to you." She tried to pass him.

"Mira, please."

He grasped her arm to hold her and his eyes pleaded for her to stay. Hadn't she learned her lesson yet? "You should be more interested in your business. You've lost your big ad. Doesn't that bother you?"

"Yeah." He nodded. "But I'm more concerned about us."

That comment caught her. He put her over the largest deal he'd ever had? "Why?"

He stalled. "Let's just say I don't want what we have to end."

"Yes," Danielle piped in, lifting a fist in the air for victory.

"Dani," she responded, "if you don't split, I'll show you what gorillas do to little sisters."

Danielle's eyes widened. "Oooh." She perked up. "Well, okay, where do you want me to look for you know who?"

She glared at Danielle. "Find Candy. She'll tell you. She should be by the lions."

"Hmmm." Danielle tapped her manicured finger against her cheek. "Better go, Gary. By the way, you should call Sam." She rushed off.

Mira hit the palm of her hand against her head. "I can't believe that girl sometimes."

Gary chuckled. "I can. She cares about you." He took Mira in his arms. "So do I."

She backed away before he could kiss her. "And I can't believe you're laughing about this. Aren't you concerned at all about your business?"

"Yeah." He peered at her with those strange, deep-colored eyes. "But I like taking care of the most important things first. Mira, go out with me. Tonight. Give me the chance to explain." He swallowed. "If afterward, you don't want to see me anymore..." He shook his head. "Then I'll understand."

She must be insane to put up with this. "Why?"

He took her in his arms, running his strong hands across her shoulders. "I love you, Mira," he said. "And I think you care for me back."

She wanted to crawl under a rock and cry. Did he know he would break her heart? "I—"

He kissed her. "Mira, just one night. I promise. I'll tell you everything. I'll tell you why I...well, why I acted like I did this morning."

She nodded, knowing their meeting could be her downfall, but in his arms she couldn't seem to find the word "no". She bit her lip. "Okay, you've got one chance, bucko. But first you have to help me find Sara."

His brow arched. "What happened to her?"

"Somehow she got out." Now she really wanted to cry. "And Burrows is blaming me. He wants me fired."

He kissed her again. "We'll see about that."

"It's a deal then?" She slid her hand against his chest and lifted it enough to look like a handshake.

He chuckled and put her hand around his neck. "Deal," he said, and sealed it with a kiss.

*   *   *   *   *

"Lions and tigers and bears, oh my," Danielle sang as she walked the pathways, looking for Candy. She glanced heavenward and said, "Thanks, Big Bud. Those two needed to get together."

The cell phone rang. "Hello?"

"Danielle? I thought this was Gary's number." Sam, again. She had been so far in la-la land she'd forgotten she had Gary's phone. She looked at the sky again, wanting to take her thanks back.

"Ah…" She cleared her throat. "Well, this is his phone. He wanted me to keep it for a few minutes." She grimaced, hoping one more lie would work in her favor and feeling bad, for some reason, that she deceived him.

"Is he there?"

She bit her lip. "Sort of."

"Well? I gave you one more chance to tell him. Have you?"

She grimaced. "I haven't had time. Sam, to be honest with you—"

"A nice thought," he jabbed.

"Ouch." She paused. "I guess I deserved that."

"You're damn right you do."

"Look, Sara's missing. The chimp we talked about."

"My star?"

"Yeah."

He grew quiet a moment. "You know, Danielle, as flaky as you are, I like your idea."

"You…you do?" His comment stunned her.

"Yeah. Where are you?"

"At the zoo. We're looking for her."

He sighed. "I'm not far. I'll be there in a few."

The line went dead. She looked upward again. "Okay, Big Guy, how much trouble am I really in?"

Expecting no answer, she walked on. Then the idea hit her. "Why didn't I think of this before?" She dialed Mira's cell number, hoping it would work. The battery had to be close to dead by now. It rang. Once. Twice.

"Ooooh."

"Sara baby, where are you?"

"Mmmm." The line went dead.

Danielle snapped the phone shut and ran to find Mira. It took almost half an hour but she found her near the polar bears. "Mira…" She huffed as she stopped her. "Where's Gary?"

"Trying to clear up the mess you made, I imagine. Your Sam found him."

"He isn't my Sam," Danielle snapped and wondered how much trouble the "boys" conversation would buy her. "Look, I have an idea. The battery still works on your cell but probably not for long."

"My cell phone? What are you talking about?"

"Mira, I know you hid it in the cage. How do you think I found out?"

Mira planted her hands on her hips. "How would you have…?"

"She's the mysterious caller."

"What mysterious caller?"

"Gary's mysterious caller. The other woman we were considering for the job."

"Danielle, you aren't making any sense. Who are you talking about?

"Sara."

"Sara? But she's an ape, not a woman."

"Oh, never mind. Look, I'm telling you, we need to get Gary to call Sara."

"What?"

"Sara has your cell phone."

"How do you know?"

"I called her and talked to her."

"You, what? Danielle, Sara's a chimp."

Danielle sputtered. "You do it all the time."

"But—"

"Look, she's fine. But we need Gary."

"Why?"

"She's enamored with Gary's voice. I think if he talks to her we can find where she is."

"How? Depending on how far she's gone, we can't hear her." Mira sighed. "I do think she's still in the park, though. She's never been one to leave familiar surroundings. When she used to escape before, she always stayed in the park. Look." Mira snapped her fingers. "I have another idea. You go get Gary. He should be near the giraffes. Maybe this will work."

"Do I have to?" Danielle squirmed.

"Yes," Mira insisted. "Might as well face the music, sis. Your meddling really messed things up. Just tell them we have a chimp to consider right now. The rest can wait."

"Okay," she replied then mumbled, "although I probably won't have a job when I get back." She hoped this facing the music thing could wait for forever. Gritting her teeth, she hurried off. At least she'd accomplished one good thing with this whole scheme. Somehow, Mira and Gary would get together. Didn't she say the risk would be worth it? Well, now she would pay, but she didn't quite relish this part. She'd hoped her scheme would have worked out more smoothly. The thought of facing Gary didn't bother her, except it wasn't so much him she worried about. She could convince him her motives were honest. Sam, on the other hand, would be another whole ball of wax.

"Certain doom," she declared, but Sara needed to be found first. Steeling herself, she rushed toward the inevitable.

* * * * *

"Look, Charlie, just get ahold of the emergency people. They should be able to pinpoint the signal, at least to some degree. Their technology is more precise these days. Since we're the ones calling, I have to know what we need to do on our end. Okay? Over." Mira rolled her eyes, her patience growing shorter with each of Charlie's questions.

"I will take care of it, Doctor Harper," he replied stiffly over the short wave. "Out here."

The sound of static met her eardrum. "Ouch." She wiggled her finger in her ear.

Behind her, she heard Danielle's voice, obviously attempting to explain her sins.

"You see using Sara for the ad…" she heard her sister say.

"What?" Mira pivoted on her heel to face her. "Use Sara for the ad? Are you insane?"

Danielle flinched.

Sam glared at Danielle. "Another lie. You told me you had the trainer in your pocket."

"Ah, I do." Danielle shrugged, smiling at Sam. "She simply doesn't know it yet."

"Argh," Mira growled and rubbed her temple, the headache growing worse.

Gary stepped up and rubbed Mira's arms. "What is it you want me to do?"

She leaned toward him, needing his strength for the moment. He pulled her into him and his arms came around her to hold her. For a second, she forgot what had bothered her about Danielle, what she needed him to do. She only wanted to revel in the warmth of his embrace.

"See what I mean?" she heard Danielle speak to Sam.

"Yeah." Sam's voice sounded rough. Mira glanced at him. Sam and Danielle had started their own conversation, ignoring them. Sam stared at Danielle in the oddest way. Did he have an attraction for her sister?

She smiled at Gary, keeping the tidbit in back of her mind. Danielle would suffer, at least for a while, because she would never tell her sister Sam was in love with her. She looked at Gary more closely. Didn't he have that same look about him?

It hit her. "You are in love with me, aren't you?" she asked.

He brushed her cheek with the pad of his thumb. "Yeah," he said and kissed her.

She kissed him back. They probably would have lingered in the embrace longer, but the radio cackled again. "Doctor Harper, come in. I have the information for you. Over."

She broke away and grabbed the radio off her belt. "I'm here. Over."

"When I give you the word, call the chimp. It should only be a few minutes. Over."

"Understood. Over."

No one spoke as the four of them waited. In a few seconds, Burrows came back on the line but Mira thought it had seemed much longer. Gary stood ready to call. "Listen for background noise," she told him. "It might give us an idea where she is."

He nodded and placed the call. Mira could only wait.

"Sara?" Gary spoke, lifting his chin in Mira's direction, letting her know he had gotten through. "Where are you, sweetheart?" He leaned over, sharing the receiver so Mira could hear Sara's moans. "Hey, you stood me up. Never had a woman do that before."

Sara "oooh'd" in response and Mira glared at him. "Just wait," she mouthed. "I might stand you up yet."

He kissed her quick. "But not tonight," he whispered. "Maybe after we're married."

She gaped. "Married?"

Danielle giggled in the background and Sara "Mmmmm'd" again, as if in agreement.

"Huh?" She lifted a finger to protest but he countered too fast, capturing her mouth while Sara "Oooo'd" and "Aaaaah'd" on the other end of the phone.

"Doctor Harper. Over."

Mira jumped as the static of the radio interrupted.

"Here. Over," she answered.

"They've pinpointed the signal as close as they can. She's in the zoo somewhere…"

"I knew it," Mira blurted out.

"Probably near the ape house from what I can tell. Scan those trees again. She's nearby. Call me when you locate her. Over."

"Received and acknowledged. Over," she replied. "She's nearby," she told the others, as if they hadn't heard. "Gary, keep talking to her and circle around the outside of the ape house. Maybe if she sees you she'll announce herself or something. Listen for ape sounds."

"Yes, ma'am," he said and gave her small salute. "Although, apparently I've been listening to those sounds for a while. Just didn't know it." He threw Danielle a warning look then looked at his friend. "Sam, you in?"

"Yeah, I'll help." He moved to go with Gary.

"No, wait." Mira stopped him. "You might scare her off. Let Gary go alone. I'd rather you went with Danielle."

"Her?" He pointed to her sister as Gary kissed Mira quickly then left, still talking to Sara on the cell.

"Yes," she insisted. "Danielle isn't all bad. She's simply…" She waved a hand in the air from frustration. "Meddlesome. Unfortunately, she also tends to grow on you."

"That's what I'm afraid of," Sam mumbled and ran a hand through his dark hair.

"You two." She scowled at her sister. "Check the perimeter. I'll go inside and look around. Maybe she didn't get as far as we suspected."

"But—" Danielle argued.

"Don't even." Mira wagged a finger at her. "If you think you're getting out of this unscathed, think again."

Miffed, Danielle walked off. Sam hustled after her, shoving his hands in his pockets as he went, watching Danielle's swaying hips from behind. For once, Danielle obviously didn't know what she did to a man.

"Good," Mira mumbled to herself. "At some point, turnabout will be fair play."

"Candy." Mira put in a call over the radio as she rushed toward the ape house. "She's by the apes, do you hear me, over?"

"Yeah. I'll meet you there. Over."

Mira took off at a run, panting when she entered the ape house. The sun had been so bright outside it took a minute for her vision to adjust to the darker interior. The apes, as usual, chatted it up, making the place noisy. Looking around, she saw Candy had arrived.

"You find her?" Mira asked as she walked toward her.

"No." Candy took a deep breath, winded herself. "Just got here too. I sent the other guys outside. Told them to fan out starting from here. You know, she's been gone for so long I didn't even think to look in here."

Mira nodded, knowing she wouldn't have either. "You look in the closets and passageways. I'll check the other cages."

"Okay."

They split up, Candy taking one end and her, the other. In less than fifteen minutes, they met in the center. "You see her?" Mira asked.

Candy shook her head.

"Maybe we're going about this the wrong way."

"Mira?" Gary opened the door, allowing the brighter light to come in.

"In here," she called.

"She's gone quiet. She's still on the phone. I can hear her breathing but she isn't talking anymore."

"Let me try." She took the phone from Gary. "Sara, honey, speak to me, please?"

A low moan sounded over the receiver.

"Wait a minute." Gary scanned the rafters. "I think I hear her. Talk to her again."

"Sara? Come home, okay?"

"Mmmm."

"I hear her," Mira shouted. "She's in here somewhere."

Gary waved at Mira to keep talking.

"Sara, it's okay, baby. No one is going to harm you." Mira studied the ceiling, trying to figure out where she could be.

"There she is." Gary pointed to a far corner where Sara hid behind a beam. "Come here, baby."

He called to her like one would a dog and walked toward her.

"Gary, talk to her like you always have. That's what she likes," Mira cautioned.

He shot her a look of horror. "I didn't know she was a chimp then."

"Pretend. You don't want her spooked."

He grimaced then swaggered closer. "Hey, baby, you want to do an ad? You've got the voice for it."

Sara's "ummm" was one of the sexiest Mira had ever heard. She'd never realized it. "Oh my." She glanced at Gary. "She sounds like a woman on the prowl."

Gary turned to Mira and shrugged. "What can I say? I'm irresistible."

Mira about choked on her laughter. "Keep going, Romeo. Coax her down. But be careful not to push too hard. She might run."

Gary shot her an "I know better look", as Candy giggled behind her.

"Okay, fine," Mira said and addressed Candy. "Radio the team to bring a net and a ladder. We'll need to get this place locked down."

The door blasted open and Sara scrambled back to her earlier position. "We couldn't find her and I'm not working with this guy any longer." Danielle stood in front of the open doorway.

Candy hurried to close the door behind Danielle but Sam Carter pushed his way through. "Any luck?" Sam asked and glared at her sister.

"She's in here. Keep the blasted door closed," Mira said.

Sam quieted and ambled toward Gary. "Where is she?"

Gary pointed to the beam Sara sat on.

"Here, let me try." Sam moved in front of Gary and spoke to her—in what sounded like Swahili or some other African dialect. His melodic voice had its own rhythm. Sara's interest was piqued. Inch by inch, she lowered herself along the wall. Finally, she dropped to the ground, the phone still in one of her hands. Everyone but Sam stood frozen. He crouched and called to her, speaking words that none of them understood, except Sara. She stepped toward him, cautiously at first then leaped the final few feet into his arms. Everyone cheered except Mira. Instead she leaned against Gary, who had come to her, and sighed with relief.

Sam carried the chimp over. "Here, I'll let you take over."

Mira took Sara from him. "How did you do that?"

He shrugged. "I was an animal trainer once. I worked with chimps like this, especially trained ones. Are you certain she wasn't part of a study at some time? She seems awful savvy."

"I didn't think so. But I still don't understand how you got her down. I've never seen anyone able to do that."

"It's a trick I learned from an old game hunter. Attracts the females every time. Of course..." He winked. "Part of it is that I'm so irresistible to women."

"Not to this woman, you're not," Danielle sputtered and walked to the door then stopped. "Gary, if you want to fire me, I understand."

Sam snorted. "I don't know how he can do that when you haven't even given him the details of this new angle you dreamed up."

"If you're talking about using Sara, forget it. Burrows will never go for it," Mira said. "And I have to say, I'd probably agree with the man for once. Whatever gave you that wild idea?" she asked Danielle.

Her sister meandered back to her and stroked Sara's head. "She did."

Sara moaned and her soulful eyes stared at Gary.

Danielle giggled. "She's been using your cell phone to dial Gary's."

"I thought so." Candy shook her head. "I knew Sara had been up to something with your phone."

Mira stared into Sara's eyes. "How could you do that?" she asked her.

"Programmed dialing," Candy cut in. "It's what I showed you the other day. Remember? You said they looked like some of Danielle's work numbers."

The chimp handed the phone back to Mira as if she understood. "Here." Mira gave it to Danielle. "Tell me what you had programmed in here."

Danielle pressed the buttons. "The first number is Gary's. I can't believe you never changed these."

"I didn't know how." Mira stroked Sara's head. "Maybe I should have asked you, huh?" She tickled Sara under her chin and the chimp laid her head on Mira's shoulder.

"Call Burrows," Mira told Candy, suddenly afraid for Sara and for herself. Neither of them might be there in the morning.

Gary sensed her angst. "It'll be all right," he said and put an arm around her shoulder. "We'll figure this out. But if Sam likes the idea, there's no reason why we can't use Sara for the ad."

Mira moved her lips to protest but Gary put a finger over them.

"Think about it, Mira. Sara's a cool chimp. Any ape that can figure out a cell phone can generate their own income. This could be a win-win situation."

"Now you're sounding like a businessman," she replied.

He hugged her. She was still in his arms when Burrows came through the door.

"Your walking papers are on your desk, Doctor Harper." He stopped and studied them, glaring at her in Gary's embrace. "What is going on?"

"Business," Sam spoke up. "And, Doctor Burrows, do I have a deal for you." He led Burrows out of the ape house.

"He can't fire you, can he?" Danielle asked.

Mira hugged Sara. "He can, but he'll have a fight. The board needs to finalize it and I won't go down easy."

"That's my girl," Gary said. "Besides, by the time Sam's through with him, Burrows won't know what hit him."

Danielle sighed. "Well, now the excitement's over, I'll be leaving."

"And I'll be calling you." Gary glared at her.

"Am...I...?" Danielle squeaked.

"How can I fire my best ad man?" Gary grinned his heart-stopping smile. "But we're setting firm ground rules. From now on, you'd better be on the up-and-up with me." He handed her the phone he'd been carrying. "And give me my cell phone. I like to answer my own calls."

She pulled it out and handed it to him.

"Now get out of here," he ordered. "I have some things I want to tell your sister."

"No problem," Danielle piped then she and Candy went out.

Mira studied him. "You aren't going to release her, are you?"

"No," he said and put his arms around her and Sara. "How can I when I intend to have this forever-type relationship with her sister?"

"Are you sure?" Mira looked at him skeptically while her heart thumped with hope.

"I'm sure." He touched his forehead to hers. "Now, should we put our baby to bed?" Gary whispered. "I've got some things I want to show her mama."

She nodded, wondering what it could be.

* * * * *

Gary waited for Mira to emerge from the bathroom. They'd stopped at her place for a few things but she insisted they eat dinner at his place and she wanted to dress special for it.

He ran a hand through his hair. It had taken a few hours for everything to settle. Thank God for Sam. He had gotten Burrows calmed down, even offering a sizable donation to the zoo, on one condition—the zoo would keep Sara and continue Mira's employment. He'd convinced the geezer the commercial would be a boon for the zoo.

Gary paced, as nervous as the lions he'd seen prowling their cages. Apparently, all the excitement had gotten the animals stirred up. Right now, the idea of being with Mira alone excited him in more ways than one. He planned to tell her his secret. Would she accept his deformity? Would it matter to her or would she be repulsed? He needed to know for sure. In the short time he'd spent in counseling with Jojo, she'd helped him through that part of things. He wanted Mira in his life. She mattered to him. In order to keep her, he needed to tell her the truth.

The door opened. Mira sauntered out in a sheer red negligee. His jaw dropped. "That's dinner-wear?"

"It is for tonight." A smile grew across her beautiful face, her hazel eyes deepening with passion. "I thought," she said as she walked up to him and slid her hands across his chest, "you ought to know where I'm coming from." Her hips ground into his. "Gary, I love you too. You make me feel things I've never had with anyone else. I don't want to lose you. And if doing wild things with you will keep you with me, then I'll do it."

"Mira." He looked at the takeout Chinese getting cold on the table. He could stall by using food as an excuse.

She stood on her tiptoes and reached for his ear. "What do you think?" she whispered. "You want to eat me or the food?"

He couldn't resist. "And here I thought you were the main course."

She giggled as he picked her up and carried her to the bedroom. Mira made him need again, made him the man he once was. How could he not take the risk?

Kissing her, he laid her on the rumpled sheets. "I need to tell you something. Be honest with you." He released her and paced the room, wondering how best to tell her.

"What is it?" she asked.

He stopped in front of her and she took his hand. "If we're together," she said, "we can face anything."

He knelt beside her. "That's what I think too. Mira, I want you in my life, but..." He stood and kicked off his shoes. Turning his back to her, he removed his shirt then his pants. Maybe he couldn't say it, but he could show her.

"Oooh, I like," she purred behind him.

"Most women do," he commented. He was naked, vulnerable. Would she accept his damaged body? He gulped then turned to face her. "It's this side they sometimes have problems with."

Mira looked him up and down, her brow arched in confusion. "Gary, what are you talking about? You are the most perfect man I've ever seen."

He steeled himself and stepped closer. "Look lower, Mira. Underneath."

She fondled his penis and kissed the head. He closed his eyes, willing to die if she didn't accept him.

"I think it feels pretty good from here," she said, her voice sultry.

His eyes popped open. "Mira, don't you feel it?"

"Feel what?" She really looked confused now.

"This." He pointed to the shriveled testicle.

"That?" She looked at him in disgust and his ego dropped to the size of a pea. Then suddenly she rolled back on the pillow and laughed. "Is...is your scrotum what you're worried about?"

He stepped back, not knowing if she was horrified, or what? "Mira…" He swallowed. He needed to know. "The wildest thing you've probably done over the last few days is have sex with a man who's half a man. I…I need to know how you feel about that, whether it matters to you."

She stopped and sat up. "You…you…" She wiggled her finger in the air at his lower body. "This is what you've been worried about?" She stood and enveloped him in her embrace. "Gary, I can't believe this would matter to any woman. I love you. You could have two horns and a tail for all I care."

He held her tight. "Are you sure?" He studied the depths of her eyes.

"Positive." Her eyes watered. "And here I worried about my body. Oh Gary." She kissed him. "You make me feel alive again. You bring out the wildness in me. Because of you, I'm confident in my physical being. What can I do to show you it doesn't matter? That you're the man I want in my life?"

He captured her mouth with his. "Make love to me, Mira. Just love me and show me you care."

He grinned that baby-come-love-me grin. When he entered her this time, Mira knew he would be by her side to stay.

Why an electronic book?

We live in the Information Age—an exciting time in the history of human civilization, in which technology rules supreme and continues to progress in leaps and bounds every minute of every day. For a multitude of reasons, more and more avid literary fans are opting to purchase e-books instead of paper books. The question from those not yet initiated into the world of electronic reading is simply: *Why?*

1. *Price.* An electronic title at Ellora's Cave Publishing and Cerridwen Press runs anywhere from 40% to 75% less than the cover price of the exact same title in paperback format. Why? Basic mathematics and cost. It is less expensive to publish an e-book (no paper and printing, no warehousing and shipping) than it is to publish a paperback, so the savings are passed along to the consumer.

2. *Space.* Running out of room in your house for your books? That is one worry you will never have with electronic books. For a low one-time cost, you can purchase a handheld device specifically designed for e-reading. Many e-readers have large, convenient screens for viewing. Better yet, hundreds of titles can be stored within your new library—on a single microchip. There are a variety of e-readers from different manufacturers. You can also read e-books on your PC or laptop computer. (Please note that Ellora's

Cave does not endorse any specific brands. You can check our websites at www.ellorascave.com or www.cerridwenpress.com for information we make available to new consumers.)

3. *Mobility.* Because your new e-library consists of only a microchip within a small, easily transportable e-reader, your entire cache of books can be taken with you wherever you go.

4. ***Personal Viewing Preferences.*** Are the words you are currently reading too small? Too large? Too… ANNOYING? Paperback books cannot be modified according to personal preferences, but e-books can.

5. ***Instant Gratification.*** Is it the middle of the night and all the bookstores near you are closed? Are you tired of waiting days, sometimes weeks, for bookstores to ship the novels you bought? Ellora's Cave Publishing sells instantaneous downloads twenty-four hours a day, seven days a week, every day of the year. Our webstore is never closed. Our e-book delivery system is 100% automated, meaning your order is filled as soon as you pay for it.

Those are a few of the top reasons why electronic books are replacing paperbacks for many avid readers.

As always, Ellora's Cave and Cerridwen Press welcome your questions and comments. We invite you to email us at Comments@ellorascave.com or write to us directly at Ellora's Cave Publishing Inc., 1056 Home Avenue, Akron, OH 44310-3502.

Cerridwen Press

Cerridwen, the Celtic goddess of wisdom, was the muse who brought inspiration to storytellers and those in the creative arts.

Cerridwen Press encompasses the best and most innovative stories in all genres of today's fiction.

Visit our website and discover the newest titles by talented authors who still get inspired — much like the ancient storytellers did...

once upon a time.

www.cerridwenpress.com